She got up and sped after them halfway across the yard, trying to get close enough to grasp whatever they had taken from Amanda. The creatures ran faster than greyhounds and quickly outdistanced her. She felt torn between chasing them and going back to help Amanda.

She turned and sprinted back to her twin, "Amanda. Amanda are you okay?" she asked, out of breath. Mira knelt, touching her; barely registering that she saw no wound and her sister's clothes were intact. Amanda's face looked slack, listless.

Mira tried to figure out what to do next. The dogs were almost at the poplars now. She watched in astonishment as a black swan streamed towards them through the mist and dove, taking the object from the dogs.

The pulsing golden thing strained to get back to her twin. Mira could almost hear it screaming. She shuddered. Whatever it was, it belonged to Amanda and somehow Mira needed to get it back to her. The swan flew through the trees swooping up and down under what seemed to be a heavy load, then disappeared into the pocket of fog halfway down the block.

The Black Opal

The Jeweled Worlds:

Book 1

Published by Metamorphosis Press
www.MetamorphosisPress.com

ISBN-13:978-0997797121/ISBN-10:0997797126

This is a work of fiction. Names, characters, places or incident are either the product of the author's imagination or are used fictitiously. Any resemblance to actual events, or persons, either living or dead, is entirely coincidental.

The Jeweled Worlds:
Book 1

The Black Opal

BY

LINDA JORDAN

Metamorphosis Press

For Michael & Zoe

Chapter 1 — Mira

Mira smelled the neighbor's lilacs as she walked down the gravel road. Stray clumps of grass and weeds splashed dew into her Crocs, and her feet squished around inside the shoes. She looked at the beautiful view of Puget Sound. It would be a gorgeous spring day, rare and sunny.

But it wasn't enough to make Mira forget her miserable life. She'd screwed up again and this time Aunt Rita had sent her to Mom's house. For good.

Mira had been crying for two days; now she just felt empty. Her life held no hope and no future.

She turned back towards the house, pausing to empty a piece of gravel from one shoe.

Then she realized that something felt very wrong. Half a block away, shadows barreled through the mist. A huge hand-shaped cloud appeared out of nowhere, passed over the sun and darkened the row of poplars beside Mom's house.

Shivering in the sudden cold and absence of all sound; she smelled the burnt air. It left a bitter taste in her mouth.

She began to run, slipping and sliding in her wet Crocs.

The shadows closed in and the creatures took shape as two huge, black dogs. They moved like one, legs and breathing synchronized, toward Mira's identical twin, Amanda. And her son, Dylan.

Amanda had her back to the hounds, absorbed in Dylan's play. Oblivious to the threat. Her three year old, golden child ran circles around his mom. She sat on the front lawn. The long, red hair tied up in a ponytail made her look younger than eighteen. She laughed, ducking the clumps of wet grass which Dylan threw up into the air.

"Amanda! Look out!" screamed Mira. She ran past the massive cedar stump towards them. "Get Dylan in the house!"

Amanda scrambled to her feet and turned towards the dogs. Dylan ran behind her. The hounds leapt at them. Saliva ran from their mouths. Amanda fell backwards on top of Dylan. He wriggled beneath her, trying to get out.

Mira gasped for breath as she ran, helplessly watching Amanda punch the creatures. Hollow thuds echoed as her sister's fists landed. Amanda screamed, but the hounds were relentless in their assault. Their jaws snapped and slavered, easily avoiding her fists and feet.

Mira was there. As she bashed them the sounds of her foot hitting reverberated in the eerie silence.

"Get away! Go!" she screamed.

She looked around for something else to hit them with. There was nothing. When she kicked one in the head, it glared at her with icy-white eyes, then returned to the attack.

To Mira's horror they ripped into Amanda's belly. No blood flowed, but something came loose. A gold object pulsed, reaching tendrils back towards Amanda, as if trying to stay with her. The dogs strained and pulled. The thing, like a golden, tropical flower, was severed from Amanda.

Mira felt helpless. Grounding herself, she tried to summon up the Earth's energy. Then attempted to move it through the dogs.

The creatures ignored her, turned and headed back the way they came. She quickly gave up on magic and chased them. She kicked harder and made a grab for the golden object. Off balance, she fell sprawling to the ground. The hound tossed the tendrilled thing to the other, yelped, and kept running.

She got up and sped after them halfway across the yard, trying to get close enough to grasp whatever they had taken from Amanda. The creatures ran faster than greyhounds and quickly outdistanced her. She felt torn between chasing them and going back to help Amanda.

She turned and sprinted back to her twin, "Amanda. Amanda are you okay?" she asked, out of breath. Mira knelt, touching her; barely registering that she saw no wound and her sister's clothes were intact. Amanda's face looked slack, listless.

Mira tried to figure out what to do next. The dogs were almost at the poplars now. She watched in astonishment as a black swan streamed towards them through the mist and dove, taking the object from the dogs.

The pulsing golden thing strained to get back to her twin. Mira could almost hear it screaming. She shuddered. Whatever it was, it belonged to Amanda and somehow Mira needed to get it back to her. The swan flew through the trees swooping up and down under what seemed to be a heavy load, then disappeared into the pocket of fog halfway down the block.

Tears streamed down her face as Mira shook her twin gently. She felt a need to keep Amanda conscious. "Amanda, please stay here." Mira didn't know what the golden thing was, but it was important. She felt worthless. Why hadn't she made different choices, ones that could have stopped the dogs?

Dylan lay beneath Amanda, whimpering.

Mira rolled Amanda over slightly and helped Dylan wiggle out from under his mom. Then he lay on top of her sobbing, "Mommy, Mommy," clasping his stuffed dinosaur, Freddie. Mira stroked his back.

Amanda looked up at Mira. Her green eyes wept, then turned completely black as if empty. She didn't speak.

Mira felt frozen. She had never seen such powerful magic before. How could she possibly counter it?

The hand-shaped cloud over the sun vanished, like smoke blowing away. Light returned. Sun blazed over the treetops and she felt arid, August heat. The air smelled clean again.

Mira's mouth went dry. She looked around sensing something, not sinister, but as great a force as the evil had been.

She looked up to see a huge, golden eagle above, starting a dive.

She pulled Dylan off Amanda, feeling instinctively it would protect him. He squirmed away from her. The massive eagle dropped down and effortlessly lifted Amanda by her clothes.

Dylan cried out, "No, Mommy come back."

Mira had no idea what to do. Her brain could make no sense out of this. The eagle flew gracefully across the acre, hovered over the massive hollow cedar stump and let go. Amanda fell, disappearing from view.

Dylan ran across the yard, tears streaming down his face. "Mommy."

Chapter 2 — Mira

Mira caught up to Dylan.

He squirmed out of her arms, yelled, "Mom," and continued running towards the fifteen-foot tall, cedar stump. He climbed faster than she could react.

"Dylan, no!"

He shook his head. "Get Mom." His face was red.

"Wait," she said, forcing herself to stop and breathe. She needed to be clear about what to do next. "Let me think a minute."

Dylan stopped climbing and stared at her; his opinion clear.

She didn't want to go into the stump. Trying to see what lay inside had gotten her banished from Mom's house six years ago. Mom had caught Mira practicing flying.

But, he was right. She needed to get Amanda out of there. Dylan shouldn't be left alone that long. She pointed to him and said firmly, "Okay, wait here."

Dylan wiped the tears off with his blue T-shirt and nodded.

She ran to the garage slamming the wide door up and open. The tall aluminum ladder lay against the dimly lit, far wall. Dragging the metal ladder across the cement floor made screeching sounds which resonated with the discordant feelings running through her body.

The ladder cut a furrow in the grass behind her. By the time she returned to the stump her breath came hard and sweat moistened her T-shirt. When she got the ladder propped up against a branch, he went right up it. She almost stopped him, then decided if Dylan fell, at least he'd land on her.

She started climbing and yelled, "Dylan stop when you get to the top." Her tight jeans made climbing difficult; all her jeans were tight these days. How good would it feel to be in shape like Amanda?

Mira gasped for breath and her legs were wobbly by the time she made it to the top. Helping Dylan straddle a branch that looked strong enough while trying to balance herself on the wide rim of the hollow stump was challenging.

"Now comes the hard part, Bucko." She looked down into the cedar. The bottom was dark. No time to go back and get a flashlight. Dylan couldn't be left alone.

"Amanda, are you okay?" Mira's voice echoed inside the rotting tree. In her head she could hear Aunt Rita's voice, "You need to think before you act. Plan before you do," as guilt at her own incompetence washed over her.

Dylan said, "Mira, magic," and pointed down.

Her neck and shoulders tightened and she almost gasped with surprise. He wasn't supposed to know. No one did, except her mom and Amanda. Not even her stepfather Elliot. Well, especially not her stepfather. Mom was afraid he'd go ballistic.

"Who told you I could do magic, you little bugger?"

"Light," said Dylan insistently.

She took a deep breath, pulled off a nearby dried out cedar twig and envisioned it burning. The stick caught fire, illuminating most of the inside of the cedar stump. She saw just enough to doubt Amanda was there. Dylan pointed to a dark spot on one side of the stump.

"Mom," he said.

"She's not there, Dylan," Mira felt torn between disappointment and fear.

"Mom. Go."

The cedar twig exploded into a small, singeing fireball and she dropped it, then sucked on her fingers. The burned twig drifted down inside the stump and went out. Mira needed to go down there, but didn't want to. She trembled.

The ladder suddenly seemed to be made of granite. It felt so heavy. On the third attempt she lifted it off the ground and slid it up the outside of the cedar, then balanced the ladder in front of her. Somehow she slid it down the inside of the stump. By the time she accomplished it, her whole body shook from the exertion and precious minutes had passed.

She got on the ladder and helped Dylan on after her.

"Go slower," she snapped, as he stepped on her fingers.

How she would get Amanda back up was anybody's guess.

They hit the bottom inside the stump and she sat down, exhausted. There was no sign of her twin. The dark spot looked like a tunnel. Dylan simply waddled into it.

"Dylan, come back here."

"Get Mom."

"I go first," she said and crawled towards the tunnel opening. Cool air wafted from it. Once her eyes adjusted to the darkness she could see a dim light inside.

"Amanda?"

No answer came back. Her voice was absorbed by the earth.

What had happened to Amanda? Mira grew increasingly afraid of what she might find. The dogs attacked her sister, yet there had been no blood.

She tried to understand, while crawling into the tunnel. Somehow, she realized, the dogs had stolen Amanda's soul. That's what the golden, curly object was. Intuition told her that; even though her mind couldn't believe it. The pain she sensed as Amanda's soul was severed from her body had been devastating. What must Amanda feel? Why would those dogs steal a soul?

Mira was born with the magic which ran in her family and she'd been studying with Aunt Rita, learning to use her own innate skills as a healer. Failing more often than succeeding. She celebrated the subtle changes of the seasons, taking in the uses of herbs, practicing spells which normal people would explain away as positive thinking. She could even do a few more complex things like making fire out of nowhere, sometimes without damaging someone's house.

Things like possessed dogs and stolen souls were the equivalent of a jumbo jet landing on the driveway at Aunt Rita's house, she thought. A sharp rock punctured her knee bringing her back to the present, but the puzzle remained. Things like this just didn't happen in her world. She'd seen a few inexplicable things, but never in her life felt magic like that of the dogs.

Mira pushed through the paralyzing fear and kept crawling. No one else could help right now and time was crucial. She wished Aunt Rita could be there. Dylan shouldn't be, but there was no one to leave him with. Taking care of a toddler was the last thing she needed.

She crawled further and further downward. Dylan was short enough to simply walk upright behind her, although he kept tripping on her feet and falling down.

The tunnel grew lighter. Rock walls and dirt floor felt cool to the touch. Her hands and knees inside her jeans grew cold from the damp earth. How long would the tunnel continue? Her legs were cramping up.

Bumping her head on a low, hanging rock she tried, unsuccessfully, not to swear in front of Dylan. The tunnel widened and they came closer to the light. Crawling to an opening in the side of the tunnel wall, she felt warmth. A whitish-silver light seemed to be radiate from everything.

She looked down onto a green hillside and a beautiful forest. In the distance lay wildflower meadows of pink and orange. The sweet scent of wild roses tickled her nose. Fields of farmland sprawled before an incredible ivory city which seemed formed from pearls. It looked perfect, like someone's painting of a fairy tale or a magical place. Beyond the towers stretched an ocean with iridescent waves. Everything glowed as if lit. A world made of radiance. She stuck her foot through the opening to climb down the hillside. Entering into that world made her feel more vibrant as if every little disfunction in her body was healed. Stress melted away. Even the air coming through the opening felt cleaner and more alive than normal air. The city pulled her towards it.

Dylan cried, "No!"

She turned to him. He pointed down the passageway which traveled still deeper into the earth. On the floor, farther down the tunnel, lay Amanda's yellow sweater in a heap.

She reluctantly crawled back into the tunnel, past Dylan to the sweater. It was crumpled and smudged with dirt. Clearly Amanda was farther down. Mira clutched the sweater to her chest, breathing deeply and trying not to cry. She looked back longingly at the pearlescent city then tied the sweater around Dylan's shoulders, to help him stay warm and keep Amanda's presence close to him. Dylan smiled, hugging himself.

She went back to the opening and broke a small branch off one of the trees near the entrance to that radiant world. As they continued down the tunnel the branch shined in the darkness, putting out a small amount of light, as if the silver leaves glowed from the inside out. Mira gently slipped it inside her T-shirt, which she tucked into her jeans so the branch wouldn't fall out. As the leaves touched each other

17

they tinkled like little silver bells, but weren't scratchy under her T-shirt, rather they felt like pussy willows caressing her skin.

Dylan followed behind her muttering, "Mom, we come," over and over again.

The tunnel floor was soft dirt rather than hard rock. She pulled the silver branch out to look. Something had dragged Amanda down the tunnel. As they crawled she could see small insects and other creepy things crawling into crevices to get away from the light. She didn't want to think about all the wildlife. The air carried a strange smell to it, like moldy houses. She shuddered and kept moving.

What would happen when she found Amanda? Mira couldn't even mend a sparrow. Two days ago she had been trying to move energy to the bird's broken leg. Instead she accidentally shattered Aunt Rita's precious crystal scrying bowl which sat on a table across the room. The one that had been passed down for generations.

Rita's face had drooped as she picked up the lifeless sparrow and said, "Go back to your mom's, go to college, get a job, anything. Your magic is too wild and uncontrolled. I've worked with you for six years and nothing has changed."

It wasn't the first thing she'd broken and failed at. So she had gone back to Mom's. Mom didn't want her. She'd never forgiven Mira for having the family 'gift'. Mom viewed it as a curse and refused to use or even acknowledge it. Mira felt worthless and didn't have a clue how to help Amanda if they found her.

After what seemed like an hour or two of going down, the tunnel suddenly curved and ended, opening up into a forest clearing.

Mira stood, slowly stretching, massaging her aching knees and looking around. Dylan followed her towards the gloomy, violet light into a new world.

It looked like no woodland she had ever seen. Trunks of towering trees stood like massive highway supports, ten feet across. Moss grew everywhere. Intriguing sounds formed a concert of new agey music. Shrieks, chirps, roars and hooting noises wove together in a such a way she couldn't tell what creatures they might belong to. The forest vibrated with unseen life. It smelled of the clean scent which comes after a brisk rain. She felt nervous, hoping the wildlife was friendly.

A trail led from the clearing, off into the misty woods. Imprinted in the mud lay tracks. Big webbed feet, twice the size of hers, with only three toes. Tangled up with the tracks was a wide, deep mark that could have been a person being dragged.

Mira's stomach rumbled and she knew Dylan must be hungry as well, but she had no food. "You up for this Bucko?"

"Find Mom," he said, puffing up his chest. She noticed his lower lip quiver slightly.

She sighed, tightened Amanda's sweater around Dylan and asked, "Can you walk or do you need to be carried?"

He looked at her and said, "Walk."

She looked back at the tunnel opening to memorize it so they could return home. The entrance stood framed between two of the most massive evergreens. As if their roots had grown around a log which had vanished over time, leaving a hole. Would she be able to spot the trees from a distance?

"Okay, let's go."

She pulled the silver branch out and held it in front of her. It glowed like a lantern making them more visible to whatever might be out there. However, it felt like the pearly light and tinkling leaves would ward off anything which wanted to harm them. The image of that beautiful, silvery land burned in her mind.

She followed the trail, worrying about just what would happen when they came upon Amanda and the web-footed thing. They walked for hours, following the tracks.

Why was the light a purple color, but the mist green? This was a very strange place. Where had the end of the tunnel put them? They must be underground somewhere. They had gone down for a very long time inside the tunnel, but if they were beneath the earth's surface, where did the light and the air come from?

After while, she picked Dylan up and carried him. He fell asleep which made him even heavier. She'd lost her sense of time. It must be the middle of the night though.

She finally stepped out of the murky woods, stopping in a meadow lit by the dim violet light. She lay Dylan on the soft grass. He continued to sleep, cuddled up with his green dinosaur. She covered him with Amanda's sweater.

Sitting on a boulder, she felt exhausted all the way down to her bones. Slipping off her shoes, rubbing her sore feet and then wiggling them in the soft meadow grass helped a little. She'd been frantic most of the day worrying about Amanda and trying to work out what happened. The light glowed a little brighter here in the meadow, but still looked dark and twilighty. She lay back enjoying the soft moss growing on the boulder. Heat radiated from the stone and she relaxed into it. The sweet, earthy smell made her feel calm.

Mira jolted back to consciousness when the rock started to move. She leapt up. It had four, stout legs, a bulbous head and a tail twice as long as its body. Now she saw the scales beneath the moss. It stared at her and hissed, then ambled slowly off towards the woods, the tail slapping back and forth like a whip, just in case.

"I'm sorry," she apologized, feeling stupid. It wasn't a tortoise, even though it lived inside a turtle-like shell. Where were they?

She groggily checked where Dylan slept under Amanda's sweater and saw with a shock, only the sweater. How long had she slept?

"Dylan? DYLAN!" she yelled.

She stood in the middle of a large meadow, no trees or bushes for Dylan to hide behind. There were no tracks through the damp grass, other than the trail they'd been following. She picked up Amanda's sweater and started running in the direction they were headed last night.

"Dylan," she called again.

She still didn't know where they were. There was no sun, although the meadow looked bright enough. Everything had a bluish, purple cast to it. Few of the plants looked familiar. She had seen a number of strange birds flitting among the shrubs. Everything dripped with moss and dampness.

Up ahead she heard a great thrashing in the bushes. Too much noise for even Dylan to make. Mira scampered off the trail to hide behind the nearest tree. The tree turned out to be too small and her pale blue T-shirt didn't make for good camouflage. She whispered to herself, "Please let me find Dylan before it does."

Men on horseback rode up the trail. Then another group burst out of the forest and entered onto the trail to join the others. She froze.

One man rode in front, leaning outward from his horse, looking at the ground. The rest followed in two columns, the trail only wide enough for two horses side by side. When the first man got to her tracks, his eyes followed them to the tree she stood behind. He stopped his horse and looked directly into her eyes.

She said under her breath, "Now that was stupid." She should have chosen a better hiding place. Too late now. She couldn't run, they were on horses after all. Where was Dylan?

Stepping out from behind the tree, she stood hands on hips. As she waited for their reaction Mira instinctively covered herself with a shield of protection, visualizing a wall of blazing fire, the hardest stone, rushing water and roaring wind, just as Aunt Rita taught her.

This time felt different, though. It mattered, not just practice. Somewhere, deep within, she found the energy, anger or fear, to fuel her magic. Mira felt amazed. Her magic never worked this well. A subtle, green aura surrounded her.

It wouldn't keep out a physical attack, but might repel any assaults on her spirit.

The tracker sat up straight, continuing to eye her, with a look on his face of either surprise or amusement.

She turned her attention to the other men. They looked like something out of a viking movie or an old heavy metal concert. Wearing leather pants and shirts with armored vests, they looked ominous. Several wore bows with quivers of arrows over their shoulders. Most of the men carried swords. Where the hell was she? There were twelve of them staring at her curiously. Some of the horses stomped restlessly. They looked like normal horses at least and smelled like normal horses, that sweet-sweaty-dusty fragrance she associated with horses.

The tracker sat quietly staring at her with his dark eyes. An older man rode his horse forward and stopped next to the tracker. They exchanged glances. The man with the gray hair and a neatly clipped goatee and mustache, got off his horse and walked forward.

"Don't be afraid, young woman. We won't hurt you."

"Who are you?" she asked. She could feel someone's power touching her, trying to find an opening in the shield. It didn't come from the older man though.

"That is not important. We are simply a hunting party. Who are you?"

She waited a moment and said as regally as she could, "That's not important either."

The older man simply looked at her and she stared back at him defiantly. There was a flash of movement coming down the trail from the meadow and she was almost knocked over by Dylan.

"Mira, cool rock," he said, opening up his hand. She could see a small red, rock in the palm of his hand. It suddenly sprouted a head and wings, then flew off.

Dylan stood staring at it and said, "Wow!"

The older man laughed. "Can we help you in any way? You must be a long way from home."

She breathed deeply. If these men had ridden far on the trail they probably wiped out the creature's tracks who had her sister. "We're hunting my sister and whatever hauled her off."

"Your sister?"

"Yes, and the thing with webbed feet and three toes."

"A quirot?" he asked.

"What's a quirot?" she asked. She hated feeling ignorant.

"Quirots are swamp people," he shrugged. "What do you plan to do when you find them? Quirots can be very fierce," he said, an amused look on his face. He put a hand on his hip and as he smiled, his wrinkles moved closer together.

She wasn't deceived. She felt patronized and really pissed off, but determined not to let him see it. He moved like a young man. Mira wished she could whip out a sword like some anime heroine or do Kung Fu and knock him flat on his back. But he was right. She had no plan. "I'll decide that when I find them,"she said with more confidence than she actually felt.

"Father," said the tracker, who looked about her age, as he smoothly slid off his horse. He walked towards them, his brown horse following like a shadow. "Back at the stream the quirot parted from whatever prey it caught. We found the tracks before you rejoined us. We could return and follow them."

She tried to keep from staring at the man. He wore his dark hair, shoulder-length and tied back with a leather thong, threaded through metal charms. His big, brown eyes had stared at her since the men rode up. From what she could see underneath all that leather and metal his lean build looked muscular. Focus, she told herself looking back at the older man. In doing so, she realized the power flowed from the younger man.

The older man glared at the son, "Ronan," he said warningly, but the son gave him a challenging gaze in return. The father nodded and turned back to her. "Your sister was not there, but we could take you to the place so you can continue your search."

"Thank you, I'll follow you."

"It would be faster if you rode," said the son.

She thought about it, but didn't trust any of them that far.

"I'll walk," she said.

Dylan pulled at her sleeve. She squatted down near him. "Don't you ever, ever run off like that again. Do you know how afraid I was?"

"Need to pee."

"Oh Jeez." She'd never baby-sat, didn't know anything about little boys, or little girls for that matter. "Can you go by yourself?"

"Uh huh."

"Good, there's a tree over there, just go behind it and do your thing."

"Kay." Dylan strutted off towards the tree and pulled his pants down in full view of everyone. He had a gleeful look on his face. He'd most likely never been allowed to pee in the woods before.

She noticed a couple of the men looking at Dylan, smiling and looking away while laughing, as if they thought he looked adorable. Maybe they weren't aliens after all.

Mira followed along behind, hefting Dylan from one hip to the other as she tired. She sensed that Ronan masked his amazing power somehow. It felt like a towel thrown over a lamp. A faint glow occasionally leaked out as if someone lifted the corner of the towel. When that happened she could feel his power looping back and touching her, still seeking an opening. What was he searching for? Mira felt glad she didn't need to focus on much except keeping her shield up and walking. She'd never really felt anyone's power before, except Aunt Rita's. It was like comparing the drip of a faucet to a roaring waterfall being held back by a dam.

Dylan remained still, looking around and taking everything in as she carried him. Only once did he speak,

"Be okay Mira," he said, confidently. The men rode silently, following Ronan who led the way.

She felt a huge difference in the way her magic worked here. It seemed clearer, stronger and easier. Did magic feel or act different here than in Seattle or on Whidbey Island, or could she simply see it better here? She didn't know where here was anyway and couldn't bring herself to ask. She didn't want to be at any more of a disadvantage.

Once they got to the stream, she couldn't see anything except mud. Ronan drifted close to her as the others dismounted, letting their horses drink downstream of the tracks. He leaned over the side of his horse, pointing out what happened. A person's footprints came towards where Amanda had been dropped. The creature's tracks led upstream and alone. It looked like the person and Amanda walked off together, although Ronan said the person half-carried her sister.

The footprints looked about the same size, but Amanda's feet were bare and the other person wore soft shoes. Their footsteps walked away from the stream in the damp soil.

"The Witch," one of the men said, then spat on the ground. They all looked uneasy, except the son.

"I could take them to her and then rejoin you," he said to his father.

The older man looked thoughtful for a minute and said, "She dare not harm you. Agreed. We will leave signs for you to follow." He and the other men mounted. "We must go before we lose the trail." The older man nodded at her and they rode back the way they came, leaving behind a cloud of dust.

"Why are they afraid of a Witch?" she asked Ronan. They walked now, his horse following along.

"She has a reputation for being whimsical. Turned one of my father's men into a dog," he said, wryly.

"Is he still a dog?" she asked.

"He died defending my father from a bear."

"Sorry." She felt stupid. His power touched her strongly now. He didn't mask it. She felt him looking at her. His eyes felt like velvet caressing her shoulders. She wondered if this could be real or some sort of glamour, a charm. As they walked up the hill she blurted out, "What do you mean, 'your father's men'? Is he a king or something?" His attention made her uncomfortable. It felt too intimate. Too intense. Too fast.

"Look, there is the Witch's home," he said, completely avoiding her question but she let it drop.

She felt something new. A sense of being searched touched her entire body. She refocused her drifting energy back towards her shield and the feeling vanished. It would seem they were expected.

They walked towards a massive evergreen tree. As they got closer she saw a wood and rope spiral staircase wind around the huge tree trunk.

Ronan said, "When danger comes or she wants to be alone, she can draw the staircase up so no one can enter."

Smoke curled out from beneath the evergreen's branches.

He said, "I must leave so I can catch up with the others. The Witch will help you find your sister." He got on his horse and rode off in the direction of the meadow.

She watched as he rode into the trees and the purple twilight. His power lingered awhile, then withdrew abruptly. "Wait, I didn't even get to thank you," Mira called after him. She felt suddenly alone.

He merely waved as if he hadn't heard her.

"Men, they're such idiots sometimes. Well, not you Dylan. You're going to grow up to be a smart cookie. Amanda and I will see to that." Looking down, she saw Dylan was asleep.

Sighing, she began to climb the stairs. She would have to meet the Witch alone.

Chapter 3 — Ronan

Ronan rode in the direction his father and the other men had taken, following their trail. His bay, Pinecone, ran through the meadow towards the stream, stretching out and picking up his pace. He knew the horse felt happy to be running. Pinecone was made for speed and Ronan could sense the wind blowing through his nostrils and mane and the power of his hooves as they pounded the earth. He felt the horse's spirit soar as the stallion sailed over the stream and roared through the woods on the other side. Branches slapped at Ronan's face before he could rein the horse in.

"Slow down there," he said. "We will catch up to them."

Pinecone shook his head in annoyance. He wanted to run.

Ronan said, "On the way back we will go on the main road and you can run until you drop."

Pinecone snorted as if to say, "Now."

"I can do no better for the time being. We have work to do," said Ronan.

Ronan felt unnerved. He could still see the redhead, Mira, ineffectually hiding behind the tree. Dressed in strange clothes, all blue. Her long hair curling down her back, she had looked so weary, he wanted to comfort her. She showed great bravado. And the child who had appeared out of nowhere, did the child belong to her? Was she joined with someone? She must be. His heart sank at that thought which kept returning. Where was her man though? Why didn't he come with her into this world. Ronan's intuition told him she was unattached, but logic said otherwise.

His father, Roderick, had done most of the talking, although he allowed Ronan to take her to Aste's home. Ronan felt like a fool, unable to speak. He should be back helping his brother, Ewan, keep his father and his men off the scent.

Ronan and Ewan had invited themselves to join Roderick's hunting party as trackers with the secret goal of leading their father away from the black unicorns. They had already misled the group three times.

Ronan asked himself why he chose to leave the hunting party, taking Mira to the witch?

He caught the scent of rotting flesh and hear snarling. Probably a woodland lion defending its kill possibly, or a couple of desperate wolves. The horse sidestepped nervously and Ronan squeezed his legs, signaling the stallion to move out of the predator's territory.

He continued worrying about his dilemmas. Many people thought the unicorn population so nearly vanished that killing the rest made no difference. Others, like his father, saw only a challenge. The unicorns held complicated magic and hunting them lay beyond most people's skills. Others simply saw profit. Ronan had a choice about his actions, but mostly he made the unpopular ones.

His decision about this woman felt different. He couldn't let her walk away, just as he could not willingly cease breathing. It felt as if she put a spell on him. Women often accused him of doing that to them, oddly enough. Even now as he closed his eyes, he saw her. The courage in her voice and actions, overshadowing her fear. Yet, somehow she was lost. If he didn't get to know her he would regret it his entire life.

Ronan shook his head to clear it. What could he be thinking? She was an outlander. Clothes like hers didn't exist in his world. The most glaring difference came from her magic. It felt exotic, like the green, asania flowers from the outer islands with their velvety petals that could perfume an entire room. Which world had she came from?

He sighed in frustration and Pinecone snorted in response. He had too much to think about and do. Mainly, he needed to keep his father from carrying out stupid acts.

Each day the Queen's reign crumbled further and a revolution sat at their feet, begging to be taken up. His father needed to be in position to accept the crown. Roderick wouldn't be able to do that if he was caught hunting and illegally selling unicorn horn. The Queen would love to have an excuse to spear him, even if he was her younger brother. There was no love lost between them. Ronan seriously wondered if Roderick would make a better ruler than the Queen. His father needed to grow up. Did he have enough empathy and sensitivity to rule well? Would the Black Opal accept him?

He reined the stallion in and looked down at the ground, following the trail of his father and the men. A broken pine branch softly brushed across his face, releasing the resinous smell in his nostrils. He pushed it aside to see the earth below and catch where half the men took another trail. Ewan would only be able to distract half the group now. Ronan felt frustrated, he should have been there. He reined his horse toward the smaller group, hoping he took the right trail.

He still felt awkward about not answering Mira's questions. He didn't want to be connected with the hunting party. For the same reason his father hadn't told her his name. Ronan felt ashamed to have anyone think of him as hunting unicorns. His father, however, was completely guilty of selling the crystalline horns to artisans instead of giving them to the Queen.

Ronan often wondered if their entire family wasn't corrupt in some way. Queen Nakia's reign consisted of bloodshed and cruelty, as her father's before her. Roderick murdered unicorns. His brother Ewan leapt between noble's homes, and the women's beds. He gathered information for Roderick and had become a windswept seed with no place to take root.

Ronan had grown into a loner. He spent long turns on the road like the nomads his people were, not long ago. With few real friends he felt lonely and incomplete; searching for some woman to complete him. An impossibility, but he dreamed. Ronan wondered how their lives would be different if their mother had lived, he'd never forgive Nakia for her part in that. He rubbed his dust-filled eyes. Better not follow that path further. She was dead, no going back. Still, one day, Nakia would pay.

Ronan stood in the saddle to stretch as Pinecone trotted down the trail, feeling the horse's gait jolting the day's events into some sort of order. He would return to the Witch's home and ask about Mira. Why had she come alone, except for the child, to find her sister? Why did the quirot carry off her sister?

There were too many unanswered questions. It was possible the outlanders presence would upset the delicate balance and tip things the wrong direction, especially if they stayed with Aste. He needed answers. He must go by the Witch's home. After his father returned home safely, without finding unicorns hiding in the uplands.

He followed the hunting party's tracks. Tall rock roses rustled on his right. A gorgeous black unicorn stallion rushed out from behind them and snorted. His sweaty body gleamed in the light. Behind him stood a small herd of mares and a few foals with their tiny, even more valuable horns. Not as many foals as mares and still all black, Ronan thought sadly. Their numbers were shrinking.

Ronan instinctively froze. Pinecone tried to look non-threatening. The unicorn snorted again and pawed at the ground. Pinecone backed up, chewing in submission. Ronan didn't want to be in the middle of a battle between the two of them, or on the end of a unicorn horn.

A deep rumbling came from the right. Probably, his father's men. Ronan sent an image of hunters to the unicorn's mind and asked him to take his herd and flee.

The stallion stood glaring at them for a moment, then tossed his head as if to say, "If I were alone...."

He sighed with relief as the unicorn turned and herded his mares in the opposite direction. They slipped around a massive stone outcrop which would hide their tracks on the rocks. Ronan rode his horse back and forth to confuse the tracks, waiting until his father and the rest arrived.

"I heard you coming. They ran off that direction," he said.

"Why did you not shoot one?" asked his father, pulling his bow off the shoulder with one hand and an arrow out of the quiver with his other hand.

"And deny my father the first kill?" asked Ronan, grinning.

His father nodded and rode past. The rest followed. Best they not stay in the area long and notice the tracks leading around the rocks. Ewan smiled a sly smile at him. He tracked much better than Ronan.

They rode until dinner, without seeing a sign of the unicorns, then made camp. Ronan hoped the unicorns kept running in the opposite direction.

They built a fire and roasted deer for dinner. Ronan sat off by himself on a rock, chewing a piece of meat and drinking warm ale. One of the men had bought a small cask in one of the villages they passed. The ale tasted good, but bubbly from all the bouncing it received on the ride.

The men celebrated nothing in particular. His father, as usual, told some entertaining story. Ronan hoped the party would extend all night. Perhaps tomorrow they would be ready to go home.

He wondered if Mira found her sister. What had happened to the sister to make her weak enough for the quirot to take her? Quirots normally preyed on small animals.

Ewan sat on the ground next to him. "You seem extraordinarily lost in thought tonight."

"Hmm," said Ronan.

"It is the redhead?"

"What makes you think that?" asked Ronan.

"How long have we been brothers?" asked Ewan, drinking ale and pushing curly, blond hair out of his eyes.

"That obvious?"

"Perhaps not to everyone, but I noticed you did not waste time in volunteering to guide her to the Witch's home."

"Just being a gentleman," said Ronan.

"In the midst of trying to lead the others astray? I think not."

Ronan sat in silence. Ewan was gifted at prying.

"Perhaps the Witch will find she has met her match if this woman bewitched you so easily."

"It was easy," said Ronan, smiling.

"Quite," said Ewan. "And you will probably inquire about her in a day or two?" He raised an eyebrow, and gnawed meat off the bone.

Ronan threw his bones into the fire. Smoke drifted his direction. He wiped his hands on already grimy pants. "I cannot think what else to do."

"Go talk to the Witch. She is a good woman and may have some advice. What will you do if the child is hers and she already has a partner?"

"If she did, where was he? If I had a woman like that and a child, I would not let them go wandering off into a strange world in search of a sister, facing danger alone," said Ronan, poking at the fire with a stick. He felt angry at the thought someone might have found the woman before he did and claimed her. He felt unable to relax his shoulders and the tension they carried.

Ronan slept fitfully that night, dreaming of Mira with her long red hair. They laughed and danced together in the fountains of the palace gardens on a summer evening, their clothes drenched. They were not drunk, just giddy. The dream lurched into another and Ronan found himself eye to eye with a white unicorn. Her blue eyes looked deep inside him as she said, "Your father is not pure enough to rule, he will not pass the test. Find another."

Ronan woke shaking. White unicorns had not been seen alive since the massacre.

Chapter 4 — Nakia

"Fool," Queen Nakia said, quietly. She would not allow herself to explode. This was more effective. Her Sorcerer shifted uncomfortably back and forth between his shrunken feet. He understood he'd made a massive mistake.

"How could you have been so stupid? You were so concerned with being dramatic that you stole the wrong soul?"

"I have no defense, my Queen," he said, his voice quavering. "I only wanted to impress you."

"Well you have impressed me, with your incompetence. I have had men whipped to death for less."

He stood silent, looking repentant but scared witless, she thought.

Nakia picked up the skirt of her long scarlet, dress, turned and walked towards the window. Her realm lay beneath her. It looked deceptively healthy with the dimming light. Only she knew the extent to which it crumbled. Crops failing, livestock dying from plague and drought, violence in her cities becoming harder to control even with more troops. Various nobles, covertly or actively waiting for her to fall. Signs of rot and decay could be seen everywhere. She did not have the strength to support her world anymore. Nakia touched her forehead. The scarlet sheath covered her horn. What remained of it.

"We must do something quickly," she said, harshly.

"I do not know what to do, my Queen."

She turned back to him and glared, "It is almost as if you wanted this plan to fail, Sorcerer."

"No, my Queen. I did not approve of this plan, as I told you, but I will always do as you ask," he said.

"Good, because if I thought you lied to me, more than your feet will shrivel."

He stood staring at her, nodding.

She felt unsure whether to trust him, but there was only one other with his knowledge. "We have little time, we must remove the other girl's soul. Then you will incorporate both souls into my body."

He looked astonished. "Even if she was not on guard, even if we could capture her soul, I am not sure that is a wise thing to do."

"Why?"

"It has never been done, adding more than one soul to a body."

"They are twins, their souls are already connected."

"True," he said, scratching his unruly, dark hair. "But I am not convinced it can be done."

She turned back to the window and gestured out towards the city. "Do you see an alternative?"

"We could use the soul we have."

"Not powerful enough to hold this land. You said so yourself. That soul's window for power has not yet come. I do not have much time before our world vanishes into chaos."

"Give this one back and take the other one?"

"No, I want them both," she turned on him venomously. Nakia let the rage flow through her, permeate her entire being. This pathetic man had no right to deny her. "Your mistake has opened a doorway. Let us take advantage of this opportunity. I need both these souls."

He took a step back and said, "As you wish, my Queen. What would you have me do?"

"Nothing right now, except prepare what you will need. I will use intimidation first. Then I will tell you where and when to take her soul, she is in my realm now."

He looked surprised. "Are you sure?"

She laughed. "Oh yes, one of my spies with Roderick, my dear brother, sent a falcon to tell me he saw the girl and a child taken to the Witch, Aste's home. It seems dear Aste rescued the soulless sister."

Nakia looked at him intently. Although he tried to mask his emotions, she saw a little twitch in his cheek. She would have to keep an eye on him. "Is there a problem?" she said, sweetly.

"No, my Queen, I am simply surprised. I did not know you had a spy with Roderick."

"Of course I do. I meant is there a problem with Aste?"

"No, my Queen," he said looking her in the eye. "That bridge was destroyed long ago."

"Good, because I would not like to think your loyalties are divided."

"I know who feeds me, my Queen."

After he left, she walked though her sleeping chambers to her study. She turned the bookcase and it pivoted, leaving an opening in front and behind it. Nakia entered her secret room. The dark, musty smell of ancient scrolls and books mingled with pungent herbs. Her workroom. Where she sifted through books on dark magic acquired from many worlds and performed experiments. Only the Sorcerer and a few of the pooka guards knew about this place.

Once a servant had discovered it. That servant was given to her special guards, Nakia remembered with a smile. The woman was peeled like an onion, layer after bloody layer, until nothing remained except bones, entrails and her secret.

A small, barred window lit the room dimly, but brighter illumination came from the long table in the center of the room. Underneath a small glass dome glowed a golden ball of light. The soul. It pulsed sporadically, proving it was not strong enough to join with Nakia and through her, to the great Black Opal that powered this land.

Nakia unlaced and removed the scarlet sheath which covered her diminishing horn. Once her horn had been long and unblemished. It had gleamed in a rainbow of colors. She gazed anxiously into the ancient mirror on the wall. These days her horn looked black, as if burnt. It too decayed, like her realm, now it was only as long as the width of her hand. Nakia covered it with a sheath so no one would know. She needed those souls.

She clenched her hands with frustration. If her sorcerer failed there was only one other she could use. That one would have to be forced. The Queen walked to the window and looked out, wrapping her fingers around the bars. She would use whatever means needed to do this. She would not give up her power to anyone.

Chapter 5 — Mira

Mira struggled up the long flight of stairs. The tree trunk was so massive it had to be at least twenty feet across. It was an evergreen, like a cedar or fir, but she couldn't identify which kind. The Witch's home sat way up in the middle of the grand tree. Very little light flowed in through the dense branches. Mira climbed the spiral stairs which swayed slightly with each step, but she didn't have any free hands to hold on with. Once or twice she caught herself holding her breath, closing her eyes and whispering, "Help me Goddess." Then she continued climbing.

Dylan was heavier asleep than awake and she felt out of breath from the climb. Standing at the top of the stairs, panting; she studied what lay around her.

The tree dripped with a luminescent yellow-green moss which lit the stairway. She heard something scampering through the branches. A pair of shining, yellow eyes moved across tree limbs, then disappeared. Mira didn't want to know what the eyes belonged to.

The Witch's house wrapped around the upper tree trunk and rested on several large branches, stabilized by vines hanging from the limbs above. It was built of logs with a thatched roof. The house looked smaller up here than from below. A shaft of purplish light streamed through the branches and lit the door. The effect was masterful.

She took a deep breath, mustered all her confidence and knocked on the door.

"Hello," she announced.

Mira waited. The closer she had gotten to the tree, the more intensely she felt watched. After a few anxious minutes the door opened. A smallish, old woman with her long, gray hair tied back and wearing a long, purple velvet robe stood in the doorway.

The old woman seized them with her gaze. The Witch was obviously used to intimidating the locals. "What do you want?" she asked, with a tone which set Mira on edge. Dylan startled in her arms, instantly awake.

"You have my sister, I believe."

"Do I?" the Witch asked, cocking her head.

"Yes, I don't know how you got her, but I want her back." Mira said.

"Careless of you to lose her."

"I didn't lose her. Amanda was attacked and kidnapped."

The old woman paused for a moment and as Mira caught what looked like a gleam of amusement in her eyes, she clenched her teeth.

The Witch said, "Come in."

Mira followed the woman into the low ceilinged room. She walked further inside before realizing the ceiling was normal height, but hung with every type of dried herb, flower and root imaginable. Some of the longer plants brushed her head. The house looked dark inside despite several windows and an oil lamp. A very inviting fireplace stood at one end and she felt curious about how it was vented, so it didn't burn the tree. She wondered at the irony of burning wood to keep warm while living in a tree house.

A huge table covered with fresh herbs and food, and surrounded by benches sat in the center of the room. This woman was a Healer. The place reminded her of Aunt Rita's house, which she'd called home for the past six years. Herbs and small glass jars filled nearly every space not used for living. Near the fireplace sat a small bed. On it lay Amanda, covered with a quilt.

Amanda's eyes were closed and even though she slept, Mira could see regular breathing. Mira felt relieved to see her twin alive, although very pale.

"Mom," cried Dylan, trying to wiggle out of her arms.

"Quiet," whispered the Witch. "She's sleeping. The poor girl is seriously depleted. I gave her some tea and bread but she needs rest."

"How did you find her?" Mira asked, putting Dylan on the floor.

"She was at the stream. I frightened off the quirot who caught her."

"What did it want with her?"

"Your sister was probably going to be dinner. Quirots will prey on humans who are helpless, but they usually eat smaller fare." The Witch glanced away.

She sensed the Witch was not telling her everything. Some sort of falsehood hung in the air.

Mira sank down on the chair next to the bed, exhausted. Her empty belly rumbled. Dylan must be even hungrier. He stood on the floor next to Amanda's head, stroking her hair and crying quietly. His life revolved around his mom. Not Grandma or Grandpa, with whom Dylan and Amanda lived. His dad was a complete no show. Dylan hardly knew Mira, because she had lived in Seattle his whole life. She was just the silly Auntie who cruised in and out of his world.

Mira didn't know what to do. Could she trust this woman? Deception ran rampant through this house, but she couldn't tell what was lies or truth. Rage at what happened to Amanda bubbled to the surface. Dislike for this woman followed. Frustration and confusion about what to do next roiled around in her mind. She visualized a green balloon sucking up all her turbulent emotions, then tied a knot in it. She needed to focus.

"Will Amanda recover?" Mira asked the old woman who stared at her.

"It's difficult to say. Her soul has been stolen. Amanda could survive without it although she would not be the sister you remember. Her chances will be better if her soul is returned." The Witch's eyebrows wrinkled together in disapproval and she shook her head.

"I don't understand any of this. How can a soul be stolen and your body still live?" Mira asked.

"Aaah, you live in a different world than this one," said the old woman, as she added more wood to the fire. "When I say her soul was stolen I'm describing a magical process. In your world you would describe it as missing a chakra, I think. It is the part of us that continues on after we die, your energetic being. Your sister's ability to love and feel compassion was stolen from her as well as her potential for carrying power. What remains is a psychic black hole in her belly," she said pointing to just below Amanda's belly button.

She remembered seeing the emptiness there when Amanda's soul was first stolen. She shuddered at the memory of the dogs attacking Amanda and ripping something golden out of her belly. "But I saw those black dogs rip her up."

"Was there any blood?"

"No."

"What you saw was powerful, dark magic. Tell me exactly what happened."

Mira recounted the horrible morning. Then she closed her eyes, put her head in her hands and said, "I'm afraid."

"You should be afraid," said the old woman, stirring a pot on the hearth.

"I'll be honest with you. We need help. I don't know what to do next. I don't know where we are. You said we're from a different world. I didn't even know there were other worlds."

"There are many other worlds. I only know a few. Only a handful of people in this land realize that other realms exist." She tore fresh basil, dropping the fragrant pieces into the pot on the hearth and added more water. "So Roderick and his men are out hunting again. That doesn't surprise me," she snorted. "I wouldn't have thought it of Ronan, though."

"What are they hunting?"

"They hunt the black unicorns every turn, secretly stalking them, desiring their power. Many of the unicorns feel hopeless their herds will ever recover from the massacre, so many dark turns have flown by with no change. Sometimes, they allow themselves to be killed," the Witch said, angrily. "Fools, what will they do when they've killed them all? The unicorns' gifts will vanish from this world, beginning the slow drain of all magic."

She went over by a window, above the sink. A small falcon perched on a branch outside the opening, taking everything in. If Mira hadn't seen it hop onto the old woman's arm, she would have thought it was stuffed. The Witch whispered to it and the bird flew out the window. She turned back to Mira and Dylan and said, "My friend will tell the unicorns to hide until Roderick and his men are gone."

Mira felt awkward about having revealed so much to a stranger. "What should I call you?"

"You can call me Aste."

"I'm Miranda, Mira. And this is Dylan." He sat on the bed, leaning his head as close as he could to Amanda without touching her.

Mira wondered if it had been wise to tell Aste about Roderick and Ronan. She didn't know if Aste could be trusted. Still, killing unicorns.... But weren't unicorns a myth?

Like dragons and faeries? She buried her head in her hands again and breathed deeply, trying to clear her mind and find calmness. That's what Aunt Rita would tell her to do. To calm herself so she could see clearly. To let her attachment to the outcome go. To simply gather information, then make a request. Only she'd never actually been able to accomplish all that.

She looked up to see Dylan standing next to a small table, glass bowls filled with dried leaves and roots. He was about to tip the table over, trying to reach something.

"Dylan, come here," she said gently.

He turned and looked at her. "Nanna," he said pointing to a yellow fruit which sat on the table.

"Oh no dear, that is not a banana," said Aste. "It is a hapberry and not for eating. Here, have this," she said, handing him a slice of bread from the counter."

Dylan looked at Mira as if to ask permission. She looked at Aste.

Aste laughed and said, "I am not going to poison you. If I wanted you dead, you would be already."

Dylan, sensing her acceptance, took the bread and began gobbling it as if he hadn't eaten for months.

"You must both be starving."

"Yes," she admitted.

"The soup is almost ready and then we can eat. It is getting dark. You can sleep here tonight. I only have blankets on the floor for the two of you. Before bed, I will try to discover who stole your sister's soul. Then you can decide what to do tomorrow."

Mira nodded her agreement, having no better plan. Feeling numb, she helped clear off the large table.

Aste set out ceramic bowls, each painted a different pattern. One with blue and white spirals, another with green waves and a third was brown with painted horses galloping around the inside. She brought wooden spoons and sat the pot of soup down on the heavy wood table with a thunk.

Aste pulled up a chair, laid her hand flat on the table and closed her eyes. Mira and Dylan sat as well.

Aste said, "Black Opal, creator of soil, bringer of water, breath of wind, source of light and the mystery within. We thank you for this bountiful meal and all the gifts you shower us with daily. Blessed be."

The soup tasted amazing. It contained vegetables and spices Mira had never tasted before, but reminded her of a curried coconut stew. Even Dylan, normally a picky eater, sat on her lap and ate his entire bowl. Amanda slept motionlessly all evening. Occasionally, she breathed heavily or moaned and Mira felt relief that her sister lived.

After dinner Aste cleared the table and they washed and dried dishes. Aste put a flowered pattern silk cloth on the table. It looked gaudy in colors of red, orange and fuchsia silk cloth. She topped it with four, unlit white candles, which Mira assumed honored the four directions. There was an amber colored candle in the center. Aste set a crystal bowl full of water on the cloth. She then blew out all the oil lamps. The only light shone from the fireplace.

"Shall we begin?"

Chapter 6 — Mira

Aste motioned for them to sit at the table. Mira tried to keep Dylan on her lap, but finally let him stand on his own chair.

The Witch walked around the table, chanting in a language Mira didn't recognize. Periodically, Aste would stop to light a candle from the fire, until all five burned and the room glowed with their warmth.

She finished casting the circle and sat at the table in front of the bowl of water. "I have made a protective circle around this house and requested the presence of helpful spirits. Now, I will ask about your sister. Please clear your minds of everything, except your love for Amanda."

She took a cloth bag from her pocket, opened it and pulled out a large pinch of herbs. Aste saw Mira staring and said, "Mint for clarity, yoala to call my guides and spirits, and sandwort to keep us grounded." She rubbed the dried leaves between her hands and over the bowl of water. Her eyes closed and her lips moved silently. Then she let the crumbled leaves drop. They spread over the water, some floating and others sinking. Mira smelled the pungent mint along with other exotic scents. Aste kept her eyes closed for several minutes. Her hands clasped together and fingers touched her forehead. She bowed her head as if praying.

Mira focused on the joy of being in her twin's company and the pleasure of simply knowing Amanda lived. She had always depended on Amanda's groundedness and compassion. Even when living in Seattle with Aunt Rita, Mira had phoned frequently to talk to Amanda and get her support.

Aste opened her eyes and peered into the bowl, stopping once or twice to stir the herbs with a finger. Mira looked at them, but couldn't see anything besides now soggy leaves. She never had been good at this, too impatient. Dylan stood entranced watching Aste and then stared into the bowl.

"The news is not good. Nakia, the Dark Queen has stolen your sister's soul because she destroyed her own."

"The Dark Queen?"

"Her official title is Queen of the Black Opal. She is the very powerful woman who rules this world. The Queen is merciless, killing some for pleasure and torturing others like a madwoman. She is destroying our world with her greed for power and immortality. She is vile."

Mira's heart sunk and fear began to fill her. They were now in this Queen's world. She'd stolen Amanda's soul; what would this Dark Queen do to Dylan and her?

Aste continued, "It will be difficult to get your sister's soul back. Nakia is protected by more than her army."

Great, thought Mira. She was in a world where a queen stole souls, unicorns were hunted for their power and she had a comatose sister and a three year old to help. What could she possibly accomplish?

Dylan, clearly bored by the lack of action, went to sit in an armchair by the fire to watch Amanda. Mira watched as he pulled Freddie out from under his shirt and hugged the dinosaur.

She took a couple of deep breaths and blew them out slowly. "What will she do with my sister's soul?"

"The only thing I can think is that she will try to make it her own, with the help of her sorcerer." Aste's face grew emotionless, but Mira sensed a deep vein of passion bubbling inside her. "This is very dark magic. They will have to do it when our moon Aine begins to wane. The dawn after Midsummer's Eve. That leaves you nine days to get Amanda's soul back."

"And what can I do? Go knock on the Queen's door and say, 'Hi, you've got my sister's soul. Return it immediately or the toddler, the zombie, and I will push you down and sit on you!'"

Aste laughed. Then she looked serious again. "You will do whatever it is your heart tells you to do." Aste looked at her as if she could see inside her heart. "It is what we all try to do."

Mira snorted.

She sat for a long time staring at the fire while Aste opened the circle and cleared things away. Dylan had fallen asleep curled up in the chair. Mira didn't know what to do.

"I will make a bed for the two of you and you can dream on the question," said Aste.

Mira helped pull cushions and blankets out of a closet that hadn't been there earlier. They made two beds on the floor. Mira put Dylan in one. He stirred briefly but didn't wake up. She lay down on the other bed. Aste added a few more logs to the fire and went through a door in the kitchen to another room. How there could be another room in this tiny building?

Mira lay awake worrying and feeling overwhelmed. She felt scared about what needed to be done. Aunt Rita had given up on her only two days ago and that rejection left her feeling worthless. After six years of schooling and work Mira's magic remained wild and uncontrollable. Rita had told her to go home and do something else; get a job, go to college, find a life.

Well, here was a job, but how could she possibly out-magic and outwit a Dark Queen? Especially when her abilities were so pathetic and courage was running short. She slid into a fitful sleep gazing into the fire, still seeing those horrible dogs and the black swan.

She woke in the morning to a quiet humming noise. Rolling over she found Dylan holding a small, glowing ball in his hands. He bobbed the ball of light gently up and down, cooing at it. Mira gasped and Dylan, startled, looked in her direction.

The ball suddenly took an almost human shape and zoomed out the open window. Dylan looked down at his hands disappointed.

"What was that?" she asked.

"Faya," he said.

She felt puzzled for a few moments, then asked "Faerie?"

He nodded as if delighted at being understood.

"You're joking." She didn't believe in faeries. Just like Witches weren't real even though it was clear she was a Witch. Her problem was she couldn't believe in herself.

Her father had believed in her, before he killed himself. But Mom had always believed her abilities were evil.

Aunt Rita had explained that when Mom was five, she got angry with a neighbor kid and blasted him with all her energy. The boy fell backwards over his bike and cracked his head open on a large rock. He became disabled and ended up in a nursing home. Rita said Mom never got over that and refused to have anything to do with magic, even shutting her own sister out of her life. Mira thought it ironic that Mom could deal with Amanda getting pregnant and having a kid at fifteen, but doing magic put Mira into exile. So she lived without her mom's support and love. Now to add Aunt Rita's rejection on top of all that made the ache worse.

Mira searched for what she could have done differently to get her mom to accept her, but could find no way out of that quagmire. She was what she was; a Witch who couldn't control her power and who didn't really believe in her own abilities.

She took the hair tie out of her hair, tried to comb it with her fingers to remove some of the tangles and watched Dylan walk around the kitchen area, looking at all the glass jars.

Yet somehow, they were now in a world where branches glowed, unicorns existed along side web-footed predators, souls could be stolen and now it seemed, faeries lived.

She could feel herself growing more vibrant the further they went in this world. It was like paint and water spread on paper. All her colors could move and mingle. But it was a long ways from doing actual magic.

Aste came in the front door with a basketful of plums, roots and herbs, which she set on the table. "I see you are awake."

"Yes," she said, looking over at Amanda, who still lay unconscious.

"She should wake up sometime this afternoon," said Aste. "I've collected herbs and roots, some you may know: Solomon's seal, sweet violets, hawthorn, lemon verbena, lemon balm and some that only grow here in these mountains: tuain, riaba and mustinwort. Your sister will need to take these until she gets her soul back. They will help boost her energy level, but most important make her less moody. Still, she will not be the same sister you are accustomed to.

"How will she be different?"

"She will not have much stamina and will be very bitter and irritable. The herbs may help somewhat, but...," Aste sighed, "Your sister will be difficult to manage and may be more interested in seeking revenge than doing anything useful to help get her soul back. She will be very angry and the closer she comes to her soul, the more that fury will consume her. Amanda will not be rational."

"If...," Mira stopped herself, then continued. "No, when we get her soul back, then what?"

"I can help return her soul to her body."

"We have no way of repaying you for any of this. We have nothing of value."

"You have yourself. The worlds work in odd ways. There are many unseen strings tying us all together. When we help others, we may not see the direct effect, but our help will enable them to assist someone else further down the road. That might come back to help us or perhaps not, but it sets up a web of intention towards goodness that stands firm against evil. We must all do our own small piece. Whether it will make a difference in the great balance of things we may never know. Life is not like a story with all the lessons and consequences tied up neatly at the end. From our point of view it is often messy and disorganized. There, that is my lecture on life," she said, rubbing her hands together as if she dusted flour off them.

Aunt Rita would have said something like 'karma' or 'what goes around comes around', but this seemed more accurate. She liked Aste's explanation better. "But what is it I'm supposed to do?"

"The best you can. Believe in yourself. Believe in possibilities. It is clear you have great power, although it is unfocused and disorderly. Act as if magic is possible, because it is not only possible, it IS. You know that deep in your heart. I see it, but your mind tells you otherwise."

"How do you know all this?"

Aste laughed and pulled two pots down from hooks on the ceiling. "It is what I do. I am a Witch. I do magic. I see the obvious. And the not so obvious."

Mira shook her head. Folding up the blankets and then stowing them and the cushions in the closet they came out of, she asked "Why do you live in a tree. Are you afraid of being attacked?"

Amused, Aste turned to her and handed Dylan half of a plum she cut as he climbed on a chair. "I always wanted to live in a tree house. So, I built one. No one has ever tried to attack me. Why would they?" she asked, with a wry smile on her face.

"Aren't you afraid of the Dark Queen?"

"No, but I have great respect for her power. I do not get in her way."

"But you will get in her way if you help us, won't you?"

"Yes," she sighed, "and I am sure she will be aware of that soon, but the trees tell me it is time for change in this world and I must do my part," said Aste. Her face looked completely empty as if she were masking her emotions. Clearly, this part of the conversation was at an end when Aste began bustling around and taking bottles off of shelves.

Mira and Dylan helped her brew up the infusion of herbs. Aste reduced the gallon of water and herbs to a quarter cup of liquid. It took hours. Aste talked to them of her world as Dylan alternately played with Freddie beside Amanda's bed and napped in the bedside chair.

Aste poured the infusion into a small silver flask. "Amanda may only have one capful a day. Best to slip it into her food or water so she does not notice."

There came a tentative knock at the door. Aste glanced into a mirror that hung by the sink. It was very beautiful, made of several pieces of mirror cut and laid at angles within the frame in such a way that they seemed to reflect each other. Mira could see the fractured reflections seemed to create a picture of trees, a stream, a dark horse by a tree and a man.

"Excuse me, I have a customer." Aste went to the door and opened it a foot and stood in the door. Mira busied herself cleaning up the table they'd been using, trying to overhear the short, terse conversation.

Aste closed the door, came back into the kitchen, rummaged through a drawer and pulled out a small bag. She filled it with a mixture of different herbs. The fragrant scent of roses, and something like sandalwood wafted Mira's way. Aste rolled her eyes at Mira as she returned to the other side of the door and presumably handed it to whoever stood there. Aste came back in and closed the door. "Difficult customer. A man who does not believe in his own strength. He needs to find the power to take control of his destiny and the courage to open himself and love the right woman. All that is intertwined in our lives."

Mira heard a moan behind her and turned to see Amanda stirring. Dylan went and knelt on the floor beside her bed.

"Amanda are you okay?" Mira asked, sitting on the edge of the bed and taking her hand.

Amanda opened her eyes and stared as if trying to understand things. Her eyes looked haunted. There lay an emptiness, a darkness that had never been there before. Mira realized Amanda's irises were still completely black.

"It's okay, you're safe," Mira said, relieved her twin was conscious.

Amanda coughed and demanded, "Where the hell am I?"

Chapter 7 — Ronan

Ronan woke instantly when the chiala began chattering just before dawn. Their red and gold plumage flashed through the mossy trees as they chased insects and each other squabbling all the while. He walked down to the stream which ran past the camp.

While washing up, the cold water slapped his face awake and he dried it on the nearby jacket. He returned as the other men began to wake with the dawn. While packing the bedroll he realized all his dreams had centered around the redhead. She had not left his thoughts since waking either.

She was no more beautiful than the court women who threw themselves at him. Mira wasn't charming, instead quite withdrawn and distrustful. Yet, he had wanted her since their power danced together, although she hadn't given any recognition of what happened. Most of the women he met didn't have that kind of power. And she came from another land, he thought, while silently eating bread and cheese with the other men, half listening to their banter. Her otherworldliness attracted him. She was mysterious. He walked over to the now cold fire pit, and pulled a chunk of dried, deer meat off the carcass. While chewing it, he tucked more meat into a bag hanging from his saddle.

It was still early as the men saddled their horses to hunt again. They would leave nothing behind. The cask from the ale was burnt last night, the metal staves bent and put in someone's saddlebag. The deer meat was divided up, the carcass buried and the fire pit covered over with moss and quickly transplanted short plants. Ewan carefully swept the entire area with branches, erasing foot and hoof prints. Once they were back on the road, their camp would look as if no one had been there.

A guard yelled out and they stood alert as hoof beats clattered on the rocks and a messenger rode quickly into their midst. Ronan recognized him from his father's household.

Roderick took the messenger aside and listened with a grim face. He motioned to James and Eric, his two most trusted advisors and spoke quickly with them.

Ronan watched and exchanged glances with Ewan. He put his face in Pinecone's mane and breathed horse scent in deeply. He wanted nothing more than to go to Aste's and find out about Mira.

Roderick got everyone's attention, announcing his need to return home. As they packed up, his father pulled Ronan aside and spoke quietly.

"One of my spies has informed me that Nakia and the Sorcerer are plotting against the dragons. This cannot happen. If humans and dragons go to war, the dragons would make us all vulture food. I have decided to seek alliance with the dragons. You are the only dragon speaker that I can trust, I wish you to go contact them and ask for their help."

Ronan felt alarmed at such news. Roderick sighed deeply, then rested a hand on his shoulder.

Such a step by the Queen and Sorcerer was suicide. For his father to ask such a thing of him meant the time grew near to act. However, even if the dragons would talk with him and not fry him alive, chances were not good they would agree to an alliance. "What do you want me to say?" he asked.

"Tell them there is a plot against them and we ask for their help in removing the Queen from power. When you are finished, come to me and I will have something for you to relate to the pooka."

He finished packing, mulling over the news. His father would finally be making the move they had planned for turns. He watched Roderick walk through the camp speaking privately to Ewan and then to each of the men in turn. He knew Roderick was arranging for all things to be set in motion.

As he mounted up and began to ride off, Ewan grabbed his leg. "Have a care brother," Ewan said. "You have the easy job. I must meet with Lady Otalla and persuade her she wants to be on our side." He dramatically shuddered with distaste.

Ronan laughed. "We will meet again," Ewan had never been able to break through Lady Otalla's distaste of young lords. He had steadily been making friends with other nobles throughout the turns, traveling around the land with the pretense of sightseeing and hunting. Ronan did the same, but with his special abilities, his mission lay elsewhere.

The trail through the Azure Mountains led directly past the Witch. If these were going to be his last days alive, he would at least learn more about the redhead, he thought while riding through the woods. He reached the Witch's home while it was still early morning.

He left Pinecone to graze beneath the tree and climbed the staircase. Knocking on the door, he searched for words. Ronan felt torn for the first time in his life between what he wanted and doing important work to depose the Queen and bring his father to rule. Work only he could do, but it would take time to pursue Mira. She would be difficult to impress. His job was to talk to dragons and pooka and do the other things Roderick would come up with. Somehow he must find a way to do both.

His turmoil was interrupted when the door opened. Aste stood in the doorway. He saw steam rising in the background, but little else. As he opened his mouth to talk, she shushed him and motioned for him to wait, then closed the door.

A few moments later she returned and said, "I wondered how long it would take you to come to your senses. The woman you seek is named Mira. She leaves here the day after tomorrow and must travel to the Tower of the Black Opal. She will need assistance on the road, especially after she passes over the mountains. Once her presence is discovered, she will have many deadly enemies. Wear this pouch around your neck and contemplate what you are willing to do to have her in your life." She turned to go.

"Please, Aste, wait."

"Ah, so you do know my name,"

"Of course," he said feeling embarrassed. "I must warn you. I know you have kept yourself isolated from politics lately, but huge changes are coming. They may effect you, because the Sorcerer is involved."

Aste spat, "That vile creature has made his own path. It will be ended. Do not worry about him. I will take care of my mistakes." She paused and looked him in the eye, "Surely, you did not come to tell me this?"

He felt his face flush. "No, you are right, I came about the redhead. Mira."

"Good, take care you choose the right redhead." She turned and went inside.

He stood for a minute looking at the closed door puzzled about what she said. He, like everyone else, didn't find the Witch's riddles amusing. As he descended the stairs, Ronan wondered what he needed to do, to change to have Mira in his life? Would she be worth him doing something he knew was wrong? No, he decided. He wouldn't go that far. Did Aste mean he needed to change himself? But, he would do almost anything that felt right to gain this woman.

Calling Pinecone, he realized the pouch was still in his hand. He smelled it, flowery, pungent and strong, then tied it around his neck, tucking it into his shirt. Instinct told him to trust Aste even as he wondered what the charm was meant for. Some clarity would certainly be welcome. Pinecone nuzzled the bag beneath his shirt as Ronan untied him.

They set off down the trail to find the dragons. While riding, he tried to understand Aste's words but realized there would be no clear answer until later. His thoughts moved towards the dragons.

There was no surety they would talk to him. When he contacted them last, several turns ago, a separatist movement had grown and gained power within their political system. They wanted no humans around.

He found the old road and Pinecone almost flew down it, so eager to run. Ronan felt his loose hair whipping behind him, tangling with the horse's mane as he crouched, his face near Pinecone's outstretched neck. The wind blew through their nostrils and the pounding of the stone road beneath them reverberated throughout their bodies. He loved times like this when their oneness was complete.

After a time Pinecone slowed to a trot and Ronan speculated about how to approach the dragons. If they had all became separatists, he'd be most unwelcome and his news and offer would be inflammatory.

His tutors had told him the problems between humans and dragons began fifty turns ago with the great unicorn massacre. Unicorns of every color , black, white, pinto, roan, bay, golden and even speckled had filled the plains. White unicorns were the most common and the herds seemed healthiest with this balance. Many unicorn horns were spotted or patched with color, frosted or roaned as well, and highly prized by humans as an aphrodisiac. Because of the danger, the horns were only taken from dead unicorns. The glorious herds had been incredible to watch, he was told. Occasionally dragons or humans preyed on them, humans for the horns and dragons for the meat. Unicorns possessed their own very alien magic and used it when cornered, making them deadly.

The dragons flew in abundance at that time. Their number increased and many bonded with humans. The two species shared a smooth relationship; fertility and ease had covered the Land of the Black Opal.

The unicorns, many of whom became so fearless and powerful that they wandered the city streets. They trespassed into the royal gardens and dined on Nakia's rare black roses, which only bloomed once a turn. The Queen, who had become mentally unstable, decided to teach them a lesson. She persuaded the dragons to join in a hunt with humans and the destruction that followed was unanticipated by all.

Nakia tapped into very dark magic and made a potion for all the human hunters. As they drank their emotions seeped into the dragons joined with them. A blood rage rose among the dragons that was insatiable. The joined pairs began the hunt. All the unicorns in the city were slaughtered. The massacre spread to the plains where they were nearly all killed as well. The only survivors were black for they ran into the Black Silk Canyons and vanished among the rocks. Even the dragons could not see them and humans were unable to flush them out. Eventually the surviving unicorns moved into the mountains far away from most humans and stayed hidden. No one had caught even a glimpse of anything other than a black unicorn since that time.

As the potion wore off, humans returned to their former selves. They and their dragons felt appalled after realizing what they had done. They had been bewitched by evil magic. The human and dragon pairs felt such despair they committed suicide by dashing themselves against the sharp cliffs near the Inland Sea until it ran crimson and amber with blood. The remaining dragons vowed never to join with humans again or to reproduce unless the unicorn population began to recover and the white unicorns reappeared. The number of dragons dwindled and the fabric of their world began to unravel.

Ronan asked Pinecone to slow to a walk. He shifted in the saddle and rubbed the horse's neck affectionately.

Many humans not only felt little regret for the devastation to the unicorns, they still continued to hunt them. One of his tutors pinpointed the massacre as the first slippery footstep down the slope to where their world was now. People gave up being nomads. The tutor surmised they stood only about three more steps from falling into a boiling pool of swampy water, from which there could be no return.

After a day of hard riding they reached Fire Pass, the highest pass in the mountains. He left Pinecone, unsaddled, close to a hidden cave. Horses felt uneasy around dragons. Pinecone looked at him worriedly. Ronan brought up an image in his mind of the horse safely grazing with a herd and sent it to the stallion. Pinecone relaxed and found a place large enough to roll. Then Ronan turned and walked up the canyon floor.

Beginning his ascent to the tallest butte, he marveled that the warm rocks looked red up close. From a distance they seemed a lavish blue, beneath the indigo light, hence the name Azure Mountains. The cliff held heat and the crunchy rocks crumbed beneath his hands, making climbing difficult. He put one foot on a large stone. As his weight shifted to that foot, it slid beneath him. His heart leapt. He regained his balance, but kept losing ground. Fear of the dragons didn't leave. He didn't want to die after finally finding a reason to live. Mira was the woman he had waited for.

Ronan began the climb again, ignoring the cuts on his hands from the sharp rocks. After much effort he reached the top. It lay wide and flat as if sheared off by some monstrous storm. The wind whipped his hair around, but was not strong enough to make him lose his balance. He put his hands to his mouth and called in the direction of the coast of the Masay Ocean, using the ritual language with the most formal tone. He stood silently and waited.

A dragon would either come to talk or kill him. Or both. He felt tension and anxiety run throughout his body. Though he sat and did the ancient calming exercises, relaxation didn't come. The cold wind made his muscles tighter. He gave up on his body and did a focusing exercise to clear his mind. His thoughts must be clear.

A beautiful, sea green dragon appeared and cautiously circled above him, probing. He called again. The dragon spiraled lower, its wings full out, gliding. He moved to the edge of the butte, giving the dragon room to land. As it got closer, the gale created by the dragon felt like a storm at sea. His hair and clothes blew backwards, threatening to tear off. The creature was close enough that its belly glistened like the inside of an old sea shell, the pearl color which looks like a rainbow. The dragon landed and the soft stone he stood on shook with its impact. Ronan sensed the dragon was female. She smelled like seaweed and the ocean.

She stared at him, flapping her translucent, pearly wings in agitation, taking his measure. He bowed at her, in the old way, touching his head to his knees, hoping she wouldn't feel his fear. She had arrived very quickly. He doubted she simply flew by and happened to hear him. It meant the dragons still sent out patrols to guard the weirs.

"Why do you call us?" she asked. She didn't give her name, which meant he was beneath her notice. So the dance began. His tutor told him it always came to this with dragons, these days. Humans needed to try their best to outwit them, a difficult task since dragons were born very smart and grew more intelligent by the day. Old dragons were very wise creatures.

"My name is Ronan, I wish to speak with the High Dragon."

After a long pause, she tipped her head sideways and said in a smooth voice, "My name is Gossa."

He smiled inwardly, although his neck and shoulder muscles still clenched with apprehension. By being exceedingly polite, he had shamed her into introducing herself.

Gossa continued, "Why do you wish to speak with our High Dragon?" she asked suspiciously, pink flushed through her wings.

That was good, she felt flustered. "It is a matter concerning both dragons and humans. My father has found a plot against you," he said, quietly, trying to stay relaxed and alert. Roderick had felt sure the dragons didn't know of the plot. They no longer any contact with the Black Opal City, not since the massacre.

Gossa thrashed her wings in anger. She said, "The High Dragon is on retreat for several days. I will give him your message when he returns." She paused and cocked her head the other way, scales shimmering with emotion. That they flickered so much with a stranger she distrusted hinted to Ronan that she must be very young. "If he should choose to speak with you, he will find you."

The fact she told him so much, made him feel the dragon would not kill him today. He breathed deeply with relief.

The statement was her way of saying, do not bother to wait.

He knew his father wanted him to speak with the pooka, but he also knew his father calculated it would take several days to contact the dragons, and that Ronan might not survive. That was the risk one took when learning to speak with dragons. Which was why Roderick had known of no one else who could do it, secretly. Dragon speakers didn't live long lives and there were few of them. His father would make plans for someone else to contact the pooka if Ronan didn't return.

With luck and a little planning, he might be able to help both Mira and his father. He wanted to do the right thing for Roderick, but couldn't stop thinking of Aste's words about Mira needing help. He tried to gauge how long it would take her to ride through the forest and over the mountains. "I will be here again in two days," he said.

Gossa nodded and said, "I will tell him." She shook her wings out and turned telling him the conversation was over.

As she coiled into the air, the wind she created nearly did knock him off the butte. After regaining his balance, he looked out across the mountains. The Opal light faded to dimness. He could see the Great Inland Sea behind the Tower of the Black Opal to the East. The City lay where the sea curved in towards the land to meet it. He sighed at the stark beauty surrounding him, so different from the lush forest. He loved them both and would do anything to protect this land.

He climbed down to get Pinecone, who felt relieved to see him, despite the tasty grass patch he found. The stallion nuzzled him, seeking reassurance that no danger existed. Ronan breathed in deeply, smelling the wind off the sea. They were too high up to smell the saltiness, but the air was fresh. His muscles gradually relaxed and he made Pinecone feel their safety.

They rode back into the forest and made camp for the night. As Ronan ate dried meat and some old bread, he thought again about Mira. What did he want from her? More than to simply have her in his bed. He'd been with enough women to know he wanted more.

Mira's magic had curled around him like soft velvet; he remembered the feel of it as he led her to the sister's footprints. The memory of it caressed his skin. She seemed unaware of those sensations, he thought. The wildness of her magic told him she didn't have much training. He knew she held powerful potential, but it felt largely untapped, like a deep underground reservoir no one knows is there.

He wanted her to look at him with the same fierce love she felt for the child. He wanted to see her strength, to know what drove her passion.

Ronan dreamt of Mira again that night. She wandered lost in the forest, afraid. He kept trying to reach her and could not. She stood just out of his sight, although he could hear her crying.

He slept fitfully and woke early. While saddling Pinecone, he chewed more dried deer meat. Dew had settled on his saddle during the night and he wiped it dry before mounting the stallion. Pinecone danced around, eager to be on the road.

They started off westward towards Aste's home. He'd spend the night in the forest near the Witch's home to be there when Mira departed the next morning.

Chapter 8 — Mira

Aste came back inside, picked up a mug and handed it to Mira and nodded towards Amanda.

"Here, drink this," said Mira, sitting on the bed.

Amanda took the cup and drank, screwing up her face. "This tastes terrible."

"Sometime medicine does," said Aste.

Amanda looked at her dubiously, then at Mira. Mira pointed to the cup. Amanda scowled as if about to argue, shrugged as if she decided not to, then downed the rest of the medicine. "Where am I and who are you?" snapped Amanda, handing the empty cup back.

"I am Aste, a Healer. As to where you are, well you are in my world, the Land of the Black Opal. We are west of the Azure Mountains in the Forest of Analla ."

"Why am I here?"

"Your soul has been stolen," said Aste.

Amanda asked, "Who the hell stole my soul?"

"The Dark Queen, who rules this world."

"You're joking," said Amanda.

"She's not joking," said Mira.

"Does this Dark Queen have a name?"

"Yes," said Aste, "but I will not say it again. To say the name is to invite her presence and she is not welcome here."

"But you said Roderick and Ronan's names." Mira was puzzled.

"They do not have her power nor her intent to do harm," said Aste, looking thoughtful.

Amanda turned to Mira, gave her a long look and said, "You're both out of your minds. If souls do exist, which I'm not even sure about, they certainly can't be stolen. I'm tired." She lay down, rolled away from them on her side and went back to sleep.

"I warned you she might be a little difficult."

"Difficult! After all I've gone through trying to find her...," Mira reached to wake her up.

"Let her sleep, she will need her rest. You must realize you will not get help from her. You may have to drag her through this whole ordeal."

"I can't do all this myself."

"You may find assistance along the way," Aste said. She nodded towards Dylan who stood by the kitchen window his hands stretched out in front of him. A foot above his upturned palms hovered three glowing orbs of light. He giggled as he moved his hands and the lights followed his movements like juggling balls. When he realized Mira and Aste watched him, his concentration broke. The balls of light swirled around him then danced out the window.

"It seems the faeries have adopted him," Aste said with a sly smile. "They will help you."

"What help will faeries be against a Queen who can steal souls and her Sorcerer?" Mira noticed that her grimy fingernails seemed to dig into her palms of their own accord.

Despair was overwhelming her. The question lay heavily on her shoulders. Her neck and head ached from tension

"Perhaps more than you know. You have a choice here. You can either have faith things will work out, that you are here for a purpose and forge ahead, or you can give up and take your sister home. Either way, your life will never be the same again." Aste returned to the kitchen, humming quietly.

She sat for a long time staring into the fire, listening to all the voices who didn't believe in her, mainly her mother's, "You aren't a Witch, I just won't believe it." Mira could still feel the pain of her mom throwing her out, even though it happened when she was twelve. Aunt Rita, disappointed in her, saying, "You'll never be any good at magic until you believe in yourself. I think you need to take a few months off, maybe a year or two. Go back home."

Mira felt like she'd been punched in the gut. Tears streamed down her face. The scent of lemon balm steeping into tea wafted over to her.

She sat and worried. She couldn't just take Amanda back home without her soul and would never forgive herself for not trying.

Mira heard the wind pick up outside and the tree groan in response. The house swayed slightly with the tree. She looked at Aste who was helping Dylan peel some sort of orange-colored, oniony thing. Aste seemed not to notice the wind.

She got up and helped Aste and Dylan prepare more potions.

"I will be coming with you for a portion of your journey, but must part ways with you after we cross the high pass. I have something I must do. A mistake to rectify," said Aste.

"How will I know where to go and what to do?"

"I will make a map for you to Black Opal City. As for what to do, I think you will have to play that by ear, as they say in your world," said Aste.

"How do you know about our world?"

"I used to travel a lot. There are portals between the lands that one can use. Of course they do change as the land is alive. I have a few other methods as well."

She felt sure Aste wasn't going to tell her what those methods were. "Why does your house seem so small from the outside, but much larger inside?"

"Magic, my dear."

"What does that mean? What kind of magic?"

"The best kind, illusion. On the outside of my house I create what I want people to see and think about me. By the time they meet me and come inside most people have their minds made up about who I am and what this tree house is."

"What do you mean the 'land is alive'?"

"In your world you see the earth as dead, static. She is not. She is a living, breathing being. In our world we recognize this and as a result she lives and breathes more visibly. Even this house is alive and growing. She grows to fit my needs," said Aste, gesturing to two extra beds now sitting by the fireplace, a small one for Dylan and a larger one for Mira

"How did you do that?" she asked.

"I did nothing. The land sees a need and grows this house for me, as I do her work, healing others."

"I don't understand, how does the land live?" she asked, cutting up some potatoes Aste set in front of her.

All this seemed hard to believe, although Mira should be the last person to doubt. She should be studying to be a Witch, a Healer. Why was believing in magic so difficult for her? She could believe in little things like synchronicity and your own ability to change your life, but this felt overwhelming. Growing houses and living worlds were Magic with a capital M.

"I think I will leave that for you to discover on your journey."

"Is this true in the other lands you know about?"

"I know of several other worlds besides yours and yes the lands are alive, although in at least one of those worlds the land is clearly male."

"Male?" asked Mira. "How can land be female or male?" This made no sense to her. Mira spent a lot of time reading books on Wicca and Goddess studies, but the whole 'moon and earth as feminine', 'sky as masculine' stuff made no sense to her. Rita always said she had too much intellect, too little intuition going on.

"I think you should ask why you think it should be neuter. When your world stopped thinking of the land as female, it became much easier for different peoples to view it as dead, just a patch of earth to be cut up, sold and abused. That culture saw the land as a commodity to sell, use up, then throw away. That is rape and murder. The things stolen from the land this way, food, shelter and luxuries are products of those crimes."

Mira realized, with a shock, that Aste described earth. The Western World, maybe the Eastern part too for all she knew, had lived this way for a very long time. Too much of the earth had been thrown away until people began to realize there was no away anymore. "So what's the alternative?"

"How much better would it be if you realized the land was alive, nourished her and helped her to create what you need to survive and thrive without the expectation of ownership and then abandonment when she became worn out? The gifts she could give would be beyond your dreams."

Mira moved on to cutting up onions, her head spinning. The onions brought her back to herself as her eyes started watering. Even as Mira rubbed her eyes, she felt herself growing sleepy. All she wanted to do was lie down. She wiped her hands on a towel and began to walk toward the fireplace, watching the room change as she went. Black tendrils moved through the air, pulling her towards the floor. She felt heavy. Sinking in a chair she vaguely heard Dylan cry out, "Go outside. Stinky."

She slumped down and rested her head on the back.

Aste cried out "Ventilate!"

She watched as the other end of the house vanished. Windows and doors that hadn't existed before opened. A strong breeze blew through. The fresh air felt bracing to Mira's face, invigorating her.

Aste stood in the center of the room, her lips moving, no sound coming out. Mira saw amber smoke swirling around her and circling out to the rest of the room. The missing walls reappeared, the windows and doors slammed shut with a bang. Dylan crouched under the kitchen table, shivering.

Mira felt alert and awake again. She rose and picked up Dylan. "What was that?" she asked Aste.

"The Queen," Aste said grimly. "She caused a potion to go wrong and tried to put us to sleep."

"Why?"

"I'm not sure," said Aste, walking to the kitchen window and peering out. She opened the window, letting the small falcon in. She whispered to the bird and off it flew. Aste closed the window and wiped her hands on a towel. "That should take care of it." Aste's face looked unconvinced.

Mira tried to get her to explain, but Aste would say nothing more.

Amanda woke up again, briefly, in the evening.

"Why did she want my soul? Why not someone else's?" Amanda demanded to know before she would drink the medicine.

"Your soul is very kind and compassionate or you may live near a portal," replied Aste, with great patience.

"So how do I get my soul back?" she wailed, holding Dylan tightly on her lap, more for her comfort than his, it seemed to Mira.

"You and your sister will need to solve that when you get there."

"How long will that take?" she asked, scowling.

"Four days."

"So if we have nine days total," said Mira, "that leaves us four days to get her soul back."

"No, yesterday began the first day and tomorrow we have more preparations to make. Amanda will not be strong enough to leave until the day after. You will have less than a day if we arrive late on the eighth day. She will perform the ritual just after high moon, which comes in the middle of that night," said Aste.

"No, I can go tomorrow," Amanda proclaimed.

"Can you walk?" asked Aste, her arms folded and a look of disbelief on her face.

Mira got up from the bed to let Amanda out. Dylan scrambled off the bed, "Walk, Mommy," he said, his face wrinkled with worry.

Amanda tried to stand but collapsed into Mira's arms and back onto the bed.

"Why am I so weak?"

"Because your soul has been stolen and you have a black hole in your psyche and your energetic body," said Aste. "It is to be expected. You will not be ready before the third day and even then you probably will not be walking without help. Now, drink this," she said, handing the cup to Amanda.

Amanda took the cup reluctantly and drank the liquid. She gave Aste a dirty look, then curled up into a fetal position and went back to sleep.

"Will we be able to travel?" asked Mira. She felt worried. How could any of this work?

"Yes, she will be weak, but the closer she gets to her soul the stronger she will become. Still, I must find some horses tomorrow."

Aste got up and walked to the kitchen window. She whispered a few words out of it. Mira heard rustling in the tree outside the window.

Dylan's face lit up and he said, "Faya?"

"No, no faeries tonight. They are busy elsewhere. But the land will provide," said Aste.

"No Faya," he said, clearly disappointed.

Dylan and Mira climbed into their new beds and Aste went off into another part of the house. Dylan bounced. He talked to Freddie. He talked to Mira. It seemed hours before she could settle him into sleep.

In her grogginess, Mira thought she lay in bed back home or at Aunt Rita's and the TV was on in the other room. Drifting off to sleep, she heard Aste laughing and could have sworn she heard Oprah Winfrey's voice in the background. Then her dreams turned dark with black tendrils invading her ears, nose and mouth, choking the breath from her. A shadowed woman laughed as Mira tried to breathe.

Chapter 9 — Mira

"You will need different clothes to blend with the trees and shrubs and to seem as if you belong here," Aste told Mira. "Try these on."

She handed pants and blouses in green tones to Amanda and Mira, brown pants and a shirt to Dylan. She also gave them simple, brown leather shoes with brown, wool socks. Capes with hoods were for the sisters and a sweater to Dylan. "It will be cold in the mountains."

Aste wore a brown split skirt with a blouse and brown cape. which made her look like a normal person from this world, Mira guessed. Aste braided her long, gray hair, coiling it on top of her head.

"I'm not wearing these drabby clothes," said Amanda. "No way."

"Fine, we'll just go home without your soul," snapped Mira, impatiently. "This isn't exactly a picnic for us either."

Amanda glared at her and grudgingly put the clothes on.
Amanda was acting like a three year old. Even Dylan
didn't act as badly. Other than running off while she slept
that once, Dylan hadn't acted out much at all. And he'd just
lost his mom.

She kept telling herself, seven more days, just seven more
days. We'll have her soul back, we'll finish it all and go back
home. If she didn't kill Amanda first.

They spent the day packing food, infusions and herbs.
Aste planned several stops to sell herbs and infusions along
the way. She had customers who lived a long distance away
and there were shops in the coastal towns where she traded
periodically. They stashed their packs with the traveling
clothes and food in a cave a short distance from Aste's home,
so they wouldn't have to carry them all down in the morning.
It meant several trips up and down the stairs, but it would
give them a faster start in the morning. She wondered how
they would carry it all. So far no horses had appeared.

Amanda worked hard to stay awake, but was crabby all
day. She wanted to try the stairs, but Aste wouldn't let her,
keeping her busy packing things. Thankfully, she collapsed
into sleep just after dinner. Dylan played with the faeries.
Aste drew a map of their journey for Mira. It seemed like a
straightforward road, but the longer Mira looked at it, the
more dubious she felt.

Mira fell asleep quickly and dreamt about hearing the
tune from Jeopardy in the background and Aste running
on a treadmill in a tropical flowered, crop top with workout
shorts. Her hair wasn't long and gray, but short and spiky.

She woke to a blazing fire. It felt a little too warm.

She snapped awake, fully alert. Flames jumped out of the
fireplace. Herbs burnt on the ceiling, filling the room with
thick smoke.

Aste screamed, "Wake up!" and pulled Amanda from her
bed. Mira got up quickly and followed Dylan to the door.

"No, the stairway is burning. Out the window," cried Aste, pointing

Mira pulled Dylan to the large open window opposite the front door. A rope ladder hung down. The window had not been there yesterday.

Dylan quickly grabbed Freddie the dinosaur. As Mira picked him up, he clung to her neck, wrapping his legs around her waist. The fresh air felt rejuvenating. Her throat burned and eyes felt raw from the smoke. She climbed down the long ladder through the dark tree, kicking branches out of the way. Shaking with fear, she went down. Her soft hands burned from hanging on so tightly to the rope. Above, she could see Aste coming down the ladder, carrying Amanda. Dylan looked up and kept silent. Then he buried his face in her chest.

It was hard going. She gasped for breath when smoke blew her way. Burning branches fell from above. Looking up she saw flames clawing out the window. They needed to get down before the rope burned.

As she descended the ladder, more fires grew visible. The tree burned near the trunk where the staircase connected, and above the house. How it could be that the stairs burned if the fire began by escaping the fireplace?

Her legs collapsed upon hitting the ground. She looked around. Who might be waiting for any survivors of the fire? As she set Dylan on the ground she gasped. He was covered with spines. He had quietly transformed into a porcupine with a tail. He spun around squealing with delight, tossing Freddie in the air with his tiny paws. She kept her weight on the ladder to hold it taut, astounded that Aste could climb down and help Amanda at the same time.

Mira's skin tingled, feeling itchy. She looked at her hands holding the rope. Hair and spines grew and her fingers shortened to become paws. She tried to keep her weight on the ladder. It took some time for her to realize Aste was changing her. Mira's eyes adjusted to the darkness. She shrank to the size of a real porcupine. She felt each individual spine and whatever it touched.

Aste and Amanda made it to the ground. Mira watched closely as both transformed into porcupines. The look of amazement and surprise on Amanda's face was priceless.

They scurried away from the large tree. It felt strange to run on all four legs. As they bounded away the tree exploded into flames behind them. Only then did Mira realize that Aste had kept the flames at bay, along with carrying Amanda and changing them all. She marveled at how powerful a magician Aste must be, yet how subtle she was about showing it.

They wove between trees, Dylan touched Mira to keep close. He carried Freddie in his mouth. It was dark, yet with porcupine eyes she could see in the murkiness. Aste stopped, rose up on two feet, looking around, her nose twitching. She ran over the rocks to the cave, where they had stored their provisions, and pushed aside the leather flap.

Mira felt the walls surround her as she ran inside the hole. It felt good and safe to be surrounded by the earth. Once they were inside, Aste chanted under her breath rearranging the leather flap over the cave's mouth. Mira transformed back into a human again. It felt as if the spines drew back into her skin. This time the change hurt and Dylan cried out in pain. Her eyes went back to normal and became night blind again. She sat, leaning against one of the packs. Aste stopped chanting and a dim light appeared in her hand. Mira thought about the packs and wondered if Aste had suspected there would be a problem. Was that why they moved everything out of the house yesterday? Was the fire intentional? She turned to Aste, who looked exhausted, yet had held all of them safe.

It was a small cave. They could sit, but not stand. The air smelled clean and Mira felt fairly safe. Amanda looked worn out and Dylan was alert. Aste seemed deep in thought, so Mira kept silent. The light went out. Outside there was a loud, long, crashing sound and Mira felt the earth shake. Dylan climbed onto her lap and she held him tightly.

"My tree is gone," said Aste, quietly.

"Who did this?" asked Mira.

"The Queen. We will sleep here tonight, her spies are out. I worked hard to ensure we went unseen. Now sleep while you can, I will keep watch," Aste said, moving closer to the opening and peering out.

Mira lay down using one of the smaller supply bags as a pillow. Dylan cuddled in her arms whimpering quietly. She tried to comfort him by humming and rocking. Eventually he slept. Something once used this cave as a den and the floor had been strewn with dried grasses that had disintegrated. It felt hard and cold. She slept badly, dreaming of fire.

They woke in the morning and ate a sparse breakfast of bread and cheese. She heard rustling and thudding nearby. They all started with fear. She felt her heart pounding.

A man's voice called out, "Aste. Aste are ye here?"

Aste sighed deeply, looking relieved.

Mira followed Aste out to find three horses with saddles, a fourth ready to be packed with bags, and a man with a heavy, dark beard holding their reins. She could barely see in the dim light before dawn. The smell of smoke lay heavily around them.

"I had a feeling you needed horses for a journey, so I brought my girls."

Mira had begun to wonder if horses would appear simply because Aste asked for them.

"Ivan, bless you. I do indeed," said Aste, taking the reins. "How is Ceela?"

"She and the babe are well, thanks to you."

"Good." Aste turned to the horses and murmured to them. Mira caught something about a long journey and then a question, "Will you carry the four of us and our belongings?" The bay whinnied, the dapple gray nodded her head emphatically, the black stared deeply into Aste's eyes and the strawberry roan snorted. Mira had never seen horses communicate like this, but felt confident they had responded to Aste's question.

"Thank you," Aste said, then turned back to Ivan.

"Aste, what happened here?" he asked, with alarm on his face.

"The Queen attacked."

He was very solemn and nodded, saying, "It had to come to this."

Aste looked surprised and said, "Yes, I suppose it did. Keep yourself safe and I will return your horses when I can." She gestured for him to wait and went inside the cave.

Returning, Aste said, "Please give this to Ceela. It will help strengthen her milk," she handed him a small bottle. "Just a spoonful with breakfast."

"Thank you. Do not worry about my girls, keep them as long as there is need," he said, bowing and walking off into the woods.

Aste and Mira packed the horses as they finished their breakfast. The bread tasted peculiar, filled with dried fruit and nuts. It seemed like granola bread. Hopefully, the chewy texture would sustain her till the next meal came, whenever that would be.

She chose the horse who looked the calmest to ride, the bay, a deep brown mare with black socks, black mane, tail and muzzle. The mare rubbed up against her and took a chomp out of her bread. Mira had never ridden much and certainly not for days on end, but she loved animals.

"I will teach you," said a voice in her head.

She stood there, shocked. The horse had talked to her. Mira didn't know what to do or say. "Thank you," she finally said out loud. The mare simply lowered her head to nibble at some clover as if it was the most natural thing in the world to talk to humans.

She stared at the horse. Did everyone and everything in this world have magic?

The mare looked at her and shook her head back and forth, mane and ears flapping, then stared at her again. "Now that's just silly," the mare said to her, then returned to grazing.

Mira continued to try, but couldn't get a straight answer to her question.

The mare simply snorted as if laughing whenever Mira asked again.

Amanda chose the dappled gray mare and Aste took the black. The roan was the packhorse. Mira felt surprised when Dylan wanted to ride with her. He clearly loved his mom, but was probably put off by her crabbiness, which didn't exclude him. He knew something was wrong with her and looked to Mira for comfort. She felt awkward, but Amanda didn't seem to notice or care.

As they packed the horses, she saw movement in the trees. The branches bounced as if alive. She noticed a few birds, but that couldn't account for all the activity. Dylan ran in circles singing. Then she saw them. Faeries. Lots of faeries. The trees almost exploded with faeries.

When they were all on the horses, Aste began singing. Her soprano carried the main thread and the faeries' voices wove in and out of hers. It reminded Mira of the music of Hildegard von Bingen, old Medieval chant. The entire forest now lit up with faeries swirling about. There were rustlings from beings in the trees who seemed a lot heavier than the faeries.

The light became brighter in the forest as she finished. "Dawn," Aste said, "time to begin. The faeries say we are safe, no enemies near." Dawn still looked pretty dark to her, perhaps because of the purplish hue of the light, which would take getting used to.

Aste rode off through the forest, leading the pack horse. Amanda followed next wearing an astonished look on her face as she stared at the trees. Mira and Dylan brought up the rear. She wondered if this could be what Aste meant about the land being alive. They rode past the burned tree that once held Aste's home. It was the only tree burned even though it fell closely to two others, they were barely singed. The trunk had exploded with the heat and a hole still smoldered where it had stood yesterday.

She shuddered thinking they'd nearly been burned alive or worse.

"Bye bye," said Dylan to the faeries.

As he spoke to them, the faeries whirled out of the tree they sat in and followed them through the forest. Every now and then, one of them would rest in a tree and she could see what it looked like sitting still. All different shapes and sizes. She'd never seen such a vast array of beings. Whoever thought all faeries looked like sweet young girls with wings about the size of a robin was so, so wrong. Some of these looked like demons, small and large. Some looked angelic. Some had rat faces combined with cow bodies. She saw kind, young faces and snake bodies. Each one seemed to be different from all the others. Then she wondered if faeries existed in her world, did they look like these or different?

Going deeper in the woods, she felt the temperature change. It grew cooler and damper, like the forests she knew that dripped with moss and were slightly moist all the time except for a month or two in late summer. She smelled clean earth, fresh and ripe, ready to grow and nurture life. It looked darker in the forest, but even here the light carried a plum tint to it. The tree canopy stood a couple hundred feet up. She couldn't recognize the type of trees. Smaller plants grew among them, frilly ferns and sometimes tiny yellow flowers. Here and there one of the giant trees had fallen, creating a meadow filled with seedlings and glossy bushes using the dead tree as fertile ground. The light continued to be dim in the small, open meadows.

Mira caught glimpses of strange creatures, but they always fled before she could get a good look at any of them. There was a feeling to this forest that she had never encountered before. It buzzed with energy. Life surged everywhere.

After several hours they stopped to eat and stretch.

Amanda said, "My legs ache. What is this we're eating?" She held up the bread, scowling as she looked at it. "Why can't we have real food? These clothes are too scratchy. I want a shower."

Mira tuned her out. Dylan stood eating his lunch, entranced by an insect on a log. Aste sat quietly on a boulder. Mira wandered away from them, walking among the trees while eating a sandwich, of she knew not what, although it was good. It tasted like chicken with goat cheese. She thought it probably contained meat from an animal not known in her world. Best to continue pretending it was chicken.

Walking past the horses grazing in the meadow, she patted the bay mare who raised her head, clearly enjoying being scratched beneath her mane. The horse felt sweaty from working and the horsey smell of her was wonderful. As she walked off, the mare returned to looking for sweet grass. Strangely, Mira could feel the stringy texture of the grass and the young, green taste of it. She turned back to look and marveled about sharing that sense with the mare. A fly landed on the bay's rump and the horse swished her tail to get rid of it. Mira felt the tickling of the insect, the expectation of the bite, then the swing of the tail aimed exactly to swat the fly away. There was a rhythm to the eating, walking and swishing which Mira found hypnotic. The mare had her head down grazing, but watched Mira. Mira shook her head in wonder and walked towards the small stream that wove through the meadow.

She stood apart from the others, eyes closed, taking in the scents and sounds of the forest. The horses grazed, an occasional snort, mingled with head shaking and tail slapping, broke the constant chewing sounds.

The mystery sandwich's flavor tingled in her mouth, tangy and rich at the same time. She inhaled the fresh, fragrant air and opened her eyes to watch bright yellow and green birds flitter between bushes while observing her. The short wildflowers looked so delicate. One had the shape of a white dragonfly frozen in time, another seemed like a red bat flying through the air. In the clearing a group of plants grew taller than her horse.

The scarlet and green leaves ended in huge, flaring purple flowers the size of a dinner platter. She watched as a bird landed on one of the flowers. The petals folded closed around the bird and she could see the shadow of the creature as it dropped down the throat of the stem. The bird fluttered against the inside of the plant, trying desperately to escape. Mira shivered and turned to go back to the others. She felt like the bird, being swallowed by this world and funneled down to an evil Queen who would digest her slowly and painfully.

Chapter 10 — Ronan

Ronan and his horse stood hidden among the pines near Aste's home. They watched Mira set out with Aste, Mira's twin and the little boy, Dylan. Seeing Amanda, he understood now what Aste meant by the right redhead. Surely, she did not mean he should be with Mira's sister? It must have been a joke.

One could never tell with wise women like Aste. Their jokes were often subtle and double edged. All he knew was that Mira's magic touched him while her sister repelled him.

He felt uneasy seeing the burned tree. The amount of magic Aste had used to shield the four of them as well as the horses almost overpowered him. What sort of trouble was Mira involved in? Only a bold enemy would have attacked someone as powerful as Aste.

He could smell Nakia's hands here, but the reason she would do this did not come to him. She was quite mad, but her schemes carried logic, however twisted.

The faeries lit up the forest. He had never seen so many in his life. Aste must truly be an amazing Healer to attract such a farewell party. Mira and the others rode slowly, so he rode around them, staying off the road until well past their party. He wanted to get to the mountains and speak with the High dragon, then catch Mira and her friends before they crossed Fire Pass.

For most of the day Pinecone ran tirelessly. When they reached the peaks Ronan hid him in the canyon full of grass.

Ronan climbed onto the rocky outcrop. He called for the High Dragon then sat, waiting. The wind shifted around him. The early corn fields of Vactona burned to clear away the first of summer crops and he smelled the clean, fresh scent of lavender harvested in Creitu. The sky looked clear and the day felt warm and summer-like.

He contemplated Aste's words and remembered the pooka's ancient stories. Was Mira the outlander they spoke of?

He had met two outlanders in his travels, but neither turned out to be the one. The first, so ancient he died soon after arriving. The other was completely foolhardy and frivolous, his goal to travel to as many places as possible, skimming the surface instead of actually seeing. That man left to travel to another land soon after Ronan met him. If Mira was the one, then somehow she would shatter the Queen's power and would open the way for his father to the throne.

The wind slapped his face as he pulled dried meat from his pack. The sweet taste of roasted deer brought with it the smell of smoke from the fire which had roasted it.

Did his father really want the throne? Roderick said several times he would like to refuse the Queen. He always seemed more interested in hunting, carousing or avoiding doing anything that seemed like work. Ronan had never really stopped to ask himself if his father would make a good king. The challenge had always been how to persuade the Queen to give up power.

Ronan wanted to have the authority to change things for the better, having heard so many songs and legends about the glorious past. He desperately wanted to undo some of the horror the Queen had created.

There seemed no end to her greed. The cream of all trade goods ended up at her court, although some spilled over into the city, to those she found deserving, while the outer provinces were taxed into starvation.

His people were not meant to settle in one place for too long. They were nomads and their world thrived when they traveled part of a turn. But the Queen had settled the majority of them near the Tower of the Black Opal.

The land could not sustain such a large static population. Nearby fields became tired, overgrazed and infertile. Disease overran food crops, animals and people. The River Angouleme ran brown with filth. Change was crucial to the people's survival.

Violence grew in the smaller cities as the Queen's armies took most of the wealth leaving people without enough to sustain them through the harsh seasons. They rebelled, turning on each other as often as on her army. Nakia's answer to the problem seemed always to end in sending more soldiers.

The land needed a new ruler, one whose power rose clean and fresh. He would do whatever needed to be done to dethrone the Queen. Yet he knew his father would have little interest in changing anything.

Yet thoughts of Mira kept returning to his mind. Did he need to change his ambitions to get Mira into his life? Or perhaps his desire to help could no longer be ignored for his father's desire for the throne. Maybe he needed to claim what he could do well. Aste's riddle puzzled him, he hoped the necessary changes would become clear. His soul told him he needed her beside him.

A graceful shape swirled through the air. The dragon drifted downward to land. Ronan stood and steadied himself by holding onto a large boulder. Still the wind caused by the dragon's huge wings made him stagger. He clung tightly to the rock to keep himself upright. Nerves tightened his throat. He had never met a powerful dragon before, let alone the High Dragon. Younglings were all he had any experience with. This truly was the High Dragon.

The dragon's scales glimmered red, blue and green. Most had only one or two colors, gaining more colors with age and power.

He bowed. The dragon returned his bow.

"You asked to meet with me, Ronan of the Black Opal City." The creature sat on its haunches and raised his right front arm, forming a circle with his thumb and forefinger.

"You are the High Dragon?" he asked, trying to get the dragon out of his formal tone.

"Yes, I am called Barinthus."

The dragon was still using formal gestures. Ronan continued anyway, hoping to overcome the distance between them. "I speak for my father, Roderick. We have heard of a plot between the Queen and her Sorcerer to harm the dragons. My father is well aware that if war broke out between the dragons and the people of the Black Opal City, humans would be the losers."

"He is her brother. Does he not represent the Queen?" asked Barinthus, cocking his head.

"No. He has come to ask the dragons for an alliance with him."

"Would your father desire to wear the crown then?" asked Barinthus, cocking his head the other direction. Ronan remembered they did this sometimes to clear their ears after flying. The gesture might mean that. It could also be a punctuation to the conversation.

"I think he would rather anyone than the Queen Nakia wear it. The Opal will make the final choice, as always."

Ronan swirled his hand in the air to indicate that this was how it should be.

"Yes, Nakia's time is over," growled Barinthus

"Are you willing to ally with us?"

"What help does he ask from the dragons?"

"None yet, other than a willingness to talk and come to an agreement," said Ronan.

"Does he have a plan to take over the rule of this land?"

"I believe he does." Ronan could feel the dragon touching his mind, feeling his intentions. He did not resist that connection.

Barinthus nodded as he felt Ronan was being honest. "I must discuss this with the other dragons. When can you return here?"

"I will be back this way in two to three days."

"That is soon. We do not rush such decisions. When we make a choice, I will find you," said Barinthus, and flew off with an explosion of wind.

Ronan watched him spiral upwards. Barinthus looked truly majestic and Ronan felt a stab of envy for those lucky humans who had been bonded with dragons. That was before his time. Before the unicorn massacre. The dragons now forbade such a connection with humans.

He longed to bond with someone that deeply. Somehow, he did not think that if Mira came to love him they could ever be so closely bonded to be able to speak to each other's minds. It happened rarely between humans, although it occurred often among pooka.

His parents had had such a bond. Ronan understood that Roderick had never recovered from his wife's death. He lost himself in frivolities to ease the pain.

Ronan needed that strong connection and had dreamt of it all his life. Did it come from spending so much time as a pooka or had he spent so much time as a pooka in hopes of gaining something to make such a bond possible with a woman?

He sighed and descended, then called for Pinecone who seemed to have traveled farther down the valley. His connection with Pinecone felt different, not as deep and compelling as a true bonding. He couldn't sense the horse's thoughts and feelings when they were not together. Ronan whistled.

Pinecone returned and nuzzled him. Ronan hefted the saddle over the horse's back. It was time to talk with Roderick about his father's ambitions. A serious talk, which Roderick could not evade with jokes; to find out where he fit in if his father took the crown?

He rode westward down the mountains. At the edge of the forest he ran into Ewan. Ewan had been out west on an errand for Roderick and was returning to Black Opal City. Ronan dismounted and stood, rubbing the horse's neck. He asked his brother to take Pinecone back to the city, keeping only his light pack.

"Are you sure you want to do this?" asked Ewan.

"I must meet up with her. I would always regret it if I did not find out who she is and give her the help she needs."

"I will give father the news that you will continue to meet with the dragons. Be safe."

Ronan continued westward on foot leaving the road once Ewan rode out of sight. Stepping behind a tree, he leaned against a massive oak to gather strength from the land.

Ronan felt his energy travel down into the roots of the tree and connect with the energy running through the soil. He bled off some of that power and filled his body with it. His senses became more vibrant. He listened and searched intently for anything nearby which did not belong in the forest. The Queen's spies were out. He felt several of them on the forest road as those spirits searched for Aste and Mira. He undressed and stuffed his clothes in the pack, adjusting the straps to make them longer, then put the pack on.

He went deep within and felt his body becoming fluid. His muscles grew longer and tighter as he adopted long legs for running and jumping, soft grey fur to keep out heat and cold, along with a short tail, sometimes used for communication. He stood upright, two heads taller than an average man, his long ears searched the forest for sounds and his eyes moved farther apart, able to see almost everything except directly behind his head. His sense of smell expanded until he caught the scent of people and horses miles away. His hands became thick and strong enough to kill a man easily with one blow, if he chose.

Ecstasy ran through veins as his body and mind shifted. Ronan had forgotten how good magic could feel, he so rarely used this most innate skill anymore. It was simply too dangerous. He gained the abilities and speech patterns of a pooka. To a certain extent, even his mind became structured the way a pooka thought. This change would allow him and his backpack to easily become invisible, which he took advantage of immediately. He went back to the road and began to run, able to keep pace with a horse.

After only an hour or two he sensed Mira, the child, Aste and the sister coming toward him. Moving off into the thickets to wait, he wanted time to think things out and understand why they traveled to the city. Heading straight toward danger.

From around a curve in the road he saw Mira riding behind Aste. She carried the little boy in front of her. The sister rode in the rear. Something about her looked vacant and terribly wrong.

Finally, he understood. She carried no soul. His mouth dropped open with horror. How could she have no soul?

Aste glanced his way and Ronan knew she saw him, even though he stood invisible. He remembered the time she spent at court. She had been a very strong witch even then. He did not know, however, if she saw the pooka or the man or both.

Mira looked so vibrant and alive, taking in the beauty of this world. He'd realized she held incredible power, but had no focus to her magic. She seemed scattered like leaves dancing in a wind storm. If Mira ever found that focus, she might be one of the most powerful magicians he'd ever seen.

Ronan knew his magic was more subtle, he could make people believe his ideas were their own. Mira's felt explosive; she could distract anyone from their purpose. They would make a good team, he thought. She exuded drama; he held secrets. Few people knew what his magic could do, he used it so rarely.

Magic was not uncommon in his land, but only one in twenty people held power enough to do more than common things like low level glamours or fix broken shovels, shattered crockery or torn leather. Maybe one in a hundred had the power to affect living things, healing or harming. Only ten people he knew of had the amount of potency Mira and he carried. Aste existed on a much higher level. She could summon more power than anyone he ever met, yet her magic remained extraordinarily subtle.

His main gift, which he tried to keep secret, was shape shifting. Even his father did not know. Shape shifters were mistrusted. If people realized he was a shape shifter, his ability to use that gift freely would be lessened.

His brother knew, his friend Stephen knew and he suspected Aste knew from her time at court. Several of the pooka realized it as they taught him about their world. The Queen was too diminished to discover his secret, although she once held great power. The Sorcerer did not know, because when he had come to court Ronan stopped shape shifting. Ronan knew he had met his match. The Sorcerer would uncover him quickly and then he would never be free to use his talent again. So Ronan had publicly sent the pooka he had disguised himself as on, a life quest. Since then he relied on luck and connections to get his information.

While following Mira's party, he noticed a very interesting thing about the child. The boy was surrounded by faeries. Not always the same ones. They seemed to turn in and out in sets of three. Ronan had never seen anyone who attracted them like that. The faeries attraction to Aste seemed more formal. This young one would be a very interesting magician when he grew older. He wondered what form his magic would take. He was startled when the child looked straight at him, cried out "Harvey!" and laughed as if he had made a grand joke. He heard Aste laugh as well. Then the boy's attention went back to the faeries.

Ronan watched them stop to eat. Aste, Amanda and Dylan settled down on a log, but Mira wandered towards the stream that cut through the meadow. He stood at the edge of the trees, invisible and saw her speak to her horse. It was as if a burst of energy floated back and forth between the mare and Mira. Then the horse returned to grazing and Mira walked up to the stream.

On impulse, he decided to show himself. He changed his fur so light could catch it and slowly became visible.

Chapter 11 — Mira

Mira stood in the meadow by the stream and trembled as the realization hit her again. She was stuck in this alien world. Plants ate birds and an evil Queen was out to kill her. She turned, moving back towards the others. The water burbled over rocks in the stream and the mossy, evergreens loomed above her almost like the forest she grew up in, but this was an altogether different place and she didn't understand it.

A forlorn voice behind her pleaded, "Please, could I have some of your food?"

Mira jumped, nearly screaming. She turned to find a large, shadowy shape with long, half droopy ears and big brown eyes in front of her. She peered at Aste, who was engrossed with Dylan. Mira couldn't easily catch her attention. Was this one of the Queen's spies Aste worried about, or a being that simply lived here in the forest?

"I did not mean to frighten you," said the creature.

"Who are you?" she asked, suspiciously.

"Edward. What a silly thing to want to know."

"What are you?"

"You do not know?" it asked amused.

"If I knew I wouldn't ask."

"Quite right. Answer my question first and I will tell you."

"Sure," she said, handing over the last few bites of her sandwich.

"Thank you. I am a pooka," it stated, then vanished.

She turned quickly, expecting to see the someone or something which frightened it away, but nothing was there. Confusion filled her and she returned quickly to the others.

Amanda was in the middle of whining, "Why are we having this bread stuff all the time. Can't we have some real...?"

Mira interrupted, "Tell me about pookas," she said to Aste.

"Ah, so you met the one who has been following us?"

"You knew about it?" she asked.

"What did he say?"

"He asked for some of my food."

"And did you give him any?" Aste asked, raising an eyebrow.

"What is a pooka and what does it have to do with what I want?" yelled Amanda as she stood up, hands on her hips.

"Keep your voice down, please," said Aste, then looked at Mira.

"Yes, I gave him the rest of my sandwich. Why?"

"Good. Now he is in your debt and will help you. Pooka always return kindnesses. They also repay slights threefold," said Aste.

"So, if I'd refused, he would have been insulted?" she asked.

"Possibly. But the important thing is your kindness to another being. Time to move on," she said, looking around nervously.

Amanda began another round of griping. Mira lifted Dylan in front of the saddle and clumsily swung back up onto the horse, her legs aching. She patted the mare on the neck and said, "I'll have to think of a name for you,"

The horse's voice spoke in her head, "What makes you think I do not already have a name?"

"You're right, how rude of me. What is your name?"

The mare tossed her head in reply and said, "I have many names, the one I like best is...," no voice sounded in Mira's head, but she saw a vision of shadows amongst tall trees in a deep forest.

"Shadow, is that what you want me to call you?"

"That is a good small part of my name."

They followed Aste down the trail. Mira looked off into the woods at the side of the trail. She saw no pooka, but a silvery gray wolf paced on top of a downed log, following them. She heard Amanda complaining to anyone who would listen about how sore she felt.

It would be a long six days, Mira thought as she fretted about the pooka, the Queen and now wolves. What else did this world have in store for them?

Chapter 12 — Nakia

Queen Nakia sat in her council chambers. The small, windowless room with stone walls felt unjustly cold even during summer. She would have to see that tapestries were made for the walls. Smoothing her black, white and silver gown, she adjusted the rayed silver crown on her head. As she touched it the lumina stones set at the tips of each ray, glowed more brightly.

"Your Highness," said Gareth running a hand nervously through his greasy, graying blond hair. "The Karsa are withholding their taxes, claiming the gold veins they mine are dwindling. The Collector for the area believes they hide their profits."

Nakia tightened her fists around the paper she held. Why were the nobles rebelling against her when she had done so much for them? She glared down the table at her Councilors, and the Sorcerer, who sat at the opposite end. When had she stopped being able to read their faces? Could she trust any of them? Could she still trust her Sorcerer, especially with his recent failure? She felt anger rising back through her like a fanned flame.

"How long has this been happening?" she asked, cooly.

"Possibly for several turns. Although we cannot confirm that."

Dripping with sincerity, she asked, "What is your suggestion?"

"I believe we should send in a couple of scouts to look around. Disguise them as men searching for work who become friends with everyone, find out what they can."

"That's a very time consuming activity," said Cameron, with the longest and grayest beard of her Council. "We already know the Rosans harbor rebels. I think we should call them out."

"No," said Antonia, Nakia's former history tutor. "We can learn more with subterfuge," she said, pushing a single, silver hair back into her austere bun.

Nakia closed her eyes and pretended to listen as they continued to disagree. She imagined various ways of torturing whoever annoyed her the most. Today it was Gareth. He would be required to bathe in water growing continually hotter until he was boiled alive. At least his hair would be clean then.

As usual, nothing happened during their discussions, except stroking each other's egos or enjoying their verbal battles. Although the meetings were a waste of time, it proved advantageous to give the illusion she shared her power.

Still, maybe the Karsa were drawing closer to open rebellion. Others would be inspired by them. They must be put in their place, firmly and soon. With no martyrs for people to rally around.

Her Sorcerer was another matter. She would have to think of a sufficient test for him to reclaim his worth. Perhaps something to do with Aste. That would be a challenge for him.

"Enough," she said rising. "I want three proposals written up and given to me this afternoon. I will read them and we will discuss this again tomorrow morning." The proposals would keep them busy, but her decision was already made. She strode toward the door, all of them bumbling to stand.

"Sorcerer," She waved for him to follow and left the room, striding down the hallway to her private quarters, hearing his long velvet robes swishing behind her. She caught a glimpse of herself in a mirrored stone and pushed the black sheath covering her horn back into place. Upon entering a small sun room off the main corridor, she motioned for him to close the door.

"Now, tell me what you have found out," she said standing with her back to the windows that overlooked the river. The light of the Black Opal was reflected back at her from the mirrored stone that lined the room. Two small, purple couches sat in the opposite corner.

"They escaped your fire," he said.

"I did not mean to kill them, merely to chase them out of hiding," she said smiling.

"Well, it worked, perfectly. They are traveling down the Forest Road toward Fire Pass."

"How many are there?"

"Aste, the twins and the young child, all on horseback."

"Good," she said, folding her hands together. "It is a pity we cannot take Aste's soul. We will just have to kill her. First." Nakia watched his face, but it looked emotionless. She knew it would be. He knew better than to show any sympathy for that one.

Nakia adjusted the scarlet lacing on the front of her gown. "I want this done. I want it to look like an accident. I want no mistakes."

"I understand, my Queen."

"Good," she said. "There is time. We will allow the twins and the child to come here and beg for the return of the soul and then we will take all their souls."

"The young child's as well, your majesty?" he asked, twisting his robes in one hand.

"Why not?"

"We do not need his soul."

"Well, then we will just kill him as well. Or perhaps I shall keep him as a pet," she said, waving her hand because the matter was of no consequence.

"I think he would be a very dangerous pet, my Queen.

She looked at him. "How can a child that young be dangerous? Surely he holds no power yet?"

"He is an outlander. He will have witnessed murder and my spies tell me he does hold a respectable amount of skill already."

"Is he a threat to you, my Sorcerer?" She arched an eyebrow in amusement.

"No, my Queen. I fear if he is allowed to grow, he would become a threat to you."

So that was it. How did such a frightened man gather the power he contained? Perhaps, he used the fear as a veil to hide how massive his capability had grown. She would find out. "The child may be a useful tool."

"Perhaps, but more likely a problem."

"Well, we will see. First, Aste must die. Soon. Do you have a plan?"

"Yes, I do. And I have just the person to send," he said, smiling slyly.

"Good, tell me when it is done."

The Sorcerer cleared his throat and continued, "My Queen, I must tell you once again, what you want is not safe."

"I do not want to be safe," she said, firmly.

"To insert two souls in your body may take your life," he said.

Nakia saw the seemingly sincere concern on his face but brushed it aside, turning her back to him. "But it also may not. I cannot hold this land with the first soul. We already discussed this."

"Please, just use the second girl's soul. It was the original plan. No one living has ever taken another's soul into their body. All we have is the one written account. I am still unsure about trying to take one soul, attempting two is...," he stammered.

Nakia watched him search for a polite word. She felt no patience for this discussion again. "No, I must have them both to overcome this. My instincts tell me this is right. I have always trusted them before and they have never failed me." She turned to face him. "If I am unable to rule because the soul I chose was too weak or if I die from assimilating two souls, the result will be the same. This land will be thrown into chaos as the scavengers fight to see who will be presented to the Opal as the next ruler. I will have them both, and the Black Opal will accept the two twin's souls as one. I will continue to rule," she said, clenching her fists.

Nakia saw the dismayed look on his face, mingled with pity. She released him with a wave. How dare he feel sympathy for her. She turned back to the window and looked out at the gleaming city, her gardens split by the River Angouleme and the Inland Sea beyond.

She felt excited. Soon she would have two new souls. Then she would be powerful enough to devastate anyone who dare oppose her, openly or secretly. This world would learn she would never lose her power.

Chapter 13 — Mira

By late afternoon they were deep in the forest. Mira didn't like the idea of spending the night there. Feeling tense and anxious, she startled at the sound of birds squawking or trees creaking. Her uneasiness spread to the mare. Shadow began to shy at leaves flapping in the breeze.

Aste was right. This land lived in a way her world did not.

The trees talked to each other. Leaves rustled, branches creaked and smacked together in a pattern she couldn't grasp. She guessed the four humans were a major topic of conversation. Something green, small and hairy with a tail five times its body length, wailed as they passed beneath it, chasing them by jumping from tree to tree.

She could hear the stream burble, it sounded like words. The earth beneath her made low rumbling noises that broadcast secrets below her hearing range.

Dylan slept in the saddle in front of her. He'd been fascinated by everything. Pointing, oohing, aahing and talking continuously to the faeries, but never to her. Then suddenly, he'd reached his limit and crashed.

Mira worried how her mom and stepfather felt about Amanda, Dylan and her own disappearance. House and garage left wide open with no one in sight. How would Mom explain this to Elliot when the three of them returned?

Mom married Elliot only three years ago. He didn't know why Mom had kicked Mira out or that she'd been apprenticed with Aunt Rita to become a Witch. He thought she lived in Seattle to study theatre. Discussions of magic were taboo in the household.

Mira wondered why she still cared about them. None of them cared about her. Mom had ostracized her from most of the family. Even Grandma had been on Mom's side, not Aunt Rita's. Except now, they all stood together. Watching Mira fail at her life. She wondered if Dad would have joined them had he lived.

They stopped for the night in a clearing. She unsaddled and brushed all the horses, while Aste took the food out and passed it around. It calmed and centered her to work. It was something she could control and made her forget the evil that had happened to her sister.

Aste said, "I'm not expecting company, but I want to be prepared if we meet anyone who wants to harm us. We will have no fire tonight." She made a protective circle around all of them, including the horses. Then she whistled quickly three times.

Shortly, the huge, silvery wolf came to the edge of the clearing and easily passed through the border of the circle. The wolf walked up to Aste and she ruffled its ears. The wolf lay down by her blankets, far from the horses.

Aste said, "The circle is for magical threats. She will alert us to any physical threats."

Mira watched the horses thinking they should be afraid of a wolf. But they simply looked at it curiously and went back to dining on the nearby grass and the small piles of grain they'd been given.

Dylan ran around between the trees and out around the meadow and back again, and again. Weaving in and out of Aste's circle, he shrieked with pleasure each time he passed the barrier. After resting all day, she knew he needed to play. He had refused to settle down and come eat.

"Mira, play tag."

"Dylan, I can't. I'm tired. I need to eat and go to sleep."

"Why?"

"Because I didn't sleep in the saddle all day. I needed to stay awake and drive the horse." Shadow snorted at the comment. Mira knew the mare laughed at her.

"Mira, come play."

"Dylan, come eat."

"No," he said, running off again.

"He will eat when he's hungry enough, let him run," said Aste.

The three of them ate granola bread, dried meat and fresh cheese. She was getting awfully tired of the bread.

Aste slipped Amanda's infusion into her tea and she drank it all. Dylan continued to run around through the trees, now and then screeching.

"I'm going to bed," announced Amanda.

"Are you okay?" asked Mira.

"Tired."

"Do you want me to put Dylan to bed, again?" she asked, glancing at him climbing a nearby rock.

"Dylan?" asked Amanda, her face wrinkled up, shaking her head in confusion.

"Dylan, your son."

"Oh," she paused, looking at Dylan like he was a stranger. "Yeah, right. Put him to bed." Amanda slipped into her bedroll, lay down and closed her eyes.

Mira watched her with sadness. She was beginning to understand how damaged Amanda was. She guessed they were lucky that despite the loss of her soul, Amanda had made it through a hard, long day of riding after an awful night.

Mira slid off her rock and stood. She'd be really sore tomorrow and wasn't looking forward to getting into the saddle again.

Dylan was having a conversation with the wolf, who patiently allowed him to crawl all over her. He said, "Ride trees, faya, coohl bugs," and the wolf yelped at him in return.

Aste sat down next to where Mira stood and said, "The pooka you met earlier is one of an ancient race. Most of them can be invisible to humans, it is dependent on how much skill a pooka has. And how sensitive the human is. Amanda saw nothing because she is so weak. Dylan saw the pooka, as did I."

She continued, "This pooka wanted to be seen. He is looking for allies. I met him at court a few times. Pooka also form the special guard at the Queen's Court. The ability to be invisible is useful for a spy. They are also great warriors and magicians." She paused. "This pooka is clearly no longer at court. He was too bedraggled. Pooka do not normally beg. It is possible he may help us."

"How can he help us, if he's no longer there?"

"I do not know. The pieces of this puzzle are not all in place yet. But it is forming. And the time is right for a shift in power."

"I understand when you talk about strategies, but when you get into this 'time is right for a shift in power,' stuff, I'm totally lost," said Mira.

"The Queen of the Black Opal has been in power a long, long time. She has refused to give up her throne to any heir. Her sisters are queens of other worlds. The Queen of the World of the Enigmatic Pearl happily handed power over to her daughter and is spending her remaining days being young again. That land is joyful and vibrant. You carry a branch from that land with you."

"How did you know that?" asked Mira. She touched the small branch which still hung around her neck on a string, hidden beneath her blouse and shawl. Days later, the leaves on the branch still remained fresh.

"How could I not sense such life and vibrancy?"

"Will it be a problem?"

"I think it is part of your future, but things are not clear, yet." Aste pulled her shawl tighter and shifted to get more comfortable. Mira could hardly see her face in the dim light of dusk.

Aste continued, "The Queen of the World of the Flaming Ruby passed the throne off to her son and has been very unhappy with the way he rules. She is still fighting him even though it has been many turns. The Flaming Ruby is very unhappy about the divisiveness between the two, and sulks. Our Black Opal is affected by the Ruby's unhappiness. The three worlds are closely woven together."

What Aste just said was so complex as to be incomprehensible. How could stones feel? How could they know what each was feeling? She let the statement wash over her and asked "How many heirs does the Queen have?"

"The next in line would be Roderick, whom you met in the forest. He would be a poor choice but he is her younger brother and closest relation in this land. However, he has two sons, either one of whom would make a better ruler. She can appoint anyone as heir. The Queen knows it is long past time to do so,. The Opal has told her as have many others. Some of them no longer living because of their outspokenness. Others have seen the truth of knowing in her eyes. Yet, she refuses and her power weakens. It festers and is corrupted, growing increasingly evil to the point where she would steal another's soul. Her healer has become a sorcerer, an evil man. He must be removed."

"I can't do that! I have no idea how to do any of this," said Mira.

"No, that is my job," she sighed. "He used to be my student. It is my work to see that the man unlearns all he knows." The wrinkles around Aste's eyes seemed to sag with weariness and sadness.

"How will you do that?"

"There are several ways. I will wait and see which one presents itself." Aste frowned.

They passed the night uneasily. Noises came from the forest and the wolf snarled periodically throughout the night. Aste got up now and then to check her circle's integrity. Faeries came and went, comforting Dylan when he woke from the wolf's growling. Other things bounced off Aste's circle with shrieking and explosions of static electricity.

"This is not good," mumbled Aste under her breath.

"Why?"

"There are too many malevolent beings trying to enter this circle. The Queen has so many spies. We must be very careful from now on."

Mira lay in the darkness looking for stars. She saw only an almost full red moon, barely rising over the tops of the trees. Could this be Aine?

In the predawn they ate some fruit left over from the day before as well as more granola bread. They packed up while they ate and were on the horses before daylight.

She still didn't know why there should be night and day here, there was no sun. When asked, Aste laughed and said, "Why should there not be a separate time for waking and for resting?"

They climbed higher and instead of the day growing warmer, it got cooler. She'd be glad for the wool cape tonight.

They left the dense forest behind. She glimpsed the pooka moving between the trees, but he came no closer. The trees grew farther and farther apart. Tall, mossy conifers were replaced by gnarled, shorter trees which looked as if they'd withstood centuries of wind. The leaves and needles looked green, but colors were deceptive here in the dim, amethyst light. Clouds blew into the clear sky and by midday they formed a continuous canopy.

Great boulders grew out of the ground. They passed by several the size of three school buses piled on top of each other. The cliffs rose even taller. She marveled at the smooth, glossy stone like polished rock marbled with black, reds, dark purples and shot through with silver. She had never seen such beautiful stones.

When they stopped for lunch, she asked Aste, "Could the pooka be a spy for the Queen?"

"I doubt it. He left while I remained at court, turns ago. Disgruntled by the Queen and her politics, most likely. Still, it is a possibility. Next time you speak with him, ask what his current connection with the Queen is. You must be very specific, leave no room for ambiguity with a pooka. Because of your kindness, this one is in your debt and must tell you the truth."

"What is a turn?" asked Mira.

"It is the way we count the passing of days. I would guess it is close to one of your years."

Mira heard a loud crash in the bushes behind them. A blur of brown knocked Aste off the boulder. It threw her up into the air again and again, claws tearing. Mira leapt up and yelled. She looked for a weapon, a stick, anything.

A bear. It was a huge bear.

Suddenly another monstrous bear vaulted into the fray. It attacked the first one. Roaring filled her ears. Mira dragged Aste away behind some bushes. Blood poured out of the older woman, spreading over her shirt. Her skin and clothes were ripped from the huge claws. Mira was surprised to see Amanda grab Dylan. They held onto the horses. The roan screamed with fear. She could overhear Shadow speaking in her mind, trying to calm the younger mare.

The smaller bear, who had attacked Aste, shimmered into a dinosaur. No, a dragon! Mira gasped, she watched the second one change into an even larger dragon. The two creatures continued to fight.

The bigger dragon growled in a deep, hoarse voice, "Leave. Run."

Mira picked up Aste. She didn't weigh much or perhaps Mira had gained superhuman strength because of the adrenaline rush. The ground shook from the monsters fighting. She heaved Aste onto her horse, then draped her arms around the black's neck. Aste's fingers reflexively curled into the mane.

"You must stay beneath her, I don't have time to tie her on," she told the black mare. Mira mounted her own horse, while holding Aste's reins.

Shadow bolted. Dylan and Amanda on the gray flew behind, leading the pack horse.

She glanced back as the smaller dragon dove in to bite the larger one in the belly, who brought a massive fist down on its head. Then they both shimmered and seemed to dissolve again.

Mira forced herself to set aside what she'd seen and focus on finding a safe place quickly. Aste needed to be tended. She hoped some of the potions on the pack horse would help. If she could find the right one.

They raced up the road. A wall of cliffs rose on one side. Turning off the main road, Shadow crashed through the brush and trees. The others followed. Faeries appeared out of nowhere, sweeping their trail away with boughs and leafed out branches.

As they closed in on the cliffs, the soil changed to stone. The horses' hooves clacked on the slippery rock. The sound echoed throughout the cliffs, causing Mira to cringe from the exposure. They worked their way through the boulders. Behind one, she found a large cave.

Slipping off the mare she called to the others, "Wait here."

Pulling the small branch out of her blouse, she took a few deep breaths to calm herself. She walked into the cave. By the branch's light she saw a space the size of Aunt Rita's huge house in Seattle. Big enough for four humans and the horses. It had no other openings or occupants. The walls were filled with intricate paintings and carvings. Someone once lived here. Now it felt peaceful, abandoned.

She went back outside and said, "Everyone in the cave, horses as well." She lifted Dylan down and gave him the reins to Aste's horse. He led the mare inside and Mira glanced at Aste's white face as she rummaged through the pack horse's bags, looking for the torch. Amanda dismounted, leading her horse inside. Mira followed with Shadow and the pack horse.

Inside the cave, she lit the torch, sending her energy into it as Aste had shown her. Outside a deluge opened up, the sound of it was deafening as it echoed throughout the cave. She lay Aste down on a bed of blankets. The old woman was unconscious. She tore the tattered blouse off her and nearly choked at the sight of the wounds. Blood stained nearly all of Aste's shirt and a great deal of her skirt.

"Build a fire," she told Amanda.

Amanda stared at her blankly. Dylan pulled at her sleeve. "Wood," he said. A look of comprehension crossed Amanda's face. She followed Dylan out of the cave into the storm.

Mira washed the wounds with water from a pouch, then found an infusion that might work as an antiseptic. The worst was a long, deep gash which ran from Aste's right shoulder across her chest to the other shoulder. Mira could see bone on that one, but the best she could do would be bind it. It probably needed to be sewn up, but she didn't know how. Other wounds needed stitching as well.

Aste woke once during the cleaning process. "Aah, dragon cave," she said, and demanded a vial that contained putrid, orange herbs. She pulled some out and chewed on them, until she slipped into unconsciousness again. Mira pulled a thick blanket out of one of the packs and covered her.

Amanda and Dylan returned with armloads of damp firewood. Amanda built a fire while Mira created a magic circle like Aste did, making it especially strong at the door. She noticed the silver wolf, dripping wet, come and lay just outside the doorway under cover of the overhanging rock, intently watching outwards.

Dylan and Amanda huddled near the fire. Mira stood and watched Aste's quiet breathing. Shadow pawed at the floor of the rock cave and Mira remembered the horses. She began unsaddling and brushing them. Amanda joined in the work, but said nothing. After grooming them, she gave them each some grain.

They ate in silence, sitting around the fire. Mira didn't feel like eating. Her belly rumbled so she ate anyway, feeling vaguely numb. She snuck the infusion into Amanda's tea. Amanda ate, then slept. Dylan sat, worriedly watching Aste, Amanda, Mira and the wolf. Then he slept, cuddled by two or three faeries. She couldn't see exactly where one faerie ended and another began.

Mira sat looking at the paintings on the wall. They reminded her of Celtic knot work. The rock walls were red like the cliffs outside. White, black and yellow ochre paintings of dragons and other creatures were interspersed with carvings. The paintings danced with shadows from the fire. Aste said this was a dragon cave; it certainly contained pictures of dragons as well as many other creatures. So did Aste mean dragons lived here, in this world, in this cave? Or did she mean humans simply painted dragons on the cave walls? The cave opening looked large enough for something huge to enter. She felt glad the opening was hidden from the road.

What would happen now? Aste needed a doctor, or a healer to sew her up and Mira didn't know where to take her. How long could the wounds wait before it was too late for stitches? The one good thing she could find in all this was that the wounds only went deep in one area, the shoulder. It could be worse.

She thought about the two creatures, the one who attacked Aste and the other who defended them. Certainly not bears. Or dragons. Unless dragons could change their form at will and talk. She shivered, despite the heat of the fire. Why had the larger one told them to run? Why did it protect them? Mira decided the only thing to do would be to ask Aste when she woke. She turned her mind elsewhere. The idea of shape changers was too frightening to contemplate in the darkness.

Mira fought off sleep by pacing. She needed to stay awake and keep the circle strong. Aste lay wounded because of her. She should have gone on this journey alone.

She fell asleep sitting up, leaning against one of the packs when dreams drew her in. She dreamt of forests, damp and mossy. Standing by a massive tree whose trunk was three times as large as the cedar stump at home. Ronan was with her. As they admired the giant tree a black unicorn came to them. She'd never seen anything so beautiful in her life. She was invited to get on the unicorn's back. They were about to run away when Ronan cried out to her, "Please don't leave, I love you."

Mira woke to find Shadow nuzzling her, the fire still going and Aste stirring, trying to get up.

Aste's wounds still horrified her. Today, they wept a red, clearish blood. Aste told her which infusion to put on the lacerations, then drank some medicine from another bottle. Afterwards, Mira and Amanda wrapped her wounds and dressed her in clean clothes. The shredded bloody ones went on the fire. Her cape they got out of a saddle bag, still whole, so at least Aste might stay warm. Aste insisted they move on. She would leave them at the pass to find a healer who could sew her up.

"You will be safer without me," she said.

Amanda and Dylan watched silently as Mira argued with Aste.

"I don't believe you. You need help until you find a healer."

"No, I don't. I've gotten worse injuries than this, my dear, and recovered alone."

Mira paused, searching for a good argument. "You were younger then."

"But I'm wiser now," Aste smiled through her pain. "I will find a healer who will help restore me faster. Then I will meet you in the City. You do not have time to stand here arguing with me. You must get riding and find your sister's soul before the Queen absorbs it into her body. You must stop her. After we reach the pass, I will leave you."

Mira knew she was right and nodded. Somehow, they got Aste on her horse.

They climbed steadily higher following the trail. Trees were replaced by increasingly smaller, gnarled plants until all that remained was lichen on the rocks and a few sickly grasses. She felt thankful they packed grain for the horses. The sky grew bright and clear, although she could not get used to the purplish hue.

By midday they reached Fire Pass, so named because it used to be inhabited by dragons, Aste said. Then disagreements broke out among the dragon weirs. Aste explained that a weir was a city that held a clan of dragons. Fewer dragons were alive now. Aste said, "I don't have time to tell their whole history here at lunch, the dragons have a long and complicated history. But I assure you, there will be another time to talk about all this."

Aste had gotten off her horse with help and lay down on a warm, reddish colored boulder with a smooth, flat top. The land behind them was forest as far as Mira could see. The trees bled off into mists in the distance. On the other side of the pass she saw mostly open country with meadows, and further on, farmland and a few towns. In the distance she saw a great city with a tall tower, from which a violet light spread everywhere.

Aste said, pointing in the direction they were going, "The Tower of the Black Opal. The Opal breathes life into this land. The palace lies beneath it. That is your destination." She pulled some herbs out of a pouch and put them in her mouth. Her face, contorted with pain, relaxed as she chewed

Mira felt naked standing on the rock staring at the large city. How would they ever pull this off? Her sister was a walking zombie. Dylan was becoming more withdrawn and spent his time whispering to the faeries, not speaking to anyone else. She guessed he missed having his mom present and his secure, routine life.

Aste pointed to the left, "That is Cossu on the Great Inland Sea. That is where I must go first." She held up her hand as Mira opened her mouth to argue "I'm tougher than you think and so are you. I will be there when you need me and you will find other help along the way."

Before they left Mira gave Amanda her infusion. It wasn't too difficult. Amanda was so tired.

"Amanda will get stronger as you get closer to the city," Aste said.

Dylan gave Aste a big hug, Amanda limply waved goodbye from astride her horse. Mira hugged Aste.

Aste said, "Remember, believe in yourself and in possibilities. Open yourself to the magic of this world and learn to use it and let it use you in return."

Mira divided the supplies she'd taken from the pack horse, between Shadow and Amanda's horse. Aste rode off on the black and leading the roan pack horse, taking the left fork of the trail downward, shadowed by the silver wolf. Mira, Dylan and Amanda took the right fork toward the Black Opal, who gleamed at them.

Mira had a difficult time understanding how a rock could be alive in the same way a human or animal or even a plant was. Aste assured her the Opal was very much alive and Mira would understand when she met the great stone in person.

Yet, since she had caught sight of the Black Opal, Mira felt as if it pierced her skin, then went deeper, reading her heart and soul, examining her and finding her wanting.

She shivered as they descended into the shadow behind a rock outcropping.

Chapter 14 — Ronan

In pooka form, Ronan followed Mira's trail to the abandoned dragon cave. He found the wolf lying in the doorway and decided they were relatively safe. His body felt drained with no more power left to help them tonight. Crawling into a smaller, cavern nearby he discovered it already inhabited by a family of fox. They cowered under a stone shelf in the far end, but settled down once he ignored them.

His wounds ached, but as any good pooka would, he licked them clean. Pooka held amazing healing powers. Changing so quickly and so often had left him exhausted.

His opponent had not fared so well. Ronan had made him so weak the man needed to return to his human self. Then Ronan snapped his neck. It would not do to leave such an enemy alive, he thought regretfully. The man was extremely skilled at shape changing, but he smelled of the

Queen. Afterwards Ronan had felt weak and nearly passed out. He lay on the hard rock until the rain restored him.

Now, inside the cave, sleep took him quickly.

The next morning he followed them, managing enough energy to stay invisible because someone else might be trailing them. They reached the pass by midday. He was puzzled to see Aste leave them, but guessed she was badly injured. The mare she rode was working hard to stay beneath her. She headed towards the coastal town of Cossu followed by the wolf. He considered following her to offer help, but the way she glared in his direction told him Aste didn't want his company.

Mira and her sister were in greater danger. If the Queen had attacked Aste so that Mira would be defenseless, then she really did need his help. Aste would be safer going off by herself, if the Queen was after Mira. If Aste could ride far enough to find a healer.

His way felt clear.

Ronan studied the child as he followed them. Which sister was the boy's mother? His magic seemed utterly unlike Mira's, yet he clung to her most. The boy approached Amanda with the sort of sad formality one saves for the fragile and slowly dying.

He wondered what form the boy's magic would ultimately take. He could access great power, would it prove too much? Most children in this land did not discover their magic until twice his age, provided they even carried the ability.

The weather grew warmer as they descended into the foothills. As a pooka his fur insulated him from warmth or cold. The cold did not help his painful wounds, although walking helped keep his body warm and healing. He'd seen Mira shivering beneath her shawl in the morning light.

That night Mira, Amanda and the boy had camped in Black Silk Canyon. He sat on a warm rock near the side of the canyon, watching them eat their cold supper, and made lists in his head of what was necessary to know about her.

He wanted to know where she came from, why she came here, did she have a lover, what she smelled like, what she tasted like, what she thought, would she stay in his land, was she going to confront the Queen? There could be no end to what there was to know about her, he thought, hungrily. He wanted to join with her mind, heart, body and soul. To stay together for life, as pooka did. Not the shallow relationships most humans he knew had. He desired a soul connection.

Ronan waited until Dylan and Amanda fell asleep. Mira was checking her circle's integrity when he made himself visible. She looked so tired. He wondered how long since she had slept, then realized that Mira was waiting to be attacked.

Screeching filled the air as an elemental hit the edge of her circle. Ronan stepped inside her circle walking the edges with her, although on the far side, so as not to threaten her. The nightly attack had begun.

Chapter 15 — Nakia

Queen Nakia sat on the high throne watching a minor noble complain about one of his neighbors. The portly noble's face twitched, turning redder as he spoke. He accused the neighbor's son of getting his youngest daughter pregnant. The noble pushed the girl out in front of him. She looked miserable. The neighbor, a merchant stood across from them, arms folded and holding his temper in. The son beside him, looked down at his feet.

Yet the noble refused a marriage, because the son's family wasn't important enough; even though they could buy him several times over. Nakia smirked contemptuously at the man, pompous, very full of himself. After all, his family had only been titled for two generations. She would have to think of a response suitable for him. He wanted the young man punished and financial reparation paid to him to bolster his bankrupt home. Nakia knew he gambled heavily.

Her attention strayed to the Sorcerer slinking in one of the side doors. His manner of walking made him look meek. She wondered if that was his intent, perhaps it was a ruse to draw people in and put them at ease. He saw her looking at him as he collapsed a little more, then puffed himself out with bravado. Interesting. She wondered what went on in his mind. Her first guess was something had gone wrong with his plot against Aste.

She tried to turn her mind back to the noble. The odious little man rambled on and she needed to think of a suitable ruling. This part of being Queen had grown boring. One day in every ten, she sat in court and made decisions about minor matters like this. A tradition her father started. But she had been Queen for sixty turns, far longer than his kingship, a paltry fifteen. In addition, she ruled only one world, so sat in state constantly. He had always traveled between the three known worlds which he ruled. On his death her father divided the three worlds between his daughters. His son by another marriage, Roderick, had been too young to rule and had been left out. Nakia worried he was plotting to take her throne.

Nakia had plans to claim all the worlds as her own. She would dispense with the tradition of sitting in court. The noble finally stopped talking and bowed to her.

He folded his arms and gave a smug look at the wealthy merchant. She stared at both of them. The merchant stated he wanted his son to marry the girl and help her care for the child. The pregnant girl and the son kept exchanging looks that spoke of a deep degree of intimacy. This was no casual union.

"You refuse this marriage?" she asked the noble.

"Yes, your Highness," he said bowing.

"And you would marry this woman," she asked the son.

"With all my heart," said the young man, bowing awkwardly.

"What would you do?" she asked the young woman.

The girl looked very young, she glanced at her lover, then at her father, then at the Queen and said nervously, "Your highness, I do not know. I would like to obey my father, but that would be untrue to my heart. I will do what you command."

Nakia felt tempted to simply have them all leave. "You should have been able to work this out between you, not bother the court with so trivial a matter. The girl will join the Caretakers and she and the child will serve the Black Opal. The boy shall enter my service, in the army." She said to the noble, "Since you brought the matter up, you shall be fined. All of your livestock shall go to the army, I think. Should you intervene in any way, I will remove your title as well. Now begone, all of you."

The young couple's faces drooped with an understanding that this was the last time they'd see each other. The merchant looked at the noble with hatred. The noble bowed, his face full of anger he couldn't hide. He'd been so sure of winning.

After they left, she turned to her servant and said, "I am finished for today. Call one of the Councilors in for the rest of the day." She stood and left the large hallway through the door behind the high throne, glancing at the Sorcerer in such a way that he knew she wanted him to follow.

When he joined her in the antechamber, she said, "You have news for me?"

"Yes. My man did not return. My spies found his body near the Forest Road. He was not able to kill Aste, but she is badly wounded and heading for the coast. The outlanders continue towards the city." He said, clasping his hands. Sweat beaded on his forehead.

She took a deep breath. How was it she seemed always surrounded by idiots who couldn't accomplish a simple thing like killing someone?

"How did it happen she killed your best man?"

"I do not know. The man was a changer. My spies found tracks from bears of two different sizes, and dragons of two sizes. I can only guess another changer was nearby, perhaps traveling with them. Aste is not a changer and surely the outlanders do not have such magic."

"Not that you know of," she said, shaking her head impatiently. "Well, send someone else after Aste and see that she is killed this time. Can you at least accomplish that? A lone, wounded, old woman?"

"I have already sent another assassin, Your Grace." He paused, looked unsure, smoothing down his dark, stringy hair. He said, "My Queen, I have been thinking. I am not sure we should attempt to put both souls in your body. It is not wise. It could cause your death. I have never even attempted this ritual with one soul before. It is also possible that those of other worlds have vastly different souls than we do."

"I will not die and I will have both their souls. If you cannot do it I will find someone who can."

"I will do my best, your highness," he said, shrinking further into himself.

After he left, she stood looking out the window. Her face twitched with anger at such incompetence. She was also worried about the trouble Aste could cause if she wasn't killed.

She felt lust at the thought of inhaling those two souls. A thought occurred to her. Why not all three? Nakia smiled at that. Surely, possessing three extra souls would make her invincible.

She took the shortest route to the tower room. Her pooka guards preceded her to ensure the room was empty. They bowed upon leaving. As she walked onto the catwalk that formed the floor in the domed room, her long skirts swirled in the breeze created by the half of the windows open to the sky. The remaining ones were covered with glass. The catwalk made of metal grates, circled the edge of the tower and extended almost out to the Black Opal. The room radiated purple from the massive Opal, who sat suspended in a wire mesh basket in the center, held at roughly eye level. The stone was larger than three of her grand carriages combined. Light began to dim, evening would be coming on. The Opal was angry.

The stone did not greet her. She walked out onto a glass extension, touching the massive stone, who shivered beneath her hand. No, she must have imagined that.

"I don't know if you still hear me, but in five days I will have new souls that will make me even more powerful than before. You must accept me again. We cannot rule if you do not help."

Nakia heard the stone make a deep rumble and saw it cloud with black. What plans was the Black Opal making? Dusk would be coming sooner tonight, the Opal was repulsed by her. She turned and stalked toward the door, then turned back and yelled, "You will have communion with me again or I shall find a way to destroy you! If I cannot rule here, no one will. This world will die."

By the time she reached the prison section of the catacombs, her frustration had congealed into rage. She found her sorcerer with Jason Karsa. The second son of four, Jason sat strapped in an uncomfortable, wooden chair, a defiant gleam in his eyes.

"My Queen, I have just been searching for a suitable beverage for our friend here, something to make him understand to whom his family owe their allegiance."

"Give him 'No Wind'. That should settle the traitor," she said, smiling.

"Perfect." The Sorcerer turned to a cupboard and brought forth a blue bottle and a larger amber one. He poured a few drops from the blue bottle on Karsa's head.

Nakia turned to Karsa and smiled sweetly to him. "It will only be a short time before it takes hold." She took the amber colored bottle from the Sorcerer. "The poison he gave you will take your breath. You will wheeze and cough until your wind is gone. Your ribs will feel cracked and anguished, your entire body spasming, unable to inhale what you need most.

It takes a long time to suffocate like that and the horror of it is inconceivable."

She smiled as his hands became fists against the wooden chair arms. "Now this bottle," she said waving the amber bottle in front of his face, "you must earn this bottle. This will return your wind, for a short time, then you will begin wheezing again, feeling your own body betray you, strangling as you struggle to breathe." She watched Karsa keep his face empty, but reveled in the terror his eyes revealed. "For every noble's name who is a traitor that you give us, you will receive a sip from this bottle."

Karsa spat, "You vile creature...."

Nakia unsheathed the small silver dagger from her sleeve and sliced him across the cheek. "I will return after I dine and see if you have something better for me than this appetizer," she said licking the droplets of blood from the dagger before sheathing it. Turning to leave, she felt much better than when she arrived. Now to deal with the outlanders.

Chapter 16 — Mira

Aste had told Mira it would take at least two days to come down this side of the pass. Now, she could see why. The trail seemed to vanish, dropping off the edge of the mountains, with one switchback after another. They walked the horses. Mira's horse slipped and slid on the slick rock. Mira sensed a stab of fear from Shadow's mind which startled her. She was still amazed the bay could speak with her. Mira kept listening to get impressions of what the world looked like from the mare's perspective. Seeking luscious, green things continued to be a big concern as well as being alert for anything that might want to eat her. She wished she could bring the mare home with her. She hoped she could even get home, period.

It was nearing the end of the day before she found the canyon Aste told her about. Slippery, black rocks, like obsidian, formed three high walls. The canyon seemed to be solid and U-shaped, but wasn't really. When they rode to the far end there lay a way out. The shiny, black rocks made the walls look seamless.

They made camp, but Aste had warned them to make no fires out in the open. So they huddled together for warmth and ate cold food for supper. The horses kept close to them, grazing on the scant grass of the canyon floor. She called a protective circle, but worried about being able to sustain it through the inevitable nightly attack.

After dinner Amanda fell asleep. Dylan, curled in his blanket, whispered to the faeries. Mira walked her circle to check its integrity. Squealing and caterwauling elementals bounced off the perimeter, setting her on edge.

She saw the pooka again. This time he was walking the other side of her circle and watching her. His fur looked nearly white as he stood against the black rocks.

"I did not mean to startle you," he said. "I followed you, wondering where you traveled with the Wise One. I am most puzzled why she left."

"I can't tell you where we're going and I don't really know where she's going. If you've been following us, then you know we've been attacked and Aste is wounded," she said, wondering if she could trust the pooka. Something large pummeled at the edge of her circle, trying to break through. The sound sent chills up her spine.

The pooka put his ears back in the same way horses did just before they bit you. He continued, "I saw the shape changers battle," he said quietly. "It is true that I am a stranger to you, so I understand your secrecy. These days it is very important to know who to confide in. Shall I explain my position to you?"

"If you like," she said, thinking this would be a long conversation. Mira felt exhausted and sat down on a rock, trying to look more interested than she actually felt. What did he want?

"My name is Edward Asao Okala Dela Rouche. I come from a royal family, although I am too far down the line for that to mean much. I have lived at the Queen of the Black Opal's Court for decades. For many turns she has been involved in things which felt unsavory to me. Torture, cruelty and other evil. I have seen it before; it is what happens when humans try to hang on to power that should slide through their fingers and pass to others."

Edward paced back and forth in front of the rock she sat on. She felt his intensity as he struggled to communicate with her. It was like static electricity raising the hair on her arms.

He turned to look at her. "We pooka believe the old stories repeat themselves throughout time. I am one of the few pooka at court who remembers such things, but I always believed and waited for the myth to come true; when a ruler is born who refuses to let go of power, the world will transform itself into an evil and sorrowful place. The Black Opal will send out a call and an outlander will come to set things right. If this outlander fails, our land will slowly be eaten alive by evil, until nothing is recognizable and our world falls into destruction."

He sighed and there seemed to be sadness in his eyes. "We who believe the legend have watched Queen Nakia, finally knowing she is the one referred to."

"Why doesn't she step down?" asked Mira.

"I do not know the answer to that. I suspect she is quite mad. I purposely left the court several turns ago, pretending to begin my life quest, while I have in fact been searching for one of you."

"What do you mean searching for one of us?"

"You are outlanders. I saw Ronan lead you to the Sacred One's home. I have never seen anyone clothed so strangely. Your magic is not from this world. I do not know which of you will set things right, but one of you will and I would be honored to assist you on your journey."

Mira took all this in. She felt Edward was concealing something big. However, his story jibed with what Aste told

131

her. "What is your current connection with the Queen?" she asked.

"I have no connection with the Queen. Except to work on removing her from the throne."

Mira didn't trust anyone, but Aste had said the pooka might be able to help them. There was too much weight on her shoulders and he seemed to be coming along anyway. She would rather know where he was than be stalked silently. "You can join us, although we don't have any more horses."

"Pooka do not ride or need horses," he said, straightening up and probably standing taller than nine feet.

"I guess not since you've kept up with us so far." Suddenly, she realized how tired she felt, everything seemed heavier now that she was in charge of the expedition. She sighed. "I need to sleep, so I can ride again tomorrow. I don't mean to be rude, but you'll have to excuse me."

"Of course," Edward said, bowing. "Pooka do not need regular sleep. I will keep watch and wake you when morning comes.

"Thank you," Mira said, going back to Amanda and Dylan. But sleep wouldn't come. How would she keep going without it? Her mind turned over and over. Did she do the right thing by agreeing to let the pooka join them? What if it was a trap? Edward. She felt curious about him and intrigued about the legend. Those were the last thoughts she had before losing consciousness.

Mira startled awake to find the pooka gently touching her arm. "It is time," he said. Dylan ran around the canyon chasing faeries and it almost took an act of god to wake Amanda. Somehow they all got food and made it onto the horses.

Aste had told her to stick to the road. If they ran into trouble they were to make up a story that they lived as part of a wandering dramatic troupe who had been separated from the rest of the family and were searching for them.

It was another hard day of riding downward. At times they got off and walked the horses. Once Dylan flew through the air supported by several faeries, giggling wildly. Edward brought up the rear.

"I don't believe there's anyone there. I think you're a fruitcake," Amanda told her over lunch, after overhearing a one-way conversation. Mira remembered Aste saying Amanda couldn't see Edward.

"Well, he's here. When you get stronger and closer to the city you'll be able to see him."

Amanda harrumphed and said, "Oh, I see we're having filet mignon tonight, how lovely," as she picked at more dried meat and granola bread.

Mira suspected Amanda was more present than she let on. She seemed to have more endurance as each day went by.

At the end of the afternoon they reached the foot of the mountains. Mira looked for another cave Aste told her about, while the others waited near the road.

Apologizing to the mare, she guided her horse through a thicket of scratchy bushes. She rode through several groves of aspen-like trees before finding a cave. "Please wait," she said to Shadow, then got off and warily entered the cave. It smelled earthy. She heard a rustling noise. Something lived there.

Mira gasped and began backing up. She pulled the pearl branch out of her shirt to light the cave and was blinded by the golden brilliance of light reflecting off the walls. A screeching sound pierced her ears. She saw movement from the far corner.

"Who are you and why do you invade my home?" shrieked the dark shape rushing towards her.

"Oh, excuse me!" Her heart pounded. Stumbling toward the cave's entrance, she babbled in fear, "I have made a mistake. I was told no one lived in this cave. I must have found the wrong one."

Slowly her vision returned and she saw a huge bird, taller than her. It had a head like an eagle covered by soft, tawny feathers and front feet with wicked talons. The back half of the creature was a lion ending with a long tail that whipped the air, furiously.

"Who are you and what are you doing in my cave?" the voice repeated.

"My name is Mira. We're looking for a place to spend the night," she said, trying not to reveal so much, but unable to stop, knowing she was in the wrong. "Someone is chasing us and we need a place to be safe. My sister is sick." She glanced at Shadow, a few feet away, who looked ready to flee.

"Who is chasing you?"

Mira hesitated. She sensed there could be no lying to this creature. There was magic at work here. Yet, how could she know if this being would be on her side? She said, "I cannot tell you."

"Then you must leave and forget you have seen this place."

She felt relieved, but where would they stay tonight? Rustling came from the bushes behind her and she jumped. Mira moved so she could see both the creature in the cave and what moved through the bushes. Edward appeared out of the brambles. He saw the creature and bowed.

"Ah, Edward, I remember you," said the creature.

"Good day Griffin. Are you well?"

"Yes, ever the polite pooka, are we?"

"I do my best," he said bowing again.

Mira sensed an undercurrent of sarcasm, and possibly hostility. She tried to remember something, anything, about griffins, but came up blank.

"Can you help us? Are there any more caves around here we could stay in?" asked Edward.

"This is the only cave larger than a rabbit in this area. Whose side are you on?"

Griffin asked him.

"I am on the side of the Black Opal and this land," he said.

"What about the Queen?" Griffin asked.

"I have no Queen," he said.

"You swear this on your father's head, and I do know who your father is," said Griffin pointedly.

"I swear on my father's head."

"What about this woman and her sister?"

"The Queen is trying to harm them," said Edward.

The creature looked thoughtful. "How many of you are there?" she asked Mira.

"My sister and her son, Edward and two horses," she said.

"Well, never let it be said that a griffin doesn't offer hospitality when it is needed. Get your companions. I do not have room for you inside, but you may stay just outside my cave and share my protection."

Mira bowed and felt relieved to leave, even to get Amanda and Dylan. Maybe they'd be safer hiding in the bushes for the night. Edward stayed behind speaking with Griffin. Could Griffin could be trusted? What past did Griffin and Edward share?

Dylan and Amanda followed her to the cave. Edward nodded at them, then vanished into the bushes.

Mira's body quivered as an eerie energy erupted all around her. It crawled on her skin and felt like being covered with insects.

Chapter 17 — Mira

Mira led the two horses to some tall, glossy bushes. She tried pinpointing the source of the energy. It felt very powerful, seemingly everywhere. The magic must be Griffin's. Why hadn't she sensed it when first arriving here? She dropped the reins, leaving the horses for Amanda to care for.

Walking a circle between the bushes and mounds of brambles, she tried to center and ground herself. She began to feel stable, whole again, connected to this land. As the life of this world rose up inside her, she felt a beetle crawling across a nearby rock and two small birds watching her curiously from the top of some brambles. Mira could feel the land's energy flowing through some scraggly shrubs and over the slow bulk of the small boulder while walking past it. Binding herself to this land, she wove in and out of the huge boulders and prickly shrubs, the dirt and the thorns, making them part of her circle.

Mira joined her circle to the wards she felt around the mouth of Griffin's cave. Griffin's magic flowed through the circle and Mira's own magic rushed into the wards around the cave mouth. The two different types of magic mingled to make a stronger whole. Griffin watched her. Was it necessary to ask permission to do such a thing? It came so naturally and unexpectedly. Griffin disappeared back into her cave.

While Mira circled, she watched Amanda pull the halters, saddles and bags off the horses. The mares rolled in the dusty soil, luxuriating in being unencumbered again.

When finished, Mira grabbed the bedrolls and looked for a place to lay them out.

Amanda stood staring, watching her work. "This is it?" she asked, hands on her hips.

Mira looked at her. "It's getting dark. There are no more caves nearby. This is the most protection I could find."

Amanda pointed to the mouth of the cave, which was glowing.

"Griffin lives there and doesn't want us inside. I think she's protecting babies. She's being kind enough letting us stay this close."

"What about my baby?" asked Amanda, agitated.

"You haven't been acting like he's your baby," Mira wanted to say, but squashed the sarcastic remark before it left her mouth, feeling very virtuous. "This is our only choice right now," she repeated, spreading out their blankets.

Dylan found the saddlebag with food and began munching on some very stale, very crunchy granola bread.

"Are we going to have a fire?" demanded Amanda.

Mira knew Amanda would continue trying to pick a fight with her. She struggled not to fall for it. Closing her eyes and taking a deep breath she walked up to her sister and stood with an inch of space between their faces.

She said quietly "I don't understand all of what's going on with you. Right now, we have bigger worries than being cold. Like the Queen is trying to kill us, for example. She already possesses your soul, but apparently that isn't enough. She tried to kill Aste. I don't know what she'll do next. Whatever pathetic magic I can do, and perhaps the pooka and maybe this griffin, might be all that saves our sorry hides tonight. Dylan deserves better, but he's dealing with it. I suggest you try to do the same." Mira glared down Amanda until she looked away. "Build a fire," Mira ordered. "At least we'll be warm. She seems to know how to find us anyway."

Edward appeared from behind some brambles. Mira had nearly forgotten about him. He carried long, cream colored roots and gave one to Dylan, and one to Amanda, who looked startled to see him, and one to Mira. "This is suenna. Eat," he said, "it will strengthen you." The root tasted slightly sweet, somewhat like a carrot, but with more of an earthy burdock flavor.

Amanda sat down on her blankets, sulking, although she ate the root while she stared at Edward. She looked stronger today than yesterday. The fact she felt willing to pick a fight was probably a good sign.

Amanda finally got up and gave some grain to the horses and brushed them. Mira watched her talking to them. She wondered if Amanda's horse talked to her. Her twin had certainly grown attached to the mare.

Mira grabbed some dried meat and collapsed on her blanket. She needed to rest while she could. She wondered why Edward lounged on a small boulder, watching the sky.

"She will attack us tonight, won't she?" asked Mira.

"Probably. She has every night you have been out on the trail. I believe she is trying to wear us down. There have been no killing attacks on you, yet. Only on Aste."

"Did she attack us last night?" asked Mira, realizing with alarm she'd slept the whole night through.

"Yes. Your circle held off the ethereals and elementals and I repelled the physical attacks she sent."

"Thank you. I didn't even know, didn't even ask."

"You were very tired," he said, gently, while looking at her with his head cocked to one side.

She finished her food and then caught herself chewing a fingernail. Even the budding faith in her own magic had not increased the power enough. Mira felt herself becoming stronger, but the Queen was relentless. There seemed to be no hiding from her. Mira didn't feel potent enough for a battle, but there would be another one tonight, nonetheless.

As darkness came, Mira watched low, damp clouds gather around them. "Is this normal?" she asked Edward.

"The weather is often foggy here. It blows in from the coast and becomes trapped close to the roots of the mountains."

"Will it help us or hinder us?"

"Who can say?" he seemed completely unconcerned.

Mira was tired of the enigmatic pooka. She felt sick of Amanda's crankiness and worn out with feeling responsible for Dylan. Her cold skin was glued with dirt and oil. Her legs and butt still ached from riding all day. She'd made one wrong decision after another since the theft of Amanda's soul and couldn't think of any way out of this, let alone a good way.

Amanda settled on her blanket at the edge of the fire and far away from Mira. Dylan slept with his trio of faeries curled up with him, Mira vaguely wondered why they always came in threes as the turmoil and fear of the impending attack roiled around in the back of her brain.

She watched sleepily as the haze and vapor wafted through their camp and made the fire seem farther away. The smoke rose clear and hot in contrast to the mist which carried a slight purplish cast making everything seem eerie. The flames and the fog danced around each other, fighting for dominance.

Mira heard a voice in the distance. "Amanda, Miranda, where are you?" called the vaguely familiar voice sounding worried.

"Mom?" called Amanda back.

Mira sat up with a start. She realized it couldn't be real. When did her mom ever worry about her? "It can't be Mom, Amanda. She's not here."

"It must be her," said Amanda, standing.

Her stomach knotted in anticipation of the attack. She stood slowly, stretching and trying to calm herself again. As she reached for the connection with the land, it slipped away. She needed to anchor her circle. She saw Amanda move away from the fire, towards the edge of the circle.

"No," said Edward breaking the silence. "The voice is a demon. Stay together and by the fire. Keep your magic tied to Griffin's."

Mira turned, but he'd vanished. Completely. Like he never existed.

Mira strode to the other side of the fire where Amanda stood and Dylan lay. She took Amanda's hands to summon whatever power Amanda had. They stood over Dylan. The faeries hovered around him, also ready for action.

Shrieking from the bushes made her heart jump. The horses neighed with fear. Mira sent a message to her mare. Calm, I'm here. Calm. Why hadn't she brought them into the circle?

She focused on keeping the lines strong and closed. Large winged shapes, about human size, battered the edges. She felt sharp pains on her head, back and arms as if their attacks physically struck her body from outside the barrier. The large, golden dome of her circle was penetrated by claws and fangs, causing streaks of blackness to drip down the sides. The scraping that accompanied the assaults sounded like fingernails on a chalkboard.

Mira hyperventilated, trying to breathe in calm. The energy flowed up through her feet but stagnated in her chest. She redoubled her efforts to not panic. Energy shot through her and out into the circle, as if the soil beneath her rushed in to help. She nearly cried with relief as the blackness on the circle returned to gold. Their shield became complete again.

The voices began in earnest. She heard Aunt Rita calling for help outside the bubble. Even her father, long dead. Mira held tight onto Amanda, who wanted to go to him. It was as if the demons picked through their brains trying to find the right lever. Their mother sounded tortured.

"It's a trick, Edward said to stay in the circle." She heard Aste, calling for her. It sounded so real, even she was tempted.

The next two or three hours Mira stood, letting go of Amanda only to add more wood on the fire to keep the energy going. She heard Edward say, "They have gone now. You can step away from the fire."

Doubt swam up inside her. Sweat from exertion and the heat of the fire ran off her forehead. She was weakening. Mira looked over at the faeries protecting Dylan and one of them said, "No."

"Show yourself," Mira yelled out.

She heard Aste scream.

Mira struggled to keep their shield intact against the demons trying to wrench it apart. Mira knew she'd already borrowed the small amount of energy that Amanda held. After a time Amanda looked at her and said, "Sorry, can't help anymore." Amanda dropped to her blanket in exhaustion, covering her head to muffle the screaming.

Once, Mira looked and saw Griffin standing in the cave door, holding something limp in her mouth, and shrieking like an eagle. Then the fog obscured her again.

Mira kept standing. Wood cracked and she heard heavy thudding. Something large trampled among the thickets. The horses screamed in pain and fear. Mira caught an image from her mare of something massive, dark and horned attacking them. She felt helpless and hoped Edward could protect the horses.

Mira closed her eyes for a moment to focus on the circle. She felt a rush of movement, then pain in her ribs. She cried out. Lying against a rock she saw the massive dark shape which had rolled through the fire and struck her.

Then something even larger and completely black attacked it.

The first beast roared and fell into the flames. A smell of burnt flesh rushed into Mira's nose. The first creature tumbled out of the blaze and faced the larger beast. The fight was now inside her circle, the defenses crumbled.

Mira grabbed Dylan and backed away from the fire, Amanda beside them. She struggled to reform the circle. The larger beast stood with its back to Mira and Amanda. They kept backing away from the fire into the bushes, but still within the circle. Mira moved the three of them towards the mouth of the cave.

Huge leathery wings, like bats, beat the air. Both beasts circled, looking for the best opening to attack. Their bodies were shaped like gorillas and just as hairy. Faces squashed flat like a bulldog with big, bulging eyes, protruding teeth and bat-like ears. The smaller one's wings were crushed and bloody.

Demons. They must be the demons Edward talked about, but why would there be a demon protecting them?

Mira kept backing up, maintaining and enlarging the circle against other invaders. The two demons circled the fire and dove, sharp claws raking each other. Where could Edward be?

She stepped in a hole in the ground near where the horses had grazed. The glossy bushes had been ripped from the earth and scattered. The horses were nowhere in sight. Mira felt her Shadow's fear. She was still alive and running.

Griffin stood in the mouth of her cave. The smaller demon dripped with thick, yellow goo. The larger demon covered with claw marks oozed the same yellow blood.

The small one lunged toward Mira. The larger demon redirected the momentum of the attack, throwing the beast against the rock wall. Stones showered from above. The demon's impact rumbled through the earth, out of proportion to its size.

The large demon stood on the small one. A tawny blur shot past her from behind. Mira cringed as Griffin attacked. Griffin flew, ripped and clawed with her beak, talons and lion claws faster than the small demon could move. The larger kept the small demon pinned so Griffin could do her work. Griffin's screeching and growling was terrible to hear.

The attack seemed to take forever. Mira smelled sulfur. Dylan tried to watch the carnage, the faeries covered his eyes.

Mira held the circle. Ethereals still assaulted the circle and the attempted intrusions sounded like glass vibrating as they continued to search for weaknesses.

The small demon thrashed. Mira watched Griffin pull back from the throat, pause for a breath then plunged her sharp beak into the back of the demon's neck. There was a sickening snap and crunch.

Mira heard labored snorts. Both Griffin and the large demon leapt back. The small demon sizzled, then exploded into flame. Ashes blew on the breeze.

The large demon looked at Griffin and some sort of communication took place before it fled into the darkness.

Griffin stalked past them and said gruffly, "It is dead. Rebuild your fire, the night is not over yet."

Mira staggered, exhausted back to the fire, carefully skirting around what remained of the small demon. Its body lay next to the fire. She took a long branch and pushed the coals closer to burn the charred remains.

Amanda piled on more wood, and Dylan threw little sticks on the fire. Everyone stayed well away from the dead demon. The glossy shrubs, battered and broken from the fight, burned well. Their smoke smelled oily and pungent, like eucalyptus. The scent helped ground her again.

She tried not to look at the demon's remains while continuing to tend the fire. Mira concentrated on her circle and calming herself. Her arms shook with fear. That thing had nearly killed them. There would have been no way she alone could have stopped it.

Her eyes met Amanda's horror-filled ones. Her sister sat on the blanket holding Dylan to rock him. The faeries circled around them, singing soothingly. This act was one of the first motherly things Amanda had done since she lost her soul.

Edward's continued absence combined with the tortured voices of family and friends, compromised her ability to be present and hold the circle.

Griffin spent most of the night standing in the doorway to her cave. She looked like a granite statue.

Amanda dozed, waking now and then, yelling. Dylan whimpered in his fitful sleep.

Mira tended the fire, pacing and holding the circle. She wondered where Edward was. Why had the large demon defended them and was it connected with Edward?

The smaller demon's remains finished roasting into charred chunks. The smell of the burning flesh and bones made her queasy.

As Mira stood against the rock wall by the mouth of Griffin's cave, she also started to doze off. Then jolted awake. The demon's carcass shifted and became engulfed in an aberrant blue flame. It sent up a screeching orange flare that lit the sky like streaking fireworks. Mira shuddered with horror. She walked around the circle, shaking. Dylan bolted awake and sobbed. Amanda tried to comfort him.

Morning birds started calling. Lilac tinted the sky, setting off coral and pink clouds. Mira heard a thud a few yards away and looked up to see Edward, dust himself off and walk towards the dwindling fire.

"Tripped," he said, trying to warm his paws by the embers in a very human like gesture. She noticed where large chunks of hair had been torn out and bloody patches of skin remained. He looked as exhausted as she felt.

"What happened to you?" she asked. Again, she wondered if he was connected to the demon who defended them.

"I will heal," he said. "And we are all alive?"

"Yes, but the horses are gone," she said.

"Perhaps they'll return."

"I hope so," said Mira. "We can't get far without them. And I want to get far far away from here."

"It is not this place that is the problem. Your troubles will continue to follow you."

She sighed. He was right, but she would still be glad to leave the demon behind. She pushed the thought from her mind and almost gagged, remembering the bloody, violent death. She wanted to never eat meat again, the smell would always remind her of that demon.

Griffin reappeared at the door of her cave. Her tawny fur marred by cuts and torn skin. "You did well last night," she said to Mira.

Mira nodded in response. Dylan wandered over to talk to Griffin, but Mira couldn't hear what he said. Griffin bowed her head, and Dylan touched the feathers of her wings with an awestruck look on his face. Griffin seemed to be smiling at him. Did beaks smile?

Amanda got up and handed her some granola bread, but Mira shook her head no. She offered some to Edward, who took it, and then some to Griffin.

"No, I won't eat until my eggs are hatched," she bowed in thanks. "I prefer more meat to grain in my diet anyway."

Mira wandered over to the mouth of the cave, mostly to get away from the fire and its contents. She was still shaky from the attack and being near Griffin felt safe. "I've never met a griffin before yesterday. Do all of you live in caves?"

"Oh no, many of us nest high in the mountains. It is a matter of preference. I like a nice, dry cave to raise babies in. And as the pooka so accurately said, there are many foul things about these days. You felt the wards placed around the mouth of this cave."

"Yes, I felt them, but they felt old and unused."

"So they would, they are not meant for you. They are meant for evil things, such as the Queen's spies and assassins."

"Why would the Queen want to harm you?" asked Mira, confused.

"Does she truly not know?" Griffin asked Edward.

He shook his head, "She does not know."

Griffin turned to Mira and said, "Since the beginning of time people have found gold and jewels in the land. Those with power gained more gold and jewels than those with little power."

Mira nodded, and leaned against a wall. She was ready for a story.

"For turns upon turns the griffins guarded the gold and jewels. Many of those riches were gathered at the Palace of the Black Opal. The griffins took their work seriously. Never did a thief get past us."

"After a time, however, it became clear to us that the Queen did not fully appreciate our work. It became ever clearer that she had no intention of naming an heir to renew the vitality of the land and keep the connection with the Black Opal fresh. We stood among those who asked her to step down."

"When she refused we left the city taking as much gold and jewels as we could carry, to hold in trust for the next ruler. We set up a network of thieves who have slowly siphoned off the rest of it for us. More than three-fourths of the Queen's Treasury has made its way out of the palace and is distributed around the country side, held in trust."

She continued, "There is an old legend that griffins always guard gold Not all griffins guard gold and not all gold is guarded by griffins. In my case, it is. Some of her spies have followed me. Over the turns, as the Queen became more evil, her treasury shrank and she became more desperate. We await the next ruler, as do the pooka," Griffin said looking intently at Edward. He affirmed this. Griffin looked thoughtful. "You have earned a right to see this. Please come in." She stood back and gestured smoothly with one of her wings, beckoning them inside the glowing room.

"These walls," said Mira, slowly understanding, "are made of gold."

"Yes."

She leaned forward and looked around Griffin's cave in wonder. Everywhere was gold inlay, mosaics of gold and decorated with gemstones. This cave looked as amazing as the dragon cave, but with completely different art work. Herds of unicorns in many colors danced across the walls, filling grasslands. Dragons in all shapes and hues wove around clouds in the purple light. Two golden moons moved across that sky. Mira was sure she would never see so much gold again in her entire life. "Did you do this?"

"Yes, one needs something to do while eggs hatch."

Mira shook her head in wonder. The horror of the night melted a little by looking at such beautiful art. "Will the Queen give up her throne, do you think?"

"Not willingly. However she will give it up. The land must have a new ruler, a new partner, or it will fail. One thing for certain, she will not be using this gold to buy more evil," said Griffin flapping her wings with great satisfaction as she settled on her eggs.

"Why are you telling us this? How do you know we aren't spies?"

Griffin gave a grim, growling laugh. "After her attack of you last night and my reading of you, I am very satisfied that you aren't. I feel a great anger towards the Queen from this one," she said, nodding at Amanda. "We clearly face the same direction."

Three faeries fluttered in through the door and Griffin looked at them as if receiving an unexpected gift. They buzzed around Dylan and then back out the cave opening.

Dylan said haltingly, "Fahy say horses here."

Mira ran outside. There stood the two mares, looking exhausted and dusty. They had a few cuts. She put her arms around the bay mare and whispered into her mane. "I'm so glad to see you safe." The mare nickered in return.

Mira and Amanda fed the horses and groomed them, tending their wounds and untangling branches and twigs from their manes and tails. Amanda's gray mare shook her whole body, then stood by the saddles, looking at Amanda.

Dylan openly admired Griffin as she talked with Edward. The humans saddled up and mounted.

As they were about to set off, Griffin handed a small, purple bag to Mira with her eagle talons, and said, "This is for you. I am sure you will use it well. Once you are in the city, if you need help, ask for Jacob the farrier. If he cannot help you, he will know others who can."

"Thank you," said Mira, looking into the bag to see several gold coins and a few things that looked like large gemstones. She tucked the jingling bag away in her pocket.

Griffin bowed at them and retreated into her cave.

They continued down the road which left the mountains and began its trek through the foothills. Most of the hills stood tall enough to hide a two-story house behind.

Mira said, "We have at least two more nights before we get to the castle. How will we stay safe?"

Edward answered, "Once we come close enough to the city there will be hordes of people around to hide in. As for tonight, we will have to do what we have to do."

They rode in silence. The ache in her muscles lessened. She felt on edge, but beyond exhaustion, having gained a second or maybe a third wind.

Up and down and around they went past the rolling hills. There were no trees. Only a few wild roses and other thorny thickets clustered here and there; otherwise mostly grasses and flowers covered the ground. The sky above spread out above them when they stood on top of a hill. She rarely saw any clouds. Only in the morning and that once on the afternoon of the rainstorm. She wondered if it snowed here or rained often. Or did plants get water some other way?

Edward walked beside Mira's horse. His head came up to her elbows. "Are you not afraid to go to the city and try to recover your sister's soul?"

"I'm terrified," she said. "I don't know what to do, or how to do it. My magic isn't that strong and I certainly don't know how to confront the Black Queen."

"Perhaps you will not have to," said Edward, his head cocked to one side.

"But I'm still scared and exhausted. I've always just wanted to use magic to help people, read tarot cards or runes and give them healing herbs. Not anything this big."

"You will help heal your sister by doing this."

"Yes, that's true," said Mira. "I just don't think I'm strong enough to do this."

"You are very powerful."

"I don't feel powerful," said Mira

"You matched the Queen's elementals last night" he said, shrugging his furry shoulders. "Surely you have, what would you call it in your world, a lover, a beloved, a consort, who could see your power and mirror it back to you? Then you would know what I say is true."

Mira laughed. "Any of my boyfriends couldn't know I did magic. My world isn't anything like yours. Those of us who do magic need to hide it, either that or we're laughed at, dismissed as fakes. They used to lock us up or burn us to death. Anyway, all my boyfriends treated me badly."

"Why is that? Surely you do not enjoy being treated badly?" asked Edward.

"I guess I felt that I wasn't worth treating well," said Mira.

Edward made a tsking noise. "You are an extraordinary woman and worth being treated like royalty."

Mira could only answer his extravagant praise with silence.

At lunch she went through the ritual of giving Amanda her infusion in the water and hoping she drank it all.

"It tastes funny," Amanda complained as usual.

"We're not in Kansas anymore, Toto," replied Mira.

Dylan was unusually quiet. "What's up little man?" she asked as she put him back up in the saddle.

"Mama," he said, wistfully, looking at Amanda who was already mounted and riding off.

"Yeah, I know, she's sick and not acting like she used to. Hopefully, in a few days we can get her well, go home and get things back to normal."

"Good," he said.

As they passed over the top of another hill, Dylan pointed to smoke coming from behind a hill up ahead.

"Does anyone live out here?" she asked the pooka.

"I do not know of any humans who do. Perhaps it is someone's cook fire. Would you be more comfortable off the road?" he asked.

"No. We were bound to meet someone sooner or later, the road feels more secure. Let's just keep going," she said, hoping she had not made another mistake.

As they passed behind the hill they saw a green stone wall the size of a huge tour bus. It turned blue, then red. Even more amazing, it moved when their horses nervously whinnied.

The stones were actually scales. The wall was a dinosaur. No. A dragon. Eyeing them, it raised its wings and head. From its open jaws the dragon shot fire and smoke straight up in the air and a terrible bellow shook the air. Afterwards, the creature dropped its head, making the ground tremble.

Mira felt Dylan jump off the back end of Shadow. The mare bolted forward in surprise. Mira barely managed to keep her seat. Amanda struggled to keep her horse under control, forcing the pooka to quickly jump out of the way.

Mira dropped her reins, sliding clumsily off Shadow's back. She turned to see Dylan walking towards the dragon, pulling Freddie out of his T-shirt.

The dragon looked at him warily, but lay still, as if waiting for him to come closer.

"Dylan, no. Come back here!" Mira started to run to him, but Edward grabbed her around the waist and held on firmly.

Dylan turned to her briefly to say, "Sick tummy." He kept walking toward the massive creature.

The dragon lay with its head down. Dylan toddled up to it, laying Freddie on top of one of the dragon's front legs as if he did this sort of thing all the time. He reached out to touch the red nose. The dragon groaned, then closed its eyes in apparent pain.

Mira tried to move forward, struggling against Edward's grip. The pooka nodded towards Dylan. She watched Dylan hold one side of the dragon's head, trying to cradle it in his arms. Slowly the dragon rolled over onto its side, the spiny back facing Mira, the hind legs and tail convulsing. Dylan disappeared behind the dragon.

Mira tried to get free from the pooka. Even if the dragon meant no harm, if it simply stood up, it would squash Dylan.

"Wait," said Edward.

Mira felt a vibrancy arise from behind the dragon. She never before had felt such strong healing energy. It flowed smoothly like water.

She felt her mouth hang open. Amanda came and stood next to her, apparently equally astounded.

The dragon's tail lashed. Grass and dirt flew up from the ground near the tail, but the dragon kept the rest of its body still. It bellowed in agony, shooting fire along the ground, scorching a trough through the meadow grass, narrowly missing the horses. The mares whinnied in panic and moved back. Then the huge beast began to tremble.

With great relief, she saw Dylan stumble out from behind the dragon's head, and totter away from it. He threw up vomit, neon, oily green. With a shock, Mira saw it coalesce, then writhe away into the grass. The dragon gave it a look of horror.

Edward finally released her. Mira sprinted towards Dylan. The dragon stood up clumsily, shaking itself like a horse after a good roll in the dirt. It stared with unfocused eyes, but seemed free of pain.

"Dylan, are you okay, honey?"

"Kay now," he said. "Hungry"

Chapter 18 — Mira

Mira watched Edward move towards the dragon and bow so deeply his long ears brushed the ground. He stood upright and asked, "Are you recovering now?"

"Yes, thanks to the little one. Otherwise I would have died."

"What happened?" asked Edward.

"Poison," growled the angry dragon, glaring at the remains of a deer-like creature.

"Who would dare to poison dragons?" asked Edward.

The dragon stared at him and said, "The Queen's Sorcerer."

"Why?" asked Edward.

"We declined an alliance with her." The dragon cocked his head at him and said slowly, "She wanted us to lay waste to the World of the Enigmatic Pearl and the World of the

Flaming Ruby. We refused to participate in such useless destruction."

"Have others been poisoned?"

"I do not know. I must find out," said the dragon. He gently picked up Freddie with one set of front claws and walked clumsily towards Dylan, the ground reverberating beneath his weight. Dylan took Freddie and clutched the stuffed dinosaur to his chest. He stared at the dragon with a look of awe and delight on his face.

The dragon said, "I am in your debt, little one. I am called Barinthus. A most gracious thank you," he said, bowing his head so that it touched the ground and went lower than Dylan's.

"Welcome," said Dylan, bowing as gracefully as he could in return. Then he ran forward and hugged part of the dragon's snout not being able to reach his arms all the way round his head. The dragon made a sound somewhat like a chortle.

"I must warn the others. Will you continue following this road?"

"Yes, we are going to the City of the Black Opal," said the pooka.

"I will return and find you. Spend tonight within the stone circle up ahead. I will see you are safe and meet you this evening." He spread his huge wings and leapt into the air.

Mira felt the ground tremble beneath their feet. The dragon flew almost as fast as a small jet, his bright scales glittering in the light.

Mira and Amanda stared at each other, then looked at Dylan. He seemed a little better after Mira gave him some bread to chew on. He had taken the poison from the dragon into himself and expelled it. She had no idea he could do such a thing.

"Have you done this before, Dylan?" she asked.

"Help dwagon?"

"Yes, you helped the dragon. You saved him. Have you ever helped anyone else like this?"

"Yes," he said, then paused and said, "No."

Mira realized Dylan had tried to figure out what she wanted to hear. Magic wasn't okay in their family, he had already learned, even though she'd been watching him summon faeries.

They started riding again. She asked Edward, "How could they be sure only dragons would get the poison?"

"Antelope are a delicacy for dragons and as dragons are occasional scavengers they often eat freshly killed animals, but I doubt very much if the Sorcerer cares who else ate the poison," he said. "If the poison did not work, they would kill them another way."

"Are there many dragons here?"

"In this part of the world alone, there are around fifty," his voice was tinged with sadness. "Maybe another couple hundred within one or two days flight. Their numbers are diminishing. It is possible the Queen is slipping further into madness, we have feared this might happen if she did not relinquish her throne to another. Humans are not made to carry that much energy for so long. That is why they pass it on to others after a time."

Periodically, they saw huge birds circling over the hills. Edward identified them as vultures. She hoped dying dragons didn't lay below the birds' circles.

An occasional dragon flew overhead. At least she thought they looked like dragons. They flew so high it was difficult to tell.

"Do you know where the stone circle is the dragon talked about?" she asked the pooka.

"Yes, we should be there soon."

"Will we be safe there?"

"If Barinthus said we will, then we will," Edward said, stoically.

Mira wondered if all pooka were close mouthed or just Edward. She really wanted to know more about him, but he was so evasive. She didn't know where to begin or how to ask. He fascinated her and she wondered about him constantly. She watched him lope alongside Shadow, his fur ruffled by the breeze, human-like speech, but beast-like exterior. The more she learned about this world, the more questions its inhabitants brought up.

After about half an hour the circle came into view. It sat upon the top of a butte, which grew up from the surrounding plains. Around its base the main road circled, like a roundabout. They climbed the hill following a smaller, straighter road.

They passed through an outer circle with a single row of tall, deciduous trees, all of which looked identical. A football field away stood the stone circle. When the dragon said he'd meet them at the stone circle, she's envisioned something like Stonehenge. This only partly resembled it. While Stonehenge lay in decline, this circle felt new and still in use. Fabric weavings hung on poles, the bright colors flapping a little in the breeze. The stones were huge, almost identical, spikes of the same glossy, almost transparent, black rock from the canyon they'd stayed in a few days ago. Unlike Stonehenge there were only vertical stones arranged in a perfect circle with no capstones. Another football field would have fit inside. At the center there lay an enormous flat rock with massive stairs carved in it. "The speaker's platform," Edward called it.

"What is the purpose of this place," she asked.

The pooka looked at her in amazement, then must have realized his rudeness. "I keep forgetting you are not from this world. This is a gift to the land to thank her for taking care of us. It is also a gathering place for celebration. For instance, in the spring humans, pooka and others, bring the new ones here to be blessed by the community." Edward removed his backpack, put it down on the grass and shook himself out much like a dog after swimming.

"Are there any towns nearby?" asked Mira, leaning up against a cool, slippery stone.

"No. We are still a traveling people at heart. We follow the herds and the seasons. This is a place we would travel to at the turning of the seasons. The differing tribes and peoples would meet here to honor this land and to celebrate and trade with each other. There used to be only a few settled places in our world, the City of the Black Opal the largest one. Although humans and pooka are becoming more settled, it does not necessarily reflect the wisest choice for our world."

What would it be like to live always on the move, with all the people you knew and loved? Always seeing new things or revisiting old ones? How would that change your outlook about life and what held importance?

They ate their usual meal of bread and dried meat then made up their beds. As she wove through the trees casting a protective circle, against whatever spirits the Queen might send, the tremendous magic which lingered in this place entwined with her energy field. The enchantment grew so strong, Mira felt her skin tingling. She felt invigorated.

As they groomed the horses, she realized Amanda had hardly spoken all day long. Amanda watched her brush Shadow. "What?" Mira asked finally.

"Nothing," said Amanda, her jaw tightening.

"No, it's not nothing. What is it?" she asked.

"I don't trust him." She nodded over at Edward playing hide and seek amongst the stones with Dylan.

"You don't trust him with Dylan?"

"I don't trust him with us," said Amanda, glaring at her.

"After what he did last night?"

"Just what did he do last night?" asked Amanda, her hands on her hips. "He disappeared and then returned when the coast was clear."

"Amanda, he was the huge demon who saved us," she said, astonished her sister hadn't worked that out. She felt indignant. How could Amanda be so stupid?

"Did he tell you that?"

"No, I didn't ask. I didn't need to." She pulled hard on a tangle in Shadow's tail and the mare stomped her hoof. "Sorry," she apologized to the horse. "I'm not mad at you,"

Amanda said, "Oh, I see. You're so brilliant, you know everything. Well, let me tell you. I don't trust him because he's up to something. He's not being entirely truthful, that much I do know. I don't trust the dragon or anyone else in this place either. Not even you. I just want to get the hell out of here."

"Aren't you forgetting something, like your soul?"

"I'm doing just fine without it!" Amanda threw down her horse's brush, stomped off to her bedroll, lay down and covered herself up.

Mira continued brushing the horses, trying to let go of anger and frustration at her twin. Aste had warned her Amanda would be uncooperative, but Mira hadn't expected combative. Most irritating was the knowledge that Amanda was right. Edward wasn't being entirely truthful, he hid something.

As twilight approached, a glowing dragon arrived. It was all sleek and silver. Mira caught the smell of fish and seaweed. The soft ground shook slightly as the dragon landed. Its head stuck inside the stone circle through the upright stones.

"Hello," the dragon said, in a silky voice.

Edward stepped behind her and inclined his head. Mira took his gesture to mean she needed to be in charge here.

"Hello," she said, noticing this dragon's head had wobbly, flesh-like appendages hanging from the massive head, almost like dreadlocks.

"Barinthus sends his regards and said to tell you he will be here soon. I have come ahead to make sure you are safe before night descends."

"Thank you," she said, bowing low as she saw the pooka do earlier. It seemed normal to bow to a creature as regal as this. "What is your name?"

"I am Bastye."

Soon there came another thump as a chartreuse, lumpy little dragon landed and stuck its head into the circle. Then a tall, dark purple dragon with two heads landed very clumsily and both its heads went around an upright and into the circle, this one exuded the aroma of cedar trees. She wondered if the smells came from where they lived, from what they ate or if the dragons simply created the aromas. She hadn't noticed one from Barinthus, although he'd been sick.

More rumblings and thumpings came as other dragons arrived. Each dragon looked different from the last. A melange of colors, shapes and even sizes. They spoke amongst themselves behind the stones, gathering like a flock of hens, gossiping about the newcomers and the events of the day. When they all began to glow it looked like fireflies on a dark night. She felt overcome with awe.

Mira was entranced by the dragons. Until Edward went over and spoke to the two horses, she hadn't realized Shadow felt terrified. Mira finally caught images of dragons diving from the sky and horses, or were they unicorns, being ripped apart with claws and teeth or roasted to death by flames. She wondered if Shadow had survived such an attack or if it existed as some sort of racial memory. Edward laid his hands on the mares' foreheads. As he did, they lay down and seemed to fall asleep. Mira felt no energy flow from him, what he did was extremely subtle and focused.

Standing inside the stone circle was like being twirled in the middle of a gaudy, glittering, Christmas light display. Everywhere she looked glowing dragons moved. They were so colorful, one the orange of a pumpkin, another the color of lilacs, yet another a respectable teal color. Every now and then one would pull its head out of the circle to make room for another to see. They each seemed to glow at will, as if they could turn it on or off. Some looked like dragons from European fairy tale books; others looked like the dragons from fancy Chinese pottery. Soon the entire circumference of the circle filled with dragons, vying for views of the outlanders.

Maybe the dragons had never seen people from other worlds before. That would explain their curiosity. She'd certainly never seen a dragon before today.

Mira glanced over to see that Amanda had crawled out of her bedroll. She and Dylan looked equally captivated. They kept turning in circles and looking at all the beautiful dragons.

Mira felt a fast wind blow behind her and the ground shook again. Right in the middle of the circle Barinthus landed. None of the other dragon seemed to carry three colors at once. Sometimes Barinthus would only be one color, then he'd add another, then he would be all three at once. It was dizzying trying to find a pattern to his color changes. She wondered if any of the other dragons could change color.

"Greetings, everyone," he said, flapping his large, translucent wings. Did moving his wings in a certain way, convey meaning as well?

"I have gathered all of you here to make an announcement. As a result of the deaths of Mirrasau and Esooth and the attempted poisoning of several other of us, we have cast our votes. It is unanimous, this weir is at war with the Queen and her sorcerer. The other weirs will give us their answer within the next day. Only if the Queen leaves her throne and gives us the Sorcerer shall we reconsider."

She felt saddened to hear of the deaths of two such amazing creatures. Why were the three humans and Edward here for this announcement? What part did they play in this secret?

Barinthus continued, "Tomorrow shall be a burning day. We will take Mirrasau and Esooth to the heights and weep and flame for them one last time. Then we will know whether the other weirs join our fight and will plan our strategy. Let anyone beware who is near the Queen in the next several days. Our vengeance will be swift and painful."

The air around her filled with smoke and heat. Until the breeze cleared it, she could hardly see. Dylan clung to her leg, not understanding the words, but from the serious look on his face, Mira realized he got the message. Amanda stood close by, as did Edward. She could feel his warm breath on the top of her head and his furry leg behind her hand. His fur felt very soft. He said, "This will certainly get things moving."

Barinthus' scales glittered even more and he began to glow with excitement. He reminded her of a spinning mirror ball. The noise from the other dragons died down. "These three humans and this most noble pooka have done me a great service. The littlest one of them took the poison into himself and healed me. The other three are on a mission that can only help us. If they are in need of any assistance, I ask you to help if you are able."

The dragons stomped their feet and Mira felt like she stood in the middle of an earthquake. She was afraid the stones might fall. How deep in the earth did their roots grow?

The meeting broke up shortly after. The dragons all had a last look at them, especially at Dylan. He seemed to hypnotize all of them.

Barinthus came to over to speak. He said, "Thank you again, for saving me," to Dylan. "As I said, I am in your debt."

Dylan nodded and then looked up at Mira. She said, "He doesn't speak well yet, but I'm sure he'd say, 'You're welcome,'."

The dragon turned to her. "I understand what you are trying to do. We can give you until Aine begins to wane, four days. After that, your attempts will be useless. We will attack at dawn on the fourth day. If you have failed, you must be out of the castle by then. We will destroy it."

"Would you destroy the Black Opal?" asked Edward.

"No, that we will save so the breath of this world can continue. Too long have we left the responsibility of caring for the worlds to humans. It is long past time we returned to our work of weaving the fabric of the worlds together. But we will destroy the Queen, her sorcerer and her army. As I said, if she names an heir, we will reconsider. The Sorcerer is forfeit."

Barinthus lashed his tail and his eyes lit up with anger. "It is time for sleep now. I will guard you. I must think." Other dragons watched the outer circle, waiting for the Queen's spies to appear. He curled up in the center of the circle and seemed to be asleep, except that his eyelids were cracked slightly open.

Dylan walked up to him and kissed him on the nose and said, "Night, nite."

Barinthus chuckled. Dylan grabbed his blanket, dragged it in front of Barinthus' front legs, then spread it out and crawled underneath, cuddling Freddy.

"Me too," Amanda said, moving sluggishly towards her own blankets.

Mira stood staring at Edward. He seemed so sad and lonely looking. He casually walked over to Barinthus and began a quiet conversation.

She went to check on the horses. They both dozed, so she patted them and said, "Sweet dreams," wondering if horses dreamt.

As she walked around, Mira felt exhausted, yet too tired to sleep. The dragon's energy, as well as the power stored in those massive stones flowed through her. So she moved around the outside of the stone circle. Some of the dragons nodded at her as she passed by, then continued their conversations. Others lay stretched out on the ground, snoring. The cool grass tickled her bare feet as she breathed in the fresh, almost salty air. They must still be fairly close to the ocean. Tomorrow they would turn directly inland. To the City of the Black Opal.

She walked around the circle of trees. The small round leaves grew green on top and silvery on the bottom. They fluttered gently in the breeze. The white bark felt smooth and silky. The trees stood the same height and basic shape. Around the whole massive circle, not one was maimed, broken or dead. Amazing. Such a thing did not happen in her world. Perfection did not exist there. She wondered if Earth still was her world. For the first time, she consciously considered the question. Would she ever go back?

She was startled out of her thoughts by the appearance of a dark shape. Her mind reached out to read its intent, and found 'no harm meant'. As the creature came closer Mira recognized a horse. No, a unicorn.

A black unicorn!

It continued to move closer. His mane hung to his knees, and tail dragged on the ground behind.

"What do you want?" she asked, beginning to feel uneasy.

No answer came. Fear rose up in her. Fear of this beautiful creature. Fear of failing her sister. A terror of failing herself, not finding her way in life. She backed up, wondered which way to run. The unicorn reared and charged.

The horn entered her belly with a sharp pain. The unicorn's hot breath hit her knees, steaming through the heavy cloth of the pants she wore. He twisted his head and a crack sounded as the horn snapped. Mira felt a wrench in her gut. He backed away. She watched his eyes open wider until the whites showed.

She stood frozen. Mira's head ached as if she'd run into a boulder and there was a throbbing in her stomach. Her feet rooted to the ground. The land's energy shot through her body.

Mira reached out to the unicorn, wanting to make sure he was okay. As she touched the silky neck, his entire body shook. His hair lightened and turned white. The unicorn's horn began to grow again, glowing from within, pearlescent. He shook his head, tossing the long mane. The unicorn whinnied, snorted, then seemed to bow his head. He turned and bolted between the trees onto the plains beyond. She quivered

She pulled her shirt up and put her hand to her stomach; there was no blood. The sealed wound felt hard, like rock or crystal. It might cause more harm to pull the horn out, even if it was possible. Then it began to glow. The horn felt warm in her belly, comfortable as if it melted into her. Mira wondered if maybe she was going into shock. Her ability to think seemed fuzzy.

She felt filled with peace and contentment, rather than fear, like hypothermia and the moments before freezing to death. Was this what it felt like to die?

"Mira," said a soft voice.

She looked up to see Edward watching her with concern.

"The unicorn...," she said.

"You changed it to a white one," he said and caught her as she collapsed. She heard him say, "Chosen by the unicorns...."

Mira dreamt about being curled up next to his gray fur. His warm paws touched her and held her naked body against his soft pelt. She sensed a shared passion between them. Then somehow she felt skin against warm skin. Mira felt him moving inside her and woke in the middle of the night to find herself alone in her soft, fuzzy blankets, fully clothed. She slipped back into dreams of the unicorn and the feeling of being in Edward's arms.

Chapter 19 — Mira

Waking with a start the morning, Mira struggled to remember what happened. She lifted her shirt to check her belly for a sore, even though she felt no pain. A round, almost crystalline scar covered her navel as if someone had imbedded quartz there. She felt happy, peaceful and full of energy.

Last night couldn't have been a dream. She remembered the part about Edward and blushed. No, that didn't happen; she knew that much.

Dylan stood talking to Barinthus. The faeries fluttered around them both. She felt strangely reassured. When had this become the new normal, she wondered.

Amazingly, Dylan conjured a bird out of midair, then a frog, then a huge, glowing emerald. These things held their shape even after leaving his hands.

Edward watched intently. Amanda still lay asleep. Mira got up and walked over to Dylan.

"Are you doing all this Dylan?" she asked.

He looked at her guiltily.

"It's fine if you are. I just want to know," said Mira.

"Grandma say no. Bad,"

She took a deep breath. "Sometimes even grandmas are wrong. This is one of those times. You just need to make better choices about who you do magic for. Like not in front of Grandma." She remembered Mom's explosive reactions to Mira's childhood magical attempts.

Mira had burned with anger at her mother. Her father had simply looked surprised. He would have accepted her if he lived. She felt a deep sorrow about his loss, even eight years later.

Dylan seemed confused, looked at Barinthus, then back to her and nodded.

Barinthus said, "I helped him understand your words."

"How?" she asked.

"I now understand how to speak to his mind."

"Can you do this with anyone?"

"No, only with a person who is my partner."

"Partner?" she asked

"I do not know how to explain this in your words. Even though I am not a dragon who believes we should separate from people and I have taken great effort to learn your language, I do not always find the right words," said Barinthus.

"Let me try," said Edward, turning to Mira. "Dragons and humans once lived in close partnerships. About half of the dragon population joined with a human partner; you might call them soul mates. They could see into each other's minds and hearts. It is a very deep, profound connection with another being. Usually a young dragon and a young child would find each other."

Edward continued, "After ten turns on the throne, the Queen's anger with the unicorns came to a peak. She claimed they overran the City, her gardens, the plains. In truth, I think it was because their magic eluded her, she could neither master it nor equal their power. Queen Nakia decided the herds needed to be thinned. She coerced the human and dragon pairs and her army to help her. The Queen held enough power to inspire them to attack the herds. She gave the humans an evil potion to awaken their blood lust." Edward paused for breath.

Mira noticed he seemed distressed.

Edward added, "All the unicorns within the City came under attack. They fought back, but eventually all were murdered. Then the battle moved onto the plains. Unicorns contain great magic, but little of it is used for defense. The blood lust raced through the humans and the dragons caught it like a disease. Once that sort of rage is awakened within a dragon it takes long to die down. The madness spread to all the weirs and every flying dragon participated in the slaughter of the unicorns. Only a few unicorns escaped. Some of them made it into the Black Silk Canyon and the blackest ones disappeared against the stones, dragons cannot see black well. In the darkness others escaped. Eventually, the survivors crossed the mountains and fled to the forests where Aste lived, far from the City."

The look on Edward's face made Mira want to cry. He felt so much for what happened in his land. She tried to imagine such an atrocity in this serene place, but couldn't.

He continued, "With the massacre of the unicorns, the dragons felt deep shame. The pairs still alive and many single dragons dashed themselves into the cliffs, killing themselves. Others struggled to live with their shame and distress. They decided there would be no more dragon and human pairings until a white unicorn could be found again, white unicorns being the most common. It would signal the recovery of the herds. So here we are with humans, dragons and unicorns all cut off from each other. It creates a terrible fissure in our world. That crack has spread to the other lands as well. The dragons link the worlds together, keeping the connections stable."

"What about the white unicorn thing?" she asked, holding her breath. Mira wasn't sure if she really wanted to talk about it. The feeling brought up by what happened between her and the unicorn was so intimate and personal, but she needed to know if it really happened.

"I think you know a white unicorn was seen by many last night," Edward said, quietly.

"But that wasn't normal. It was really black and turned white before my eyes. That doesn't mean the population is recovering from the massacre."

"I think it does. I think it is a sign for us and to the dragons," Edward said.

It felt good to know she hadn't imagined the encounter with the unicorn. Mira touched her belly.

"Ride," screeched Dylan in excitement.

"What did you say?" she asked, turning quickly to Dylan.

Barinthus grabbed the back of Dylan's jacket with his mouth. He stretched his long neck around and neatly placed Dylan on his back, between two spines.

"No!" she cried.

"I will take good care of him. We will return shortly," said Barinthus as he lifted slowly into the air, his wings creating a wind that blew Mira backwards and created a cloud of dust.

Dylan yelped with joy. She just cringed.

"He will be fine," said Edward touching her shoulder.

"Well, there's nothing I can do about it, is there?" she said, annoyed.

"No. It is a great honor for him to be joined to such a dragon."

She understood, but felt jealous. "Why can't I be joined with someone in that sort of 'deep, profound' relationship?" she mumbled to herself, rustling through a saddlebag.

Edward must have overheard her. "Your time will come, have faith in that," he said, quietly.

Mira grabbed some food. She had grown really tired of stale bread and dried meat and vowed never to eat granola again. She put some of the infusion into water for Amanda.

Amanda finally woke up. She ate, drank, and grumbled. Her typical morning routine. The two of them packed up the horses. They saw Barinthus fly over several times, accompanied by three other dragons. Finally, they landed, the earth shaking with their impact.

Barinthus helped Dylan down. Dylan gave him a hug and shouted, "Mom, Mira, Eddy, I fly." He jumped up and down, flapping his arms. She couldn't help but laugh.

Barinthus bowed his head at them. "I wish you luck on your journey. We will meet again soon. If you need to get a message to me, you may tell Dylan." The dragons flew off, spiraling into the air.

"Are all dragons that abrupt?" asked Amanda.

The pooka said, "Barinthus is long winded for a dragon. Come, we will need all day for the long ride to the City and then to find a way into the castle."

"Just how are we going to do that?" asked Amanda, haughtily brushing her long hair out of her eyes.

"We're going to look for Jacob, the farrier and hope he can help us or knows someone who can," said Mira

"That's your plan?" asked Amanda. "That's just ridiculous," she said, glaring at her. "The Queen must be expecting us. She attacks us every night. Let's just march through the front door."

"No," said Mira. "There's not enough of us. We need to be more stealthy. Sneak in."

"Like she won't find out we're there? She has spies out in the boonies who find us. How many spies do you think she has in the City? Your plan is pathetic; it's not even a plan!" she said, crossing her arms.

"Please let me know if you come up with a better one," sniped Mira. They must be getting closer to her soul if Amanda was this angry and argumentative. "C'mon, we've got to get going." She lifted Dylan up onto Shadow and got on. Amanda got on the gray, still shaking her head in disbelief. As they galloped down the road, the pooka paced tirelessly beside them.

Dylan amused himself by making small rocks appear in his hands and throwing them off onto the side of the road. His magic seemed effortless. He was having so much fun playing. Did that make him more powerful?

Dylan told her he'd healed spiders before and once a bird. Theoretically, size shouldn't matter. So a dragon shouldn't be harder than a spider. Maybe to him size meant nothing. Most of what he did was circus tricks. That's how she'd started as well. If she'd been allowed to follow her own magic, without interference from Mom, would she be plagued by her current lack of control?

Things had changed when she entered this land though. Her power came in straightforward and strong and she noticed a small bloom of confidence creeping into herself. She continued to ponder the nature of her own magic, and Dylan's, as they passed out of the rolling foothills.

Finally she could see plains stretching out beneath them. In the distance lay the Tower of the Black Opal, gleaming purple light. The road looked straight all the way to the City. But the distance must be misleading if it would take them till late afternoon to get there. A mirage, she thought.

Their path joined the main road from the north that followed the River Angouleme. The river was too wide and deep for horses to cross, Edward told her. The trees on the other side looked like match sticks. The clear water ran mostly straight, through the city and out into the Great Inland Sea. At least that's what Aste's map told her. She'd hardly needed the map.

They ate lunch as they rode. When they got to the main road, they paused to feed, water and rest the horses. Dylan waded into the river a few inches and squealed as the coldness of the water filled his shoes.

"Dylan," snapped Mira, grabbing him before he went in any further, getting her own shoes wet. It felt good. "Don't go in any deeper, the current's too fast." Mira sensed the horses' joy for the fresh water to drink and wade in.

An incredible scent drifted past her, sweeter than honeysuckle, more luscious than ripe peaches. Mira turned and saw a stand of tall plants across the road. Amanda stood in front of them. Edward patted Mira's horse, his head buried in the horse's mane. He rested, still breathing hard from running alongside the horses.

She walked across the road, drawn by the exotic smell. The plants grew tall with massive stems. Fuzzy leaves about nine feet across were green streaked with red. The flower stalks stood three feet higher than the leaves and looked like huge, fancy orchids of fuchsia, orange, red and yellow. The flowers made her dizzy just looking at them. She walked up to the plants and touched the leaves, inhaling deeply. Her magic wanted to know this plant, but her senses wanted to become one with it. She felt herself enveloped by the fuzzy leaves, wrapped cozily like a velvet blanket.

She looked across the road and saw Dylan wading back in the water. A huge green creature that looked almost like the Loch Ness Monster floated in the river talking to Dylan. She couldn't hear the words, but she saw it lift one of its front paddle-like legs to give Dylan a way to scramble on its back. She tried to cry out, but her voice wouldn't come.

Edward yelled, "Dylan, no! Jump off!" as the creature swam downstream in the fast current. Soon Dylan disappeared from sight behind tall bushes and around a bend. She couldn't move and part of her didn't really want to.

Dylan's abduction must be a hallucination.

As she drifted off, someone called her name. Edward, it was Edward. Calling Amanda and her. She dozed off again, curled into the soft cushy foliage.

When Mira came to, she lay on the ground with Edward kneeling over her waving something stinky past her nose.

She stared at it and recognized a fresh horse turd. Amanda also lay passed out. A strange man knelt over Amanda giving her the same aromatherapy treatment.

She sat up and heard crackling. Four other men were setting fire to the group of plants that had seduced Amanda and herself. A fifth man held the reins of everyone's horses further down the road.

The smoke swirled thick and black with an almost caramel fragrance as the plants burned like dry firewood. She could almost hear the plants screaming.

"What is happening?" she asked Edward.

He brushed her cheek with his clean hand and said in a worried tone, "It was my fault, I thought you knew about 'sweet death'. You were almost eaten by a clump of it. They lure you in with their scent and beauty then trap you. They slowly digest you, leaving nothing behind. Then they catch the next traveler."

"They didn't catch you."

"I'm a pooka."

"What about them?" she asked, gesturing to the men.

"They arrived shortly after the plant captured you. I bewitched them so their sense of smell wouldn't work. They recognized the plants. We burn these plants wherever we find them, but they seed rampantly and grow quickly. This clump was probably only two days old. I am so very sorry." His ears drooped, dejectedly.

Edward got up, padded to the river shore and stared off into the distance. He seemed anxious. She couldn't understand why, but could read the tension in his body. She clenched and unclenched her fists. How could he not have told them? She and Amanda had stood in front of the plant for a long time. He should have noticed. They could have died! She gritted her teeth until her jaws hurt.

Mira looked over at Amanda and the man who woke her up. They talked animatedly. She recognized him from Roderick's hunting party. The man's hair was blond and curled around his shoulders. He had an open, handsome face. No demons haunted him, his life was easy and carefree.

He looked over at Mira and asked, "Is everything well with you?"

"I think I'm okay," she said, not really feeling okay.

"We'll be just fine, thanks to your help," said Amanda, giggling. "We obviously picked the wrong place to stop and give our horses a rest."

"We needed to do the same," said the man.

"Who are you?" asked Amanda, ogling him.

Mira realized Amanda was flirting with him. Was she channeling all that anger into lust now? She had certainly found more energy as they closed in on the City.

"My name is Ewan DiAntok. Prince Roderick is my father."

"So Ronan is your brother?" asked Mira.

"Yes, I see you have met him," he laughed, a clear bell like laughter that made her want to hear more of it. "But obviously you did not fall in love with him. Most women do. A put down would do him good." As he said this, he glanced at Edward, who ignored him.

"You were with the hunters. Hunting unicorns," Mira said, angrily. The intensity grew out of her fury with Edward. Her mind felt all jumbled up, something was wrong, but she couldn't quite pinpoint it. Was it an after effect from the plants?

"I rode with the party. My brother Ronan and I went as trackers, but to hinder the others, not help."

"Hinder?" asked Amanda.

"We do not believe in killing unicorns. We scout ahead, make false trails while covering up the real ones. So far our father has not caught on," he said to both of them. His blue eyes carried a smile in them. Ewan turned to Amanda, obviously returning her stare, but not in a challenging way, "Who are you?"

"I'm Amanda Sullivan. This is my sister Miranda. We're on our way to the City in search of our parents. Edward here has adopted us and become our tour guide."

"Amanda," what a beautiful name. We are also on our way back to the City. My father has called us home. He says the dragons are out and there is talk of a war. I think he is imagining things. There has never been war between us and the dragons. They are such sensible beings. But I go home all the same. And tomorrow is Midsummer! I missed the festivities last turn and am looking forward to enjoying them. Would you like to ride with us or do you have other plans?"

"We'd love to ride with you," gushed Amanda.

Mira still felt something was wrong or missing. Edward stayed silent, withdrawn. He wouldn't meet her eyes, but paced along the river bank. She got up, staggering at first, then found her balance. Walking over to Edward she touched his shoulder. He turned to her and said, "I have failed you."

"What," she said, confused, then understanding, "Oh my god, where's Dylan?"

"He has been taken," said Edward, his voice hoarse.

"By whom? When?" She felt like a volcano just erupted in her belly and was spreading to her entire body. Everything turned red.

"I would guess the Queen. Alanos do not normally approach humans and they certainly do not let people ride them. A boat under enchantment I would guess. I could not see it. I tried, but the enchanter held more powerful magic than I." Edward's face twisted up, but she couldn't tell which bothered him more, losing Dylan or meeting someone with more power. She didn't ask. Mira looked over to Amanda flirting with Ewan. She clearly didn't realize Dylan had been kidnapped.

"I remember, I stood inside the flower and saw him leaving. I tried to call out, but couldn't," she said.

"I should never have let us stop near the sweet death. I forgot you would not know what they were." He looked at her with such sad eyes.

"It's not your fault," said Mira in a small voice, unsure whether she believed it herself.

She stood looking at the river, her nails making bruises on the palms of her hands. She wanted to hurt someone and settled for herself. How could she have left him standing there by the river with no one watching him? Now the Queen had Amanda's soul and Dylan.

"What does she want with Dylan?" she asked, rubbing her aching forehead. How would they be able to rescue Dylan and find Amanda's soul?

"I do not know," said Edward. "Perhaps she wants more power over you. Maybe she wants Dylan's soul or his power? If her spies followed us then she must know that he and Barinthus are joined. Although it is not completed, this would give her some leverage over the dragons. I simply do not know."

Chapter 20 — Nakia

Queen Nakia sat in her garden eating breakfast. Eggs fried with vegetables and cheese, ham, a sweet roll, fruit juices from the far south, and tea. She watched Dylan, who chased butterflies, attended by one of her ladies.

Earlier, she had politely asked the boy to do magic for her. He refused and she slapped him. After another refusal she hit him again. The child stared defiantly at her, tears in his eyes. Through those tears she saw dragon's eyes and heard a deep voice within her mind say, "We are coming for you," Nakia shuddered. No, it had simply been the child, finally using his magic. Still, she left him alone with her ladies.

The Sorcerer entered behind her and stood waiting, clearing his throat.

"What?" she asked impatiently.

"I wonder what you intend to do now," he asked.

"Wait."

"For the girl?"

"Yes. It is her turn to make a move." She sipped her tea, pretending to a calm that was not there.

"What about the dragons?"

She sighed. "If it is true that they are joined, which I doubt, it would be very exciting. Think of the possibilities," she said, rising from her chair and walking further into the garden. "We now have what the dragons want most. There has not been a joining since the unicorns were thinned. And this one, although incomplete, involves a young boy from another world and the High Dragon. We have power over them," she smiled in the way reserved for those who were clenched within her fist. Sweet, but with poison behind it.

"What if they attack?" he asked.

"Attack, why would they attack?"

"They are dragons. Who understands why they do anything? And they will fight once they realize you will not give up the boy alive."

"Well, if they fight, the child dies and I take his soul. After that I will have the soul and the High Dragon will be joined to me. However as I will then have two other souls in my body, I will be the more powerful partner and will rule the dragons as well."

She watched him as he walked silently by her side. His face twitched as emotion moved across his cheeks and eyebrows. He was probably trying to find a way out.

"You must see," she said,"there is no other way. This will help us contain our world and move out into the others.

"What if something does not work? This plan is based on too many small pieces all flowing together smoothly. What if one does not?"

"We will improvise. If things do not work perfectly, it only makes things more exciting. How can you not understand that?"

"Yes," he said, "I understand that is your view, I am not as courageous as you, my Queen. And, since my neck is at stake

if things go wrong, I like to see plans made ahead of time."
He smiled at her.

"Fine. All you need is arrange for the child, the girl, the
captured soul and the two of us to be in the Opal Tower on
the deep night of High Summer. Then you may take the
other two souls and insert all three in my body. How we
make that happen does not matter."

"What if the Opal will not allow it?" the Sorcerer asked
quietly.

"How could the Opal not want this?" The look on his
face said everything. He clearly thought she was mad. She
waved his reply off. "I am Queen, it will make me stronger,
thus making the land stronger. That the Opal should object
is impossible," she said. The thought of the potency which
three more souls would bring made her body tingle with
excitement. Nakia wanted it all now.

She would absorb all three souls, be joined with the High
Dragon and rule with more power than even her father. After
she crushed her enemies in this world she would move on to
take control over other realms. Nakia wondered if there was
any limit to the number of souls she could consume. Time
enough to consider that later.

She sat watching Dylan run, jump and fall. She wondered
whether to gather in the World of the Enigmatic Pearl or
the World of the Flaming Ruby first. One existed in stability
and perfection, the other unstable.

She would attack the Pearl first. Let the Ruby fall on its
own and she would pick up the easy pieces. She needed to
consider how to bring instability to the Pearl Realm.

A servant knelt before her, interrupting her thoughts.

"What?"

"Your highness, Councilor Gareth is here to discuss the
Festival," he said.

She sighed and walked back into the castle towards the
council chambers. Nakia said to the Sorcerer who followed
her, "Go. You must have things to plan. This will be trivial.

Food, music, decorations. Why he thinks I must be involved in these petty things is beyond my understanding. But I will humor him. He is useful."

A pair of pooka stood guarding the door leading to the more public parts of the castle. One moved and opened the door for her. The other followed her to the council chamber.

Then again, the World of the Flaming Ruby was so ripe that once she had control of that, her power would be greater and there would be nothing the Enigmatic Pearl could do to stop her from controlling it as well.

The three Jeweled Worlds would be united once again, as her father had done. After that, she would decide what to do about the peculiar world of those wretched girls.

Chapter 21 — Mira

Mira stormed over to her sister, who stood flirting with Ewan. She grabbed Amanda's elbow and pulled her away. "I need to talk to you."

Amanda giggled. They both staggered, still dizzy from the sweet death.

When they were far enough away from the noise of the men laughing at Ewan's jokes, the fire crackling and the splashing of the horses in the river, Mira asked, "What are you thinking? We can't go with them. We don't know who they are. That could be the Sorcerer for all you know!"

Amanda yanked her arm away and glared. "That's not who stole my soul!" She turned her head to gaze at Ewan. "Although I'd gladly give it to him."

Amanda couldn't stop looking at him. Ewan met her glances while talking with Edward. Mira's face flushed with rage. "Could you focus for one minute. Dylan's gone!"

Amanda looked puzzled, then met Mira's eyes. "Dylan, where's Dylan?"

"He's been taken."

"Who would take Dylan?" She paused, then Mira saw the realization hit her, "That bitch." Amanda began to pace back and forth.

Mira felt the same rage burning inside.

Amanda said, "You don't really have a plan to get into the palace. I'm going with Ewan and we'll get in, either that or I'll walk in the front door alone. The Queen wants me or she wouldn't have taken my son. She'll let me in."

"Amanda no!"

"Yes," she yelled, pointing a finger at Mira, "You and Edward can follow your lame plan. I'll go my way. One of us will succeed."

"What good will it do if we get your soul, but you're not around?"

"I'll be around. I'll find you."

"I don't think splitting up is such a good idea," said Mira, grabbing her sister's arm.

"Well, I do," said Amanda, shoving her away. Mira nearly fell. "So give me that nasty medicine you've been slipping into my tea, so I can keep taking it."

"How long have you known?"

"A few days," said Amanda. "I understand why you did it, but I'm still pissed." Amanda grabbed Mira's hair.

"Oww. Let go."

"Give me the medicine."

"Let go of my hair."

Amanda let go. Mira fished the medicine out of her pocket and tossed it to Amanda who caught it easily.

"I gotta go and get Dylan."

"Amanda, let's stick together."

"No. I'm doing things my way now."

Mira moved towards her.

"Don't touch me. I don't want any of your touchy-feely stuff right now. I just want to kill somebody or screw that guy. Those are the only emotions that monster left me."

Amanda strode away, then snatched, the reins to her horse. She said to Ewan, "I'll ride with you. My sister will go with the pooka."

The men mounted their horses to follow. Ewan had a worried look as he met Mira's eyes. "I'll take care of her," he said, just before their horses raced down the road, leaving a cloud of dust behind.

Mira felt like someone punched her in the belly. She knew Amanda was doing the best she could, but that didn't stop the pain. Aste gone. Dylan kidnapped. Now Amanda deserted her. Mira felt afraid and alone. She would have to do this all herself. Find Dylan, Amanda's soul and now Amanda, get out of the City before the dragons attacked and in the middle of everything, locate Aste to return Amanda's soul to her body. Her mind reeled.

Shadow nudged her. The mare's muzzle dripped with river water. "Come, get up, we must go."

Mira looked at Edward, who waited patiently, but seemed lost in guilt about Dylan. She sighed and mounted. Amanda, Ewan and the others were lost in the dust cloud ahead.

"You did the right thing to let her go," he said.

"How can you be so sure?"

He shrugged, "Some things I just know. You are the key to getting her soul back. Ewan will take care of her."

They trotted in silence for miles.

When they slowed to a walk, he asked "What will you do when you have your sister's soul back?"

"I don't know. Go back home, I suppose."

"You do not wish to explore this land?"

"Yes, of course I do. This is an amazing, mystical place. I would love to see more of it, but I don't know what will happen with the Queen and I have to get Dylan and Amanda back home."

"You miss your home?"

"Not really. I just feel bad for Dylan. Amanda hasn't really been able to be his mom since her soul was taken. His whole world is shaken up and I feel for my mom and step dad. We left without leaving a note, just ran after Amanda. I know they're worried."

"But now Dylan has Barinthus. He is exploring his own magic. He would not have those if he stayed in your world."

"I suppose so," she said. "I wish I could say I was getting something as useful or as wonderful out of this ordeal." She stood in the stirrups, stretching her legs, the leather of the saddle creaking with the movement.

"Are you not?"

"I'm seeing beautiful, wonderful things. But there's nothing tangible I can take home with me. My magic is clearer now, but who's to stay that won't end when I leave here? I wish I had a deep and profound connection with another being, like Dylan and Barinthus. I still have no idea what happened with the unicorn. I don't feel complete, just more unsettled. And I have a headache." She felt shrunk in on herself, feeling very small and helpless.

"Be careful what you wish for," said Edward. "You may receive it in unexpected ways."

People always said that. What did it really mean? Nothing, she thought.

They traveled in silence for a while. Through the throbbing of her headache and the flashes of light that accompanied the pain, she watched the countryside slide past. The rolling grasslands seemed uninhabited by large animals. A few, small creatures darting furtively about reminded her of rabbits or gophers. A large hawk or maybe an eagle circled overhead. Edward told her these plains once lay rich with forest and living creatures. Before people settled there and stripped them.

She wondered where Aste might be. Was she recovered from her wounds enough to do whatever business on the coast had been so urgent? Aste had brought along infusions and rare herbs to sell, but Mira knew there had been another purpose which Aste didn't confide to her. She hoped Aste was on her way to the City tonight. Otherwise what would she do with Amanda's soul when she got it back?

The wind began to pick up and it seemed to push them closer to whatever awaited them in the City. The Tower of the Black Opal loomed larger.

Faeries swirling in and out of the wind, almost as if they body surfed on the currents. These were the first she'd seen since Dylan was taken. Had they followed him? It comforted her to think they kept him safe.

The pooka watched them also and smiled as he trotted along side. There were five faeries, two very small, one medium sized with a goat's head and two larger than Edward. None of the faeries she saw previously were nine feet tall or even close. The large ones wore black and looked very serious. Hoods covered most of their heads, but they had beautiful male faces with dark hair and goatees.

They spoke simultaneously to her, their voices vibrating and sounding almost like a recording, "The Queen is having a party tomorrow night, a feast to celebrate midsummer's eve. She will announce her choice of a consort, something she has never done before, so the feast will be well attended. You must get into the castle by then if you are to stop her."

The two large ones stopped speaking and immediately vanished. The three who didn't speak slowly spun backward into the force of the wind.

Mira looked at Edward to see if he heard the message.

"We can do this," he said, nodding.

"I got tricked and captured by a plant. How am I going to take on an evil Sorcerer and a mad Queen?" Finding three people and a disembodied soul sounded easier than confronting the Queen. But how would they get into the castle?

185

Behind them massive storm clouds welled. Shadow grew skittish. She flinched at the debris that blew past them.

An enormous clap of thunder crashed through the clouds. Lightening flashed behind them. Mira wrapped her cloak tight and put the hood up, tying the strings. She felt as if the wind chased them. The earth beneath them seemed to rumble in response.

Edward said, "The dragons are talking to the land and she is speaking back."

"What are the dragons saying?" asked Mira.

"War."

"What is the land saying?"

"I do not know, I cannot understand her," he said, looking dejected as he ran beside trying to soothe the mare.

Mira wished she knew what lay behind his deep sadness. But she could hardly hear his voice above the wind and the rumbling earth. It wasn't the right time for conversation.

It was time to run.

The next few hours seemed to take forever. She couldn't see much of what lay beside the road, but got an impression of fields of grasses, maybe wheat or some other grain. And trees, possibly fruit trees. The wind blew dust into clouds around them howling and baying in their ears. She strained to see even the road ahead.

The tall black marble wall, which encircled the City, loomed ever closer. Huge arches stood in the wall at regular intervals. They were wider than necessary for a gate. Mira decided the walls existed merely for ostentation, as if to say, 'No one would dare to attack us here, for we are mighty.'

There stood several towers on top of the wall, but they looked more like they would be used for information gathering, rather than defense. The tops looked exposed and she could see people. Unlike medieval castles in her world, the walls were covered with artwork. Mosaics, she thought. The light dimmed, so she couldn't be sure, but she thought there were shiny, mirror-like bits here and there on the towers.

Clustered just inside the walls she could barely make out tents and wagons.

"The traveling people," said Edward. "They are not human or pooka, a totally separate people. They carry the true wisdom of this land, for they live out on her and see our world in all her many forms. We used to all be nomads," he said, his ears drooping.

"Even humans?"

"Yes, most humans travelled and lived out on the land. A few of most races settled here by the Black Opal and in other important places to maintain them, but nearly all peoples traveled. We moved according to the seasons, so we did not wear out one part of the land. When more people settled, including our rulers, we ignored the land's wisdom and slaughtered unicorns, broke with dragons and exhausted the soil, putting filth in the rivers. As Nakia's reign crumbles, even more huddle closer to the Opal for safety," His eyes burned with a quiet anger as his voice sounded weary and melancholy.

"Would you have everyone travel again?"

"Yes, I would make it so. Although it may be too late," he said looking down. He began to fade. She could feel him brushing her knee where his hand lay on the mare, gently guiding her. She wondered if he became invisible to hide from the city or to hide his sadness and anger from her.

Mira saw a face or two peek out from the tents. She couldn't make out the features, but the faces looked strange. They were a different shape and didn't look as if the eyes, nose and mouth in the same places as humans. She wondered what they really looked like, who they were and how they lived.

"What are they doing here?"

"Selling their wares. They collect rare stones, black pearls or other works of nature. Ironically, people in the City buy them and have them made into fine jewelry or beautiful things for their houses to remind them of the land."

The wind had died down as they passed through the outermost wall and approached the City inside. It was as if the City had a will of her own and could control nature. Even the whitecaps on the river calmed here as it flowed smoothly underneath one of the massive arched gates. Slowly and warily, Mira and the invisible Edward entered the City of the Black Opal.

Chapter 22 — Mira

Mira felt the energy of Black Opal City swarm around her. So many bodies were packed into that space. Many people lived in Seattle as well, but here magic coursed through the air. She sensed that many beings in the City held minor amounts of power. Perhaps the high-level magic was masked, which was why she couldn't feel it. Aste certainly disguised her abilities.

Close to the wall lay quaint thatched roof cottages which suffered from disrepair. They were fronted by wilting roses, nasturtiums covered with black aphids and many weeds. As they drew closer to the center of the City, the houses were larger and made completely of stone, but they too looked uncared for. She rode as Edward walked through the noisy streets. He told her the City had really only existed for the last forty turns, but had grown quickly. It must extend for miles. Thousands of people lived here.

"How will we find this Jacob the farrier? This city is huge."

"I know where to find him," said Edward.

"Why didn't you tell me?"

"You did not ask."

Mira felt annoyed. Would she ever be able to understand the pooka? What else did he keep from her because she hadn't asked?

It grew close to dark and she felt ready to drop. The only thing holding her upright was the crust of dirt encasing her. She sighed, letting Edward lead the horse. Her stomach rumbled. She hoped to find something more interesting than granola bread and dried meat.

The river ran along the same route they traveled. Several bridges spanned the Angouleme's width. She wondered if the City had indoor plumbing or a sewage system. She was tired of squatting behind bushes and hoping the leaves she used weren't this world's equivalent of nettles. She also really wanted a bath after that windstorm and not have to settle for a piece of wet cloth. Again. Thinking about trivialities kept her mind occupied, away from the overwhelming thing she must do tomorrow.

The diminishing glow from the Black Opal reflected down onto the darkening City. She could see it leaking out through the Tower and the clouds above reflecting it back onto the land. She felt a bit hopeful looking at the light. It warmed her soul

Lamplight shone out from a few windows of homes and apartments. The landscape deepened to a purple. She was losing her sight in the growing darkness, but could still see dim outlines of buildings containing businesses. An occasional tree used the remaining light to cast long shadows.

About hour had passed since they entered the city. The market stalls were covered with tarps and blankets. As they continued to walk through the street market area, the mare stopped abruptly. Mira asked, "Why are we stopping?" but received no answer.

She heard footsteps, rustling of fabric, and an invisible hand thrust an apple into hers. "Did you steal this?" she asked in amazement.

"Pooka do not steal. I left money in its place," said Edward, and they continued on.

The apple tasted better than any she'd ever eaten. Sweet and tart flavors collided in her mouth. Juice ran down her chin.

The mare tossed her head. Edward gave her half of another apple and Shadow munched happily, then waited, lips open and neck stuck out, for the second half. Mira could taste as the sweetness exploded in Shadow's mouth.

They came to a part of the city where lamps hung on metal poles lined the streets. Horses stood grouped outside buildings as if chatting. Mira saw several fantastic and elegant carriages pulled by creatures she could not name, with a llama's face, a draft horse's body, and long and upright, twisting horns, the strange creatures pranced beautifully in front of the fanciful carriages. The wooly fur changed patterns, glowing with pinks, blues, greens and maybe even orange. It was difficult to tell their color in the dark. Mira wondered if the colors and patterns were natural or dye or magic.

Edward led her to a dark stable. The upper story was lit. "Stay on your horse and wait here."

Walking close to the building in the shadows, he removed his pack then bent over to take things out. Then he stood and seemed to shake himself out. She detected a surge of magical energy and watched in awe as his silhouette shrunk in height several feet and became smaller in bulk. She felt frustrated with the darkness, wanting to see more details yet feeling awkward watching this moment. It was almost too private. Still she stared harder. He crouched down as if in pain, then came upright again and made a few clumsy movements which Mira couldn't figure out. Maybe picking up the things from his pack. When she realized he was dressing, she looked away.

Mira could see his outline in the streetlight as he walked to the door and knocked. He seemed to be in human form, wearing clothes.

She heard a banging noise from the second story as a window above opened. A red bearded face stuck out. "Who are you and what do you want?"

"We're looking for Jacob," said Edward.

"You found him."

"Please, we need your help. I'll be happy to tell you our business in private."

"All right. I'll be down shortly." He pulled his head back inside and closed the window.

Edward walked back to Mira's side and guided Shadow forward.

The large door to the stable opened and Edward led the horse inside. The stable was dimly lit, by a single oil lamp. Mira stared at Edward with his tan skin, short dusty, blond hair and scruffy beard. He'd blend in nicely with the few men she'd seen in this world. She stretched her stiff legs and shifted in the saddle for long moments. Only then could she move enough to get off the mare. Edward held the saddle for her, balancing her weight to make it easier on Shadow's back.

"Now, who are you?" asked Jacob, a very large, burly man. Edward gestured to her as if to say, 'take the lead'.

"I'm Mira and this is my brother, Edward. A few nights ago we spent some time with Griffin. She suggested we ask you for help."

"Aaaaw, Griffin. How is she?" he asked, getting a bucket of water for Shadow.

"She's doing fine, sitting on four eggs."

"Good for her. What would you be needing help with?"

"We need to get into the palace."

"The palace," he said, scratching his beard. "That's a tough one. Let me think on that. I was just up having some supper. Let's put this tired gal to bed," he said, taking the mare's reins, "and then you can come join me for dinner. It's not much."

"We would love to," said Mira.

Jacob, unsaddled the horse and Mira removed her bag from the saddle. Edward reached out to carry it. She patted Shadow and said in her mind, "Thank you." The mare simply stuck her nose towards the water bucket. Jacob slid the halter and reins off. Shadow shook herself out and snorted with relief. The stall was large enough for her to have a good roll. He gave her more water, hay, and filled a bucket with grain, then closed the stall door after giving her a nice pat on the rear, from which a cloud of dust rose.

"She'll be fine till morning." He knocked on a door and a boy who looked a couple years younger than Mira appeared. Jacob gave him directions about taking care of Shadow and the boy grabbed a box of tools that looked like brushes and such. He disappeared into Shadow's stall.

Mira felt sure a cloud of dust could easily rise from her as well. She may have needed grooming more than the horse.

They followed Jacob up the narrow stairs to his home. The stew cooking smelled wonderful. Jacob pulled out two wooden bowls and spoons and handed them to Mira and Edward. "Dish up however much you want. I made a lot. Somehow, knew I'd have company tonight."

She dove into the stew, which tasted like beef, and had carrots, onions and other root vegetables she couldn't identify. She didn't look up again until her bowl was empty.

There was ample light and she could clearly see who Edward had changed into. A medium height man with blondish hair and green eyes. Actually, quite a good-looking man, despite the raggedy beard.

Everyone else was equally as quiet, intent on their food. After dinner they gravitated to the other side of the room, where a wood stove burned, its little door open. The evening had grown cool. It must have been the breeze blowing off the sea.

"Now," said Jacob, leaning back into his chair, "you want to get into the castle. Do you know what part of the castle you want to get into?"

She looked at Edward questioningly.

He replied, "We're not sure, but most likely what we're looking for is in the Queen's private residence."

"And what is it that ya are looking for? I may know where it is."

Mira said, "The Queen stole my sister's soul and her child."

Jacob looked appalled, then shook his head. "I guess it should not surprise me. She has been doing strange things lately. I cannot say as I know where she would keep either, but the soul would likely be in her private quarters, as you guessed, and they're the most heavily guarded. That is where it gets to be a problem. I could easily get you into the public parts of the castle, especially with Midsummer Feast, but her private areas, there are only a few entrances. Most of those have been sealed off. But if there is any way to get inside, I know the man who can tell us. We will have to wait an hour or so. He will not be around just yet."

Could she trust Jacob? What if he ratted them out and spent the next hour delaying them for the Queen's guards? Griffin said he was trustworthy, but how well did she know Griffin? Her thoughts spun as Jacob asked the boy downstairs to go find the man.

If she could trust him though, Jacob didn't say it would be impossible. How could she find both Dylan and the soul? It was unlikely they'd be together. She'd always assumed she would just know, be able to sense her sister's soul. What if she couldn't? What if some barrier shielded the soul? And what about Dylan? Jacob hadn't speculated on Dylan's whereabouts. What if the Queen sat in her quarters and wouldn't leave? What if too many men guarded the soul's hiding place? She felt overwhelmed with worry and couldn't shut her mind off. It felt like a hamster running on a wheel inside her head.

Edward and Jacob discussed the latest goings on in the city. She should be listening, but felt too tired. She stared into the hypnotic, flickering blaze of the fire.

Edward touched her arm gently and he said, "Mira, wake up please."

"What?" she said, almost jumping to her feet. "What's wrong?"

"Nothing is wrong. Jacob's friend, Essail is here. I thought you would like to hear what he says."

Essail was short, skinny and covered with grime.

"Would you like some supper?" Jacob asked Essail.

"Na, my woman would skin me alive if I did not come home with an appetite. Now, what can I do for you?" he asked them.

Edward said, "Do you know how we can get into the Queen's private quarters?"

"I assume you mean unnoticed." Essail stood looking at them for a good while. He glanced at Jacob and asked, "Can we trust these two?"

Jacob replied, "Word came from Griffin just a day ago that we could."

Essail smiled as he turned to Mira and Edward and said, "Well, there used to be the servant's entrances, the back doors to all the Queen's rooms but they blocked those off after an assassination attempt. Pity that. We used to make good use of those doors. Then there is the door to the Opal Tower, that one is so heavily guarded a flea could not get through. You could try sneaking past the guards during the festivities tomorrow night, but that would be very tricky and not a guaranteed way in." He paused, thinking for a while.

"There is one other entrance, the one from the Catacombs. You can get in there and make it all the way up to the Queen's Quarters. Most of us will not risk it, not for a piece of jewelry. It is a terrifying place and most people say haunted by more than ghosts.

"What do you mean?" asked Mira.

"They say the ghosts who haunt the catacombs are sorcerers who still have their power," said Essail.

"Have you ever been there and how long does it take to get to the Queen's quarters?" asked Edward.

"Nope, I always have someone else do the leg work, even with the servant's entrances. I am just the man who got the gold or jewelry cleaned up and to Jacob here or another rescuer. If you you start at dawn, it should not take longer than half the morning. Provided you do not meet with any problems," said Essail.

"Can you get us into the catacombs and point us in the right direction?" asked Mira.

"That I can do. When do you want to go?"

Edward looked at her, "Tomorrow morning?"

Mira nodded, relieved. She couldn't face it on no sleep. Her forehead throbbed.

"Yes, tomorrow morning, that will work. I will draw you a map of the palace so you know where to go," said Essail. "You will have to get into the graveyard and sleep in the crypt tonight. Tomorrow there will be too many pooka roaming around."

Mira dreaded the idea of sleeping that close to the catacombs, that close to the Queen. She ran her hands through her hair, irritated that most of it hung in her face. She finally yanked the hair tie out, gathered up her tangled hair and stuffed it all back in the tie again. It was a mess and would just have to stay that way. The catacombs would hardly care.

Jacob found heavy paper and a rough pencil. Essail drew them two maps, one of the catacombs and the route they should take to the stairway up to the royal quarters. It became clear the catacombs were designed intentionally as a maze or by someone severely drunk. The second map was a floor plan of the Queen's Quarters. He pointed out the rooms where he'd look first for Amanda's soul. He didn't know where to look for Dylan, since they didn't know the Queen's plan for him. Essail also drew them a route to get out to the public areas so they could disappear into the festival crowd in case they couldn't escape through the catacombs.

Her body felt numb. She grew more exhausted. And scared. She tried her best to pay attention and memorize the maps in case they got separated, but the whole palace seemed to be designed to confuse.

Jacob gave them a loaf of fresh bread and a chunk of cheese to pack in her bag. Mira left him with instructions to send her horse to the general area where Aste's home had been, in case she didn't return for the mare.

They went down to the stable and Mira said goodbye, hugging the mare while she chewed contentedly on hay and whinnied goodbye in return. Shadow said she could find her way home from where Aste's tree lay, perhaps even from the City, but Mira didn't want to take chances that someone might capture the mare. She wondered if it was possible to steal a horse who could speak to you.

Jacob promised to explain Essail's absence to his wife. He refused to take any of Griffin's gold.

"No, this is my gift, my part in what we are all trying to do here," he said, closing the stable door behind them.

Essail led them through the city. They walked for about an hour, past homes, shops and parks. It was a beautiful city, even in the dark. A slight breeze drifted by, but nothing like the wind of yesterday out on the plains. Mira didn't get her bath or even a wet cloth, she still felt as dusty as her clothes. At least she'd had a great meal.

The streets stayed nearly empty. A fancy carriage passed them by once, the people riding in it laughing and drinking, the driver solemn. A wagon full of wooden boxes, pulled by two stout horses drove past them going the opposite way. Essail and the driver tipped their hats at each other.

The old graveyard stood surrounded by dark, metal fencing. Edward and Essail whispered to each other. The gate to the graveyard was open. Essail stood outside it, stopping to pull out a bottle from which he drank and then passed to Edward. Edward drank from it and they laughed. Mira smelled it and declined a drink. Taking a sip of alcohol that strong on top of being exhausted, was a perfect recipe for passing out. They walked a few feet past the entrance and stopped. Essail said, "Now, we wait and see what happens."

After a few tense, silent minutes Edward said, "Now."

Essail and Edward ran quietly through the gate, dragging Mira by the hand. They darted off the path and hid behind a hedge. Edward peered back the way they came. He seemed satisfied and motioned Essail to lead them on.

She smelled sweet-scented, night blooming flowers on the breeze and asked Edward quietly, "Do people bury their dead in this garden?"

"No, we burn our dead in the City and scatter the ashes so the River takes them out to sea. People still have monuments made for their beloved. The catacombs are filled with bones, but that is a custom long since ended."

They followed Essail to the center of the garden. She whispered to Edward, "I don't see any guard around."

"You cannot see them," said Edward. "They are pooka guards. Invisible. We slipped past one at the entrance, while the guard changed. We will be coming upon one soon, though, so quiet."

Mira shook herself, trying to focus. Essail or Edward must have used some magic to slip them past the pooka unnoticed. All the magic swirling around had made her senses less acute, as if she were drunk on it. She would have to be more careful.

"You are very good, sir," whispered Essail, looking appraisingly at Edward. I don't know what line of work you are in, but it you are ever in need of employment, let me know."

"I will," said Edward. Mira couldn't tell if he felt insulted or amused or both. They became silent as they slipped past the next two crypts. As they stopped and squeezed behind some bushes, Mira heard a quiet cough, then footsteps. Her heart seemed to pound almost as loudly as the footsteps. She felt only a slight breeze past her as the nearly silent, invisible pooka walked by.

After a time Edward moved and they left the safety of the bushes. Essail stepped up to one of the monuments, which looked like a very formal, small house. He opened a side door. Inside was all stone and Essail used a long piece of metal to pry up one of the larger tiles in the floor.

"You can sleep out here, although sometimes pooka check in here. I would sleep at the bottom of these stairs. There are robes in a wardrobe down there. I would wear them were I you, they are the same as those worn by the mystics who tend the Opal. It might help you mix in."

They said their goodbyes and she followed Edward down the stone staircase. It felt really creepy, cobwebs, dust and who knew what sort of crawly things. She heard the stone scrape across the gritty floor until it sat over the staircase opening. Her jaw tensed with fear. There was no turning back now.

She careened into Edward and stopped. The room below was lit by a dim glow of purple. The stairs had small treads, half the size of her foot. She hung onto the metal rail after nearly slipping. They stirred up dust while descending. She struggled not to sneeze. At the foot of the stairs stood the wardrobe.

Edward opened its doors and Mira took out a robe that smelled musty. He took two, but didn't put them on and motioned for her to follow him. He turned left, not right as Essail told them and entered into a small room which smelled even dustier than the stairs.

"We shall sleep here," he said.

Mira looked around. In the dimness from what she could see, it looked like a mostly bare room, with a few pieces of statuary in it. Edward pointed to the far corner and spread the two robes on the floor. "I need to change back to a pooka," he said and walked across the room. She turned her back and heard him undressing and stuffing his clothes in the backpack.

Then there was silence. Mira felt embarrassed and sat down on one of the robes he spread out, taking her time trying to cover herself with the dusty, velvet robe she'd taken. At least it felt soft.

"Why are you changing back so soon?"

"I am of more use in pooka form in these catacombs, than I would be as a man," he said quietly. She could hear the fatigue in his voice.

"Does it hurt to change?"

"Not if I take my time, but it does drain one. Especially to change often in a short period."

"How long can you stay in another form?"

"That depends on the form. Some are more difficult to maintain than others. It is different, I believe for everyone."

"Have you met many shape shifters?"

"Only two."

"Are you really a pooka, or is your natural form different?"

"You have too many questions tonight. I think I will answer that one another time, I am too weary."

"I'm sorry. I'm just afraid. Talking about something else helps me to keep from thinking about what I have to do."

"We are safer here than you have been since you went to Aste's. The Queen is unlikely to hunt for you in a storage room in the catacombs."

After a time he lay down beside her and said, "Come put your head on my shoulder, I will warm you."

Mira hadn't realized her teeth were chattering. She had felt that way all night long, even in front of Jacob's fire. Exhaustion did that to her and her head roared with an unrelenting headache. Her warm bedroll lay tied on the saddle at the stables. She felt strange cuddling up to Edward, but could think of no logical reason not to.

She also felt uncomfortable in a room of carved monsters. Even after nights of sleeping in caves and forest floors, this unseen space filled with cobwebs and whatever else did not feel like a safe place to sleep. Still, she needed rest to meet whatever the day would bring.

She curled up with Edward and buried her face in his chest. Mira didn't think sleep would come, but her next coherent thought came waking from a dream and blushing at its contents. She lay alone on the robes.

The towering form of Edward stood in the doorway with his back to her.

Her head still throbbed. Touching a hand to her forehead, she felt a big knot there. She sat up quickly, filled with panic. Had Edward heard something? How long had she slept? Did they still have time to find the soul, Dylan and Amanda?

Chapter 23 — Edward/Ronan

He realized Mira was watching him, and whispered, "It is midday. Time to eat and make our way into the catacombs." He returned to the door and listened again to the voices that occasionally echoed from the cavern and the noise of people moving about.

He heard Mira pull out the bread and cheese.

"How long have you been awake," she asked, quietly.

He turned and spoke softly, "Since morning broke. Pooka do not normally sleep as long as humans, but I felt tired from the changing."

"You must be really worn out."

"More than I can say," he said. He noticed her forehead.

The bump on it had expanded overnight and became a protrusion. Yesterday, it had been red and angry looking. Today it looked a pearly cream color. Was it what he suspected?

She put on the velvety, black robe, drawing the hood up to cover her fiery hair. He pulled his pack on. She followed him out into the hallway and he wrapped his shield around both of them, so their magical energy would not leak and betray them. In the hallway he slowly become invisible.

The tunnel smelled of dry, musty earth. No life grew here in this graveyard. Edward stopped once before they finished descending. "Now we are in the passageway to the castle. This is where trouble will begin if there is to be any. I know you have many powerful magic, but you must save yours for finding Dylan and your sister's soul. I am more familiar with the castle's magic and, as a pooka, may be more powerful than you."

She nodded. He felt relieved there would be no argument.

The tunnel widened until it was as large as a small sized room. The facade here was carved of square tiles from the Black Silk Canyon. They gleamed in the dim light which filtered down the tunnels from the main cavern of the Black Opal.

He stopped once at a relief room so they could empty themselves. Mira looked more relaxed afterward. He felt bad for not thinking of her needs earlier. He usually traveled alone, without being responsible for anyone else.

The magic felt stronger the closer they came to the Opal. It also felt subtle, more devious. What had caused the change?

They came around a corner to find a black iron screen with a door in it. He had never used this corridor as a guard and was unfamiliar with it. The door was locked. He made several physical, then magical attempts before finally opening it. "Let us hope there is no alarm on this door that tells someone we are here," he said. They went through. He put a good sized stone block to keep it open, but as they walked away, the door slammed shut. Clanging echoed throughout the tunnel.

"A door that wants to be shut," she said.

"And announce our presence." Someone must have heard the door. He hoped they'd simply think a pooka used it and let it clang shut.

As they continued down the corridor, he bowed at the row upon row of skulls set into mortar between stones. A waist-high row was made of arm and leg bones. Near the floor were foot bones set in the mortar. The further down the hallway they walked, the more elaborate the mosaics became, including glossy tiles and cut stones. Edward never tired of looking at the art his ancestors made, however grisly it might be. It puzzled him, though. Did they worship death or create this to be the ultimate affirmation of life?

"All these stones and skulls are attached to the actual cave walls. For centuries our predecessors worked the caves down here, digging new rooms and adding the stonework," he whispered.

"Pooka did this?"

"And humans."

As they snuck along he watched her touch the walls, admiring the work. The elaborate mosaic made from pieces of old bones, gems and other stones represented parts of his world. On this section of the wall was a scene of the open ocean, with seabirds circling above and strange creatures swimming beneath the waves. On the other wall, mountains were lit by the Opal while glowing orange and red dragons artfully whirled above.

The hallway emptied into an enormous cavern with several other corridors radiating out from it. In the center of the cavern stood pillars and arches which met high in the center. One was composed of skulls, another of ribs and the third of backbones.

Mira whispered, "This is amazing. I don't think I've ever seen anything so creative in my life."

"There is a profound beauty to these caverns," he said quietly.

"It's all about the shortness of life, isn't it? The need to appreciate life while we have it." She stood staring up at the ceiling and whispered, "It takes my breath away."

As Mira started to step out into the cavern, Edward stopped her and gently turned her face down to look at the center of the cavern.

A man stood, positioned between the three pillars, looking upward, his arms raised in ritual. He recognized the Sorcerer. The man wore black velvet robes and stood bathed in a radiant dark, purplish light flowing down from the Black Opal

The Sorcerer seemed unaware of their presence. He continued to absorb potency from the Opal.

Fury churned in his stomach. The man had no right to do such a thing. The Opal's power was only for her chosen rulers. Others would be incensed at his actions if they knew.

The Sorcerer put his arms down, bowed and began to slowly walk out of the cavern towards the first passage. At the last moment, just as Edward was about to breathe in relief, the Sorcerer spun towards them.

A bolt of energy shot through the air towards Edward. He turned it around and bounced the energy back to the Sorcerer, adding some of his own.

The Sorcerer recoiled as the blow punched him. Then he attacked again, quickly before Edward could ready himself.

Edward felt his body crumple and become visible. He was not strong enough to remain a pooka, shield himself along with Mira, be invisible and fight.

"Run," he gasped at Mira, "I will find you." Edward tried to add a sense of urgency, pass it through to her mind, hoping she understood.

Mira ran for the corridor that would take her into the palace. He shielded her from attack. Assaulting the Sorcerer again with an undulating, cold current, he hoped Mira would not look back. He shifted out of the burden of maintaining Edward.

In the transition, he heard the Sorcerer say, "Do not run away little one. Do you not want to see your friend die?" The Sorcerer was distracted enough to give him a little more time.

Edward was caught in flux. Pain burned through his bones, muscles, nerves and skin. The metamorphosis was taking too long, but there was no choice. It happened just as the Sorcerer's next attack came, a hard, hot blast to his stomach. The agony became unbearable. Ronan/Edward countered with another attack, but knew it was weak. He needed more time to regain his energy. The Sorcerer was simply too fast, aided by the power he stole from the Black Opal. The Sorcerer sent the final blow to his head and Ronan passed out of consciousness.

Upon gaining consciousness, he surprisingly found himself back in pooka form. Edward was being carried on a wide board by four pooka and escorted by two others. He suspected they moved towards the dungeons. He was not certain if the change had been incomplete or if he changed back to a pooka for protection. Pooka healed faster. It would be troublesome for Ronan to be caught sneaking into the palace and treasonous to attack the Queen's Sorcerer. It could not be much better for a pooka to be caught doing it, but at least it would not bring unwanted attention to his father. He felt the numbness in his arms and hands leaving. He had not known he could shape change while unconscious.

"Ahh," said one of the pooka at his feet. "It seems our friend Edward is awake."

The other pooka laughed. Edward shifted his weight, feeling the lumpiness of the pack beneath his back.

One of them who walked near his head said, "Do not struggle, my son. Simply pretend you are still knocked out. We will remove you from this predicament." Edward recognized the voice but could not fully place it.

He went limp and stayed that way, struggling to clear his mind. He trusted the pooka. They felt no love for the

Sorcerer and would be appalled at what the man was doing. Perhaps they knew. How did the Sorcerer steal potency from the Opal? She carried the strongest magic in their world. The Opal must be allowing the Sorcerer access to her, but why?

As he was carried deeper into the catacombs, he worried about Mira. Did she get away in time?

"Mira," he whispered, "did she escape him?"

"Shhh," one of the pooka warned.

Edward's back, arms and hands itched terribly. It felt unbearable to avoid scratching his burning skin. Unbathed or not, he had never felt like this before and didn't know if it was part of the attack from the Sorcerer, or something else.

One of his carriers greeted a jailer and they were led around a corner and down some steps. Keys jangled and the darkness deepened. The pooka set his board down on straw which was most likely infested with vile, biting insects.

One of the pooka said, "We will question him and call you when we are finished."

The jailer grunted and left, shuffling away.

He sat up slowly, feeling very stiff. His head still hurt a great deal. A dark mood surrounded the other pooka. "What is wrong?" he asked.

"Dragons circle the castle. They mean to make war on us unless the Queen releases the boy," said one.

"What is her response?" he asked, rubbing his head and trying to clear it. He felt dizzy.

"The Queen laughs. She is mad."

"Has Mira been caught?"

"The woman has escaped so far," said one of the pooka," but I think she is lost in the catacombs. After we leave you, we shall try to find her and help her into the palace. We assume that is her destination."

"Yes," said Edward, slowly getting to his feet. He leaned against the stone wall of the cell and breathed heavily.

"She is the one we wait for?" asked one of the pooka, young enough to still have streaks of black in his fur.

"Possibly. If she is, Mira could use all the help any of us can give her."

"That she will have," they agreed.

"Where does she need to go in the palace," asked another pooka. Edward recognized him now that his head had cleared. Arron. He had spent many evenings with him, guarding the catacombs. Arron remained one of the pooka vehement in the belief the Queen should step down.

"She seeks her sister's soul and the child whom the Queen stole."

"The Queen had stolen a soul?" asked the youngest one.

"Yes, and the kidnapped child is joined with a master dragon." He winced while trying to walk. His right leg ached.

The pooka murmured among themselves. They were outraged and appalled. The shortest pooka, Marcus stayed silent. Edward knew he communicated what they learned to the elders, who lived on the other side of the City.

Edward asked, "Were you aware the Sorcerer communes with the Black Opal?"

A silence followed and Arron said, "We have long suspected it, but there is no proof."

"I have proof. Mira and I saw him, standing between the Pillars of Life, Death and Mystery, bathed in the light of the Opal." He still felt horrified at this. It was forbidden for any but the ruler chosen by the Black Opal, to join with the stone in this manner. What the Sorcerer did was an obscenity, undoubtedly why he chose to hide in the catacombs and steal power instead of going to the tower.

Anger burned in their eyes. "This cannot continue," said a rangy, brown pooka, whom Edward barely knew.

"No, it cannot," said Marcus. "By revealing this knowledge to us, the Black Opal has asked for our help. The Queen and her Sorcerer must be made powerless this night."

Nods of agreement circled among all the pooka.

"Is your father coming to the feast tonight?" asked Marcus.

"I suppose he is, I have been out of touch with him for several days."

"We should not make that presumption," said the brown pooka.

"We have never interfered with the rule of this land, but it is time we did so. We have been satisfied, until Nakia became Queen, to serve the Black Opal. The Queen is under the impression we have become tame and are no longer great warriors, simply because we remain silent and seem subservient. The young among us have wanted this for a long time. Now our elders say it is time to act. Roderick is next in line, he should be prepared for the test," said Marcus.

The pooka talked amongst themselves for a few minutes before agreeing. Arron turned to Edward and said, "We took you from human guards, saying we recognized you as a renegade and would take you to the dungeons so the Sorcerer could deal with you at his leisure. He should not return tonight, and tomorrow will be powerless."

They motioned for him to become invisible. He did so and one of the pooka pushed straw into a pile and threw a velvet robe from the catacombs over it. In the darkness it looked as if someone lay face down on the floor.

"Jailer, we are finished here," yelled one of the pooka.

After the door was unlocked, Edward wedged himself between two of the pooka who carried the board back out and followed them down a corridor towards the royal quarters.

Marcus whispered to him, "Leave us at this next turn and go upstairs. When it is safe, become Ronan again and warn your father to be ready. We will find the woman and lead her to the Queen's quarters."

"Thank you," he said.

"Our thanks will be if everything turns out well tonight," said one of the pooka.

As they rounded the corner, he saw two pooka guarding the door to the stairs leading up.

His pooka guard stopped to speak with the others. Edward knew the pooka watching the door saw him, but they gave no hint of it. Finally, one of them turned, opened the door and looked inside as if he heard a sound. After he did so and found nothing, he held it open just long enough for Edward to slip past.

"May you feel the wind through your fur," the pooka whispered to him.

He felt honored. This was the highest blessing one pooka could wish to another. It spoke of freedom. Although humans might not be able to see through his disguise, the pooka always did.

The news about the Sorcerer would spread quickly to all pooka before he even reached the upper levels of the palace. Remaining invisible, he reached the public part of the palace. The guests had begun to arrive for the feast. He did not see his father yet, although he saw Ewan and Amanda. His father joined them. Edward almost left to find a place to shift when one of the Queen's human guards spoke to this father. His father looked relieved and he, Ewan and Amanda followed the guard out of the ballroom.

In a corner, Edward saw his friend Stephen drinking ale and watching the crowd, no doubt looking for some beautiful woman to flirt with. Stephen knew his friend could become a pooka, but not the true extent of his abilities. Still invisible, he walked up behind Stephen and said, "Do not move, I am not here."

"Playing games again, are we?" asked Stephen behind his mug of ale.

"Hopefully, the last game. Where did my father go?"

"He requested an audience with the Queen. He is worried about your whereabouts, as you should have returned days ago, according to him. Since Ewan brought your horse back long before, Roderick is concerned something may have befallen you and is requesting her assistance," said Stephen.

"Thereby assuring she is not involved in my disappearance."

"You do catch on quickly for a young whip." Stephen was a week older than him.

"When he returns, please tell my father to be ready to face the Opal tonight. The dragons will help us, as will pooka and many others."

"You have been busy," he said, eyebrows raised. Stephen could masterfully hide his emotions, but this surprised him.

"You have no idea."

"What shall I tell him about you?" asked Stephen.

"You may tell him I am here and will be in touch with him, but I must be going now. I have work to do." Upon seeing the Sorcerer enter the room, he slipped out another door and headed for the royal quarters. Several pooka guards passed him along the way and either ignored him or gave him a simple twitch of the ear.

When he reached the royal quarters, he slipped into the rooms reserved for family members. These rooms were set aside so they could live in the palace or stay after imbibing heavily at a party. The rooms lay empty of servants. Edward went into the rooms his father kept and found some clean clothes, then entered the bathroom. He removed his backpack and shook. Still feeling burning skin, he shifted very slowly back into Ronan. He felt relieved to be human again. To hold another form always meant bleeding off some of his energy, even if it was an easy form to hold. His head throbbed a little, but his leg had healed.

Ronan drew a bath and cleaned himself, puzzling over scaly, greenish iridescent skin on his hands and arms. When he stood in front of the mirror he saw the same thing on his back, forming a slight ridge along his spine. Three things came to mind. It could be part of the Sorcerer's spell. It could be from an incomplete change from fighting with the other shape shifter or the demon. The third alternative he refused to consider.

After dressing, he collected himself for some time, filling up again. Then he left to find Mira.

How could he explain Edward to her?

Chapter 24 — Mira

Mira fled down the tunnel, away from the Sorcerer, feeling like a coward. She had left Edward to die.

Gasping for breath she slowed to a stagger. Her legs wobbled. How had she gotten so out of shape? What did she think she could do here? How could she accomplish anything? Her thoughts grew deeper, darker and more cutting. Sweat drenched her face, her head pounding.

She was alone, faced with an impossible task. Finally stopping and slumping, Mira took a ragged breath, then a deeper one, she tried to imagine all the negative thoughts blown away by a cool breeze.

After five more breaths, clarity returned. Danger. Hide.

She slid into the dark room on her left. This room, too, was filled floor to ceiling with bones. She pressed herself close to the cold wall inside the doorway. Foot steps came and went.

She shuffled back to the open doorway. It didn't feel right. She moved inside the room again. More footsteps, slower this time.

Her concealment spell came easily, once she thought to even use it. She focused on becoming part of the rock wall. Heat grew in her belly, where the unicorn horn had entered. Was this a gift she received from the unicorn? She could feel the age of these rocks, and a deep, slow power that lay beneath thinking. She felt herself meld with them, actually becoming stone. A feeling of being loved and cared for, of joining with others through the creation of beauty. It felt as if the mosaics made by humans and pooka had awakened the rocks. She struggled to shake herself back to an awareness of being human.

She lost track of which direction the last footsteps had gone. This room echoed more than the hallway. She felt along the wall moving still farther away from the door, then around a pile of bones. There were less bones than other rooms she had passed. She sensed a draft of cool air. After a few minutes she found a second door which led to a different corridor. It seemed to run parallel to the first.

More shouting and footsteps echoed down the first tunnel. She backed into the room again. Instinct told her to stay put. Sweat made her cold and clammy underneath the heavy velvet robe. According to the map this new hallway led to a part of the palace close to the Queen's quarters. Provided the map could be trusted.

The old corridor she'd traveled was now a very busy arterial. She couldn't understand the voices, too much echo, but it was clear they were searching all the rooms.

She went deep inside herself for guidance. The answer came back from her intuition, move down the new tunnel while you still can.

Leaving the bone room, she ran down the new twisting and turning hallway, past rows of skulls which grinned in the dim light. Side corridors crossed in several places, but she stayed with what looked like the main thoroughfare. She ran, walked to catch her breath, then sped again over and over, for what seemed like hours. The light grew so dim she could barely see, which must mean she was going away from the Black Opal and the central cavern. Hopefully, toward the entrance to the Queen's Quarters. There seemed to be no end to this place, but she heard no voices or footsteps.

She felt exhausted. Her stomach rumbled so loudly it seemed to echo on the tunnel walls. Finding another bone room, she slumped down to the floor and pulled out her half of the bread and cheese, glad Edward had insisted on splitting it up. He had said, "Normally, I could go without, but my powers are weakened right now."

Edward. There was no way she could have helped him. She hadn't even gotten a chance to say goodbye. He had been right though. Her job was to get Dylan and the soul. She had to stop the Queen. If she could rescue Dylan and retrieve the soul, she wouldn't have to face the Queen. That realization made her feel slightly bolder.

She felt thirsty. Her water pouch was with the saddle in Jacob's stable.

After eating she began running again. The path crossed over an underground stream with a little wooden bridge. Was it a branch of the River Angouleme? Mira wondered if there could be something about the crossing of this river and the Black Opal that gave this place its power.

She wished there could have been more time to explore the cavern beneath the tower and those amazing columns, but she needed to find Dylan and free Amanda's soul. Then somehow find Aste and get the soul back inside Amanda. And get away from the palace before the dragons came. All seemed impossible.

After another couple hours of walking and running, she heard a keening noise. It sounded ghostly. Was it in front or behind her? The noise grew louder.

She moved into the next open room and stood still again, slowing her breathing and focusing on becoming one with the stone wall. The noise echoed unevenly, sounding closer one minute and much father the next. Dogs. The guards had brought dogs down here to look for her. The map said the tunnels ran parallel, fanning out from the central cavern, each corridor leading to a separate part of the palace. As she listened more, the dogs seemed to be ahead of her.

Unless the map was wrong. After all, Essail said he'd never been down here. Had she become lost in the darkness?

She ran again, then walked when she couldn't run any more. As she touched the front of her velvet robe Mira realized she'd torn a hunk out of it somewhere along the way. That would give the dogs something to work on. She ditched the robe, to hell with any camouflage it could give her. It was too hot. Passing an open room on the far side of the tunnel, away from the first one she'd come down, she tossed the robe inside. She hoped it would leave someone as confused as she felt. Did dehydration cause confusion?

She heard water running again. Rocks glowed neon green and sickly yellow above her as they did in several of the darkest parts of the corridors. Were they uranium or something awful and was she now getting five lifetime's worth of radiation? Her hair would fall out, her skin would peel off.

She climbed onto the same wooden bridge as before. She knew because the gashes on the wooden handrail were in the same places. She was going around in circles.

Panic filled her. She was lost.

She'd failed utterly and was unable to help her sister or Dylan. They were all doomed. She crossed her arms in frustration and ragged fingernails cut gashes in the skin..

She remained frozen on the bridge. Below her, white fish swam slowly through the water. Their long flowing fins streamed behind them. They helped her remember to breathe and gradually she released herself from the panic and frustration to think again. Out of her pocket she pulled a few bread crumbs and put her hand in the water. The fish swam towards her and eagerly sucked at the food and her hand. Their mouths felt like vacuum cleaners. The fish swam through her hands and let her pet them. It was clear they were used to being fed.

She took a handful of the water, tasting it. It was crisp, clean and refreshing. She drank only enough to wet her lips and mouth, in case it was poisonous. Rubbing some water on her face, she tried to clean it and cool down. The lump on her forehead had grown ever larger. It stuck out about two inches now. This was no simple bump from hitting herself. How fast did brain tumors grow? She trembled. It explained her constant headache. Maybe Aste would know what to do about it. If she ever saw her again.

There was no use trying this corridor again. Edward had the map and she was afraid to go back down the other tunnel, even if she knew the way. She might run into the dogs

The only thing she could think of was to go the other direction in this hallway and try to get back to the Opal Cavern and start again. Perhaps the men and dogs would have moved on by then. They wouldn't search rooms they had already looked at. It might work.

Fighting her exhaustion, she forced herself to stand up, then turned and went the opposite direction this time, alert for any tunnels which crossed it. She listened for guards and dogs, but heard only her own heartbeat. She kept moving towards the purplish glow at the end of the corridor.

Finally, she was at the cavern. The stone wall felt cold on her cheek as she leaned and waited, listening. No guards speaking and no dogs. Perhaps they were in one of the other corridors like herself, watching and waiting.

She stood for some minutes. Mira gingerly crept out into the cavern, sticking as close to the wall as she could. She went a couple of feet and stopped. Nothing happened. No movement. No alarms raised.

Moving a little further towards the second corridor, she stopped again. She looked at the bone columns in the center of the cavern. The warm, purplish light pulsed as if calling to her. She felt it had a message for her.

She moved to the center of the cavern into the purple light beneath the Black Opal. She looked up at it. The Opal was massive, perhaps twenty stories up inside the otherwise empty tower. It lay suspended in a net of metal rope, glistening and swirling in a rainbow of colors against a black-purple cosmos.

The Opal's potentiality flowed into Mira's body as the stone's voice vibrated within her mind.

"Welcome Mira, my child. Long have I waited for your arrival. I understand your confusion. To help bring clarity to you, I must first explain my long history."

Images flooded Mira's mind: the volcano that birthed the Black Opal, exploding and dying, the ancient peoples who found the stone in this massive underground cavern. Mira saw a small group of humans and pooka cleaning and anointing the Black Opal with herbs and wine. They kept her hidden for a long time, but that was not the Opal's intent.

"I needed to be seen and shared with every creature in this world."

Eventually, she cracked and eroded the crust above with her longing and people began to understand her plans. They gained the knowledge necessary and over many turns built the tower, so the Black Opal's light could be seen everywhere in their land.

Mira felt the land rise up in her blood and claim her.

"You need to live in this land," the Opal told her. "You belong here. That is why your magic never worked in your world. That was the unicorn's message for you."

Mira began to weep with joy and gratitude. Her feet molded to the stone floor and she felt grounded. Her mind and priorities effortlessly reorganized themselves in ways that seemed completely natural. All excess baggage simply fell away. Confidence and faith in her abilities filled Mira's being. Doorways opened and new knowledge flooded in from the Opal. Now, uncovered in her mind, lay the ability to be disciplined about her craft. Love and compassion emerged from a very deep place. She felt whole for the first time.

"You must hide! Hurry! Behind my columns. I will conceal you from the dogs."

"I don't want to leave."

"You will always have me with you now, can you not feel it? We are part of each other."

Mira moved out of the radiance and behind the columns of skulls. The lump on her forehead became caught on it. Mira realized the lump now stood out four inches. She could actually see it when she looked up, red and angry.

A human guard came out of the tunnel from the graveyard. From the same opening that she and Edward used to enter the cavern earlier. The guard was pulled by three huge, black dogs. The same kind of dogs that had stolen Amanda's soul. Noses to the ground, they followed her original trail. She spied a piece of her black robe in the dog handler's hand. He put it to the dogs' noses to keep their memories fresh.

The man and dogs rushed off into the first corridor she had gone down. If she hadn't stayed just now, to speak with the Opal, they would be moving down that same corridor right behind her. She sighed with relief. But only for a moment.

Mira watched as the Sorcerer slyly followed in the wake of the handler and dogs. Apparently waiting to see if something moved after the dogs left.

She stayed still. Mira watched the Sorcerer slink into the center of the cavern, clenching his fists, punching the air, angrily. A pooka ran from the corridor the dogs had just entered and towards the Sorcerer. Mira quietly extricated the lump on her forehead from the column of bones.

The pooka whispered quietly to the Sorcerer. He yelled at the pooka, threw up his hands in frustration, stalking back the way the pooka come from.

The pooka turned to her and smiled.

Mira felt filled with fear.

Chapter 25 — Mira

From the middle of the cavern, the pooka came to Mira and bowed. "We must wait here a little longer. The guard are attempting to rescue your companion. I will escort you into the castle safely. You will be on your own from there."

"Why are you helping me?" This dark, gray pooka reminded her of Edward, but how did she know she could trust him?

"Because it is necessary. You must retrieve the soul from the Queen and overthrow her. No one else can do this. Dragons are circling the Tower, threatening to kill everyone, unless the boy is released."

"Why me?"

Did Edward tell him about her? No, probably not. He must know from the Sorcerer. This must be a trap.

"Chosen by the unicorns, Blessed by the Opal," he bowed.

She recognized the verse when he said it, but couldn't grasp any context. The Opal had transferred an amazing amount of strength and knowledge and Mira knew she could now do things without really understanding how. Her mind and body were still trying to make sense of it all.

Cupping her hands together, she imagined a stone that glowed. A golden gemstone the size of a plum appeared in her hands. Its glow lit the pooka's face.

"You will do it. We are sure of that," he said.

"What about the Sorcerer?"

The pooka grinned. "He will be taken care of." The expression sent chills through her. "Come, we must go now," he said.

She slipped the stone into her pocket, still feeling its warmth in her hands. Mira hadn't realized how cold her body had become. She sent heat throughout it and soon needed to unbutton the top of her blouse and roll up her sleeves. Sweat began to drip down her face. Her hand caught on the lump on her forehead. If it wasn't for the massive headache she could almost have forgotten it grew there.

She followed the pooka. He would think she trusted him, but she would escape when the moment presented itself. Right now he watched her. Better to take him unawares. He led her to the fourth tunnel, on the far side of the two she already used.

"Isn't this the wrong hallway?" she asked.

"We will cross over to the correct one at the end of the corridor. There are too many guards in the other one. All the tunnels connect, eventually."

"That's not what the map said."

"Ah. Perhaps your informant has spent less time learning his way down here than we have," said the pooka, smiling at her again.

That smirk made her even more nervous. She wondered if perhaps he really meant to help her. This hallway looked just like the other two. Farther on, she noticed the skulls looked red. Not blood, the color was too vivid. They were decorated with red paint. It didn't look gruesome, more like gaudy. Like the sugar skulls from a Day of the Dead Festival.

They traveled down the tunnel, the pooka padding along slowly and Mira running faster just to keep up. Already tired, she became more and more exhausted, then decided to try shifting energy to her muscles. It worked. She felt them fill with energy and begin move more efficiently. She focused so much on her new found power that she ran into a wall, where the tunnel curved. Landing flat on her bum, she was amazed and startled at the rush of so much power.

"Are you all right? I am so sorry. I should not run so quickly. You must be tired," said the pooka, extending a hand to help her up.

"I'm fine, just not paying attention."

She stood up, very embarrassed, and brushed herself off. The magic felt intoxicating. Like a fine dessert wine, sweet and full of fruit, masking all that alcohol, then wham. She could get drunk off all this power. It would be best to use it sparingly.

They took a turn into a small, side passageway. This tunnel looked darker than the others. They had to pick their steps carefully as the ground lay littered with bones and fallen stones. The side corridors, clearly, weren't kept up as well as the main ones. She could hear the faint barking of dogs all around them.

As they neared the other main passageway, the familiar sounds of pursuit became audible. Dogs and guards. The pooka stopped and waited. Soon the echoes diminished.

The pooka turned to her. "We are almost at the entrance to the palace. You must go up three stairways, passing the first two doors. Then go through the third doorway and turn to the left. Enter the second door on your left. A pooka will be guarding it, but will take that moment to turn away and check a disturbance in another room. That will let you into the Queen's Quarters. We do not know where your sister's soul is. That is for you to find. The child will find you."

She paused for a moment, astonished. He hadn't turned her in. The pooka really did mean to help her. She nodded in answer and followed the pooka as he sprinted for the door. He unlocked and opened it. She ran for the stairs saying, "Thank you."

"Our thanks will come when the Queen is deposed," he said, smiling broadly.

Air whooshed by as the door closed behind her. She started up the black, glossy stairs. They felt slippery, despite the inset red tiles, so she hung onto the railing. At the top of the first flight she passed by a heavy wooden door. The stairs turned and became brilliant red stone inset with black tiles. As she ascended more light came in. After so long in the dark it took awhile for her eyes to adjust.

She passed a second door and started on the third stairway of black stone and tiles. What time was it? Had the feasting started? Better not think about food, she thought. At least she didn't feel thirsty now.

She reached the top of the third stairway. This wooden door was painted gold. She cautiously opened it and peered around. The hallway stood empty except for the pooka guarding the second door to the left.

He caught her eye and gave a slight twitch of his ear that reminded her of a wink. The pooka walked to a door across the corridor and opened it, looking inside. She walked into the hallway, past one door on the left and went inside the second one.

A sumptuous seating area sat in front of her. She felt humidity and the powerful fragrance of sweet flowers. Shining blue and silver tapestries hung on several walls. A large shallow pool, with a fountain splashing in it, lay in the center. The ceiling contained several skylights and luscious, tropical plants grew everywhere, some twining around the pillars and many fragrant flowers in pink, red and yellow bloomed. The room also contained a few small trees to fill the tall, vaulted ceiling. Three doors opened into the lobby. She saw no one.

She chose the door on the left. Inside lay a slightly smaller room, decorated the same way but only occupied by several silky, green couches. The room stood open to the outside with large doors and a breeze blowing through gauzy teal curtains. Twilight had arrived, but of which day? What if she was too late? How long had she wandered in the catacombs? What if the Queen had already inhaled Amanda's soul?

She tried to breathe deep and remain calm, to listen to the Opal's voice inside herself for directions, but it felt very difficult. Tension crept up her back. She stretched, trying to release the muscles.

She went deep inside again and asked for guidance. Finding it, she slipped through a door into a second room, lined with scarlet, gauzy curtains. Inside lay a huge pool of steaming water filled with rose petals. The room felt warm, humid and fragrant.

She heard voices from an adjoining chamber and found a cluster of huge potted plants to hide behind. She visualized putting a cloak over herself to hide her power. The door must have opened because the voices became clearer.

"Hurry," said a woman's voice. "We must put the asania petals into her bath so they can steep.

There was chattering, punctuated by a deep and strong, feminine voice that commanded, "Tonight must be perfect. All of you out, out." Then there was a sound of rustling. The woman said, "Turn your back until I am in the bath. The feast must be flawless. Tonight, I will choose a consort." Someone quietly splashed water.

"Do you think that wise your majesty? Why not wait until the souls have truly become yours at dawn. That way your new souls can help you choose," said a slippery, slimy voice.

She recognized the Sorcerer. She heard deception in his voice. Did he not intend to give Amanda's soul to the

Queen? Or did he hope to add a little spell in addition, that would give him more power over her, perhaps so the Queen would choose him? She wondered if the Queen could hear the deception.

"When has a soul or a heart helped anyone choose a consort wisely? No, I need a clear head to do that, then all the new souls will help me love him."

The Queen sounded strange, although Mira had never heard her voice before. She seemed manic, maybe slightly deranged. Very deranged.

"As you wish."

Had Mira heard correctly? 'All the new souls'? Had the Queen stolen more that one? Fear crept up the small hairs on the back of her neck. Did the Queen steal Dylan's soul as well? No one could do that to a child, could they?

"Now, why have you kept me waiting so long?" demanded the Queen.

"Nothing terribly important, but something I wanted to take care of before it became a larger problem."

Mira realized she could catch glimpses of the Sorcerer. She watched as he sat on a stool, his back to her.

"What?"

"Just a couple of burglars in the catacombs."

"Burglars! Tonight of all nights there must be no problems. Could not my pooka take care of that without you?"

The Sorcerer fidgeted as he spoke. "I happened to be down there when the burglars arrived, so I stayed to help catch them. The pooka seemed to be having some problem finding one of them."

"But you caught them?"

"One. He is in the dungeons. The other man is still in the catacombs, but will be caught shortly, we brought the dogs down."

"Only one?" she said. "Well, he will have to do. Let us have a little sacrifice before dawn."

Mira shivered, trying hard to become one with the wall behind and mask her emotions and power.

"I do not think that would be a good idea, your Highness. Blood sacrifices, midsummer and new souls, it is a clash of intentions. And I have not the time to question the prisoner properly."

"Nonsense, there is time before the feast. Time enough for a great many things."

Mira felt embarrassed. That sounded like a seduction if she ever heard one.

"Ah, but I have other visitors. My mother and brother have come unexpectedly."

"The old witch. She's not dead? You do not think she suspects you tried to kill her?"

"No, I do not. She arrived this afternoon. I put her off, but I must speak with her and find out exactly what she wants and what she knows."

"Yes, do that." The Queen gave a deep sigh. "I suppose the sacrifice will have to take place another time. Relatives are tiresome. My brother has requested an audience before the feast. I assume he will bring Ronan and Ewan and we will have another nice little chat about me giving up the throne. If he was not my brother, I would kill him."

Mira nearly fainted with relief to hear the sacrifice would wait. It would give the pooka time to help Edward escape. She desperately needed to get out of this room and find the soul and Dylan.

The Queen dismissed the Sorcerer and finished her bath. Servants returned and the Queen complained to them about the temperature, that they pulled her hair, soap ran in her eyes, they didn't hurry fast enough and on and on. The Queen and Amanda would have gotten on perfectly.

Mira did not feel impressed. She could sense the Queen's power, although oddly enough, she felt that Aste or Edward held more power. Did most of the Queen's power came from other people, such as the Sorcerer, or from her bearing and appearance? Well, hopefully she'd never find out. She'd just find the soul, Amanda and Dylan, then get out of the palace and hopefully the City, all before dawn when the dragons attacked.

The Queen left for another room to dress and Mira sighed. Now she needed only to wait a while for the Queen to depart and for the servants to clean up and get out.

She poked her head out from behind the plants. The room looked empty, but this was still a good hiding place. There were several rooms left to search before she left this area. She wanted to wait a little longer. She wished for some food. That should be the least of her worries.

Mira sat down. She could stay here awhile and rest while waiting. She would have liked a bath in that huge pool and to change out of her dusty clothes. She was almost surprised the servants couldn't smell her.

She scratched her face, a little less dusty now, after washing it somewhat in the stream. The lump on her forehead had grown even longer. It felt hard and round, very symmetrical. Again she worried what caused. What if it was from some horrible magical accident?

It would take all her attention to find Dylan and Amanda's soul and get out of here. She must focus on that and forget about baths and food and lumps on foreheads.

Chapter 26 — Mira

Mira must have waited an hour while gossiping servants had come in, lazily cleaned the entire room and left.

She crept out from behind the pots, walked past the now empty bath and into the third room. It stood empty of people, but full of clothes. The huge room was a walk-in closet that looked like an upscale clothing store with only one size and style, dramatic. Nothing casual existed in this room. She toyed with the idea of borrowing some of the Queen's clothes to blend in with people at the feast, it might make her escape easier. However, Queen Nakia was clearly much taller and thinner. She'd have to wear her own filthy, funky clothes.

Looking at the far mirrored wall, her mouth gaped open. A horn six inches long and pearlescent protruded from her forehead. Somehow the unicorn's horn was growing out of her head. She touched its smoothness in fascinated horror.

No longer could she pretend it might be a lump or some strange magical accident that could be removed by Aste. There would be no removing this. Was she actually becoming a unicorn with this being the first step? How would that fit into her old life? She wanted to curl up in a ball and cry, but forced herself to keep moving and find Amanda's soul. It took several minutes of deep breathing before she could focus again.

Within the mirrored wall stood another door, also covered with mirror and outlined in gold with a golden doorknob. Which way to go? She sent tendrils of her energy through the surrounding rooms, trying to be subtle, drawing them back whenever they touched someone else's aura. She didn't want to awaken anyone to her presence.

Mira sensed Amanda's soul. It was close. What would be guarding the soul, she worried? She walked to the mirrored door, but could perceive no living being.

Opening the door and peering inside, she snuck in. The room stood open to the outside with a long wall of open windows. A huge, oval bed with dark green silk sheets lay in the center. Candles were placed everywhere, ready to be lit. Masses of fragrant, red and orange flowers sat in vases on most of the flat surfaces. A smaller bath lay beside the windows, just right for two people, not ten. It was obviously the Queen's bedchamber.

She sought again for Amanda's soul and followed her intuition to the next room. It contained two doors. Out the open windows the river meandered through the palace gardens and lighted boats floated on it. She could see that the palace stood just on the edge of the sea, an amazing view of the City lay in the opposite direction. The Queen's Quarters must cover much of the entire floor of the building. She could feel the Opal's presence behind her. If she went out on the balcony and turned around, its Tower would loom above her.

The view below captivated her, making it harder to concentrate on the search for Amanda's soul. She felt so tired. The sky was growing dim. Unlike the previous night, the whole City was lit up, glittering like starlight on water. People with bright, flickering torches walked the grounds below, it looked very festive. She saw fanciful carriages pulling up and people getting out. Some wore truly amazing head gear which reminded her of peacock's plumage, combined with massively antlered, elk heads that hung in mountain lodges. Each one was different, but equally stunning.

Mira forced her attention back inside the room. She could feel Amanda's soul nearby, but couldn't see it. The soul's tortured pulse made her chest tighten and ache.

The room itself was plainly furnished, consisting of an easy chair, a couch, a coffee table, a desk and chair. The walls stood lined with books. A ladder waited so someone could reach the taller shelves. She noticed that most were about magic. Some were written in English, some French, German, Spanish, others contained languages she didn't recognize. A few held symbols she'd never encountered. This room seemed to be the Queen's private office.

How did the Queen come by books from the U.S. and Europe? Then she realized if the Queen could steal a soul through a portal, knocking off a bookstore would be no problem. One of the titles sitting on the coffee table read Codependent No More. Somehow she couldn't picture the Queen of the Black Opal as codependent. Although she'd never actually seen her. So who knew?

Mira was startled by the sound of the other door opening. She dove under the desk. Sandals with glittery gems topped with silky turquoise pants which flowed like a skirt passed by.

She held her breath and realized the soul felt like it was behind her. Not in this room, probably in the next one.

She could feel it pulsing. The other person in the room was mumbling.

"Where did that horrible woman hide it?" grumbled the husky, female voice.

Mira heard the coffee table crash and saw books fly through the air. "I hate this, how could it happen to me? I'm going to kill that bitch!"

The voice sounded familiar, but not quite right.

"Amanda?" she asked, peering out from under the desk.

"Who's there?" asked Amanda.

Mira crawled out from under the desk in front of Amanda, who stood brandishing a huge sword.

"Geesh Amanda, put that away before you kill someone."

Amanda wore a silky, white blouse and a long kimono-style, turquoise jacket that made her red hair glow. Her long hair curled down her back and around her arms. Clearly, she had gotten a bath and cleaned up.

Amanda relaxed, but said grimly, "That's exactly my plan. Have you found my soul yet?"

"No, I just got here. How did you get in the castle?"

"I came with Ewan and his father. I followed them up here when they came to talk to the Queen, I said I'd meet Ewan back at the feast. I haven't found my soul, but it's nearby. I can feel it." Amanda stared at her, "What is that thing on your head?"

"What does it look like?" Mira felt embarrassed and defensive.

"A horn. You've got a horn growing out of your head. It's either gross or really cool, I can't decide." But apparently Amanda wasn't too impressed. She turned her attention to the bookcases, looking for her soul, behind the books.

Mira felt something strange about Amanda's energy. Her aura hadn't looked like that before. Amanda's energy felt volcanic, like she'd erupt any minute.

She realized with horror what felt wrong about Amanda. Taking a steadying breath she asked, "What happens after we get your soul back?"

"I kill the Queen and her Sorcerer and then I don't really care. Maybe something will happen with Ewan, maybe not.

Maybe I'll go home, maybe not. Maybe I'll find some decent coffee. I'll deal with that later."

"You took all the potion, didn't you?"

"No, of course I didn't. I thought about it, but didn't. Nope, I took you at what you said, so I only did my capful in the morning," she said, pretending to look for the soul by looking inside the books.

Amanda was acting too casual and trying to change the subject. Mira knew she lied.

"Where can it be?" Amanda asked, her expression coy.

"Why did you do it, Amanda?"

Amanda turned to her.

Mira noticed her sister's pupils were oddly dilated and drops of sweat beaded on her face. Amanda said venomously, "Because I'm tired of being the good girl who does what everyone says. I'm smart enough to run my own life. I know what I'm doing and if you don't trust me, that's just too bad."

"But what if you're wrong? What if you don't have enough energy left to take your soul back inside?"

"Well, then I'll die. I don't care anymore. I can't let anyone else run my life."

"What about Dylan?"

"Dylan. Oh I don't have time for him. He's been cramping my style."

"He's your son. He loves you. You will break his heart if you leave him."

"I need to take care of myself. The mother gets the oxygen mask first," Amanda said, her voice suddenly shrill, almost manic. "There's got to be another room on the other side of this wall. I'm going to find the entrance. I know my soul's near." She turned away.

"Amanda, wait! Can we stay together?"

"Well, hurry. I don't have all night. I want to get my soul, then go snog Ewan. He is some amazing man." A dreamy look flowed across Amanda's face.

Mira muttered, "Bipolar, she's bipolar."

She followed Amanda out the opposite door which opened back into the hallway she had entered upon coming to this level of the palace. No pooka stood guard at the next door. Amanda practiced swinging the sword like she would swing a baseball bat. It looked very strange, even for her sporty sister.

Mira muttered to herself, "It'll all turn out. Somehow I have to believe that."

No doorway existed for a room that might lie behind the Queen's study. There was a room at the far end of the hallway, but it looked like a small audience room with a throne. She followed Amanda inside. Possibly it was used for private meetings with the Queen. It felt like they had passed by where the soul was hidden. The entrance to that room must be concealed somewhere in the Queen's office.

Voices came from outside the door of the audience room. Amanda and Mira slipped behind the heavy, velvet curtains to the rear of the throne. Mira worked on making their energy invisible.

She recognized the Queen and Sorcerer's voices.

The Queen asked, "Well, what did she want? Does she know?"

Mira heard the door close with a bang.

The Sorcerer said, "No, not even a hint of it. Although she healed rather quickly for one so old. Said she was attacked by a wild beast. She plans to retire and go on a long trip, although she would not tell us where. She holds some strange notion one of her sons should replace her. As if I would leave the court to make potions for sick peasants in the forest."

"Fool. We are surrounded by fools. Roderick came to speak to me. It seems Ronan has disappeared and he wants my help finding his son. I will probably help him so he does not think I was the cause of his son's disappearance. I need to keep him in my debt. I should be watching my family more closely."

"My Queen, you are a brilliant strategist."

"Did you find the other burglar?"

"Not yet," he said, "but we will. I will join the search as soon as possible."

"It is time to go to the feast," she said. "And name my consort. I think I shall give him a turn to father a child with me."

"And if he cannot?" asked the Sorcerer.

"Then he shall be sacrificed at my next betrothal."

The Sorcerer laughed a nervous laugh. "Is there any hope that a mere magician would ever be on your list of candidates?"

Mira heard an awkward silence. Apparently not.

"I had no idea your ambitions traveled in that direction, my Sorcerer."

"How could they not my beautiful Queen?"

Amanda pointed to her own mouth and made gagging motions. Mira looked away, appalled by her sister's lack of fear. She did not want to be discovered, especially by those two. She refocused her efforts on masking their presence.

"I will give it some thought," the Queen said, her gown rustling as she moved.

"Thank you," he said.

"Now, we must go."

"Yes, my Queen."

Mira heard the door open. It seemed to stay that way. She could hear servants, the movement of guards and unidentifiable sounds. Finally, the hallway grew quiet again. She and Amanda came out from behind the curtains and crept to the door.

"I think the answer to where your soul can be found is back in that office."

"What do you mean?" asked Amanda.

"There must be a hidden room and the entrance must be in her office," said Mira.

"What, like you take a certain book out and the bookcase spins around?"

"Yeah, exactly."

Amanda snorted with laughter. "You are crazy. There's no way she would do something that cliché. You've been watching too many bad movies."

"I think it's worth checking out."

"I don't," Amanda scoffed. "I'm following them. The Queen will lead me to the soul."

"Amanda no! Her guards will stop you!"

"No. They won't stop me," she said, swinging the sword again. "And I am so tired of being told no! Don't ever do that again!" she said, pointing the sword at Mira. Amanda turned away and stormed out of the room.

Mira followed her to the door, watched Amanda walk down the dimly lit hall and turn right at the end.

A cool breeze blew past her. It carried the scent of sweet, tropical flowers. Flowers like she had never smelled before. It was ambrosial. She walked out into the hallway, trying to follow the perfume.

I need those flowers, was the last thought that came to her as she slid down the wall to the floor.

Chapter 27 — Nakia

Nakia was dancing with yet another suitor. This time, Lord Montaine. Tall, handsome and ruthless. Rumor said he murdered his brother, who had claimed the lordship because Lord Montaine had been overdue from a fishing trip on the Wild Craggy Sea.

A good match for her, provided she could keep him in check. Nakia had forgotten about him. He lived in the Outer Islands and seldom traveled to the City of the Black Opal, but had made this journey in hopes of winning her heart, or at least a place on the throne. Definitely a man to be considered.

So was her Sorcerer. She watched him move through the crowd, like a woodland lion slinking through a herd of sheep. He listened and watched, sometimes speaking and putting someone at ease, others on edge. A predator, trying to decide exactly which sheep should be his prey.

The dance ended and Lord Montaine, Rufus, escorted her to the side of the room. "Would you like a glass of wine?" he asked.

"Yes."

"I will return presently," he said and moved through the crowd to the tables of food and spirits

She touched her forehead and the sheath covering her crumbled horn. Just a small, black bump remained. She felt ashamed of her loss and wore the sheath even while bathing, so her servants wouldn't see. After the ritual she'd have three souls and the Opal would help her grow a new horn.

The Sorcerer came to her side, "Your Highness?"

She said, "I have told the faeries who entered the castle for the festival to guard my private quarters and catch any intruders."

"Is that wise? Faerie cannot be controlled."

"The pooka and the Royal Shields are guarding as well. They will catch the girls when they come for the child," said Nakia

Lord Montaine returned with two glasses. He and the Sorcerer began a heated discussion about trading rights. Nakia felt chills of excitement at the knowledge they were really arguing over her. Many turns had passed since men dared to do such a thing. Long ago she had closed and locked that door. She smiled into her wine glass. It felt exhilarating to open those emotions again.

The entire room glowed from candles inside colored glass chimneys. A gentle breeze wafted though the open windows, just enough to keep the air fresh from waxy smoke and the cloying perfume worn by both the men and women.

The light reflected the gaudy costumes worn as a traditional part of the midsummer's festival. The clothes echoed the lush, extravagant flowers and vines of reds, oranges, pinks and purples that filled the room. Small yellow and blue birds sang sweetly along with the music, flitting among the vines. The designers had outdone themselves tonight, with fountains running by magic; she would need to think of a suitable reward. It was rare her servants could do anything right.

Some of the impressive fountains streamed as tall as three men. Sparkling fish in a rainbow of colors leapt between fountains while couples walking underneath their arc received playful splashes of mist. The sound of water formed a backdrop to the laughter, music and conversation. Entire trees and flowering shrubs filled the edges of the room and scented the air. The massive room wore a feeling of ease with an undercurrent of burgeoning growth.

She watched Marco Amalia walk underneath one of the fountains with his much younger wife on his arm. Marco was one of the nobles who always lied to her. She twitched her little finger, but nothing happened. She flashed her hand and a ripple moved across the fountain. She finally had to flap her entire arm in the air, as if she were swatting flies, simply to make the fountain momentarily stop so that a red and white fish dropped on his head. He jumped out from under it, brushing it off his head and swearing. A magician's assistant popped the fish back in the fountain and dried up the mess with a flick of his wrist. Marco glared at him, grabbed his wife's arm and huffed away.

Nakia snorted. The atmosphere would be completely different in the Commoner's Room. Much more boisterous.

Before she could go, tingles crept up her back as a hand touched her arm gently, but firmly.

Her sorcerer asked, "Would you dance with me?"

"I didn't know you danced" she said, raising an eyebrow.

"Most certainly," he said smiling. The smile would have been frightening, had she been a sheep.

The Sorcerer took her wine glass and handed it to Lord Montaine with a triumphant smile. Lord Montaine did not return the smile. The Sorcerer whirled her out onto the floor.

He surprised her by being a fine dancer. She hadn't expected to find such strength and grace in him. Perhaps she could find a way to keep both of them. Now that was an interesting idea.

Afterwards, the Sorcerer escorted her to the Commoner's Room. Fully four times the size of the Throne room it was packed with people. The music played louder and faster. People spun and stamped around the room, showing little restraint.

The leader of the band spotted her and stopped the music. She lifted a cup and cried out, "Glad Midsummer." With difficulty, she made yellow and blue butterflies appear from her cup and flutter throughout the room. Such things had once been child's play for her. Anger bubbled up inside at the weakening of her magic.

The crowd echoed the toast back to her, and she motioned for the music to continue. The dancing began again. The Queen noted how many nobles had spent all evening in the Commoner's Room. She found it interesting that they were also the ones who distanced themselves from her, except of course her brother, Roderick.

He kept as close to her as possible. However, she knew that he followed their father's belief; "You keep your friends close and your enemies closer." He probably knew she was his enemy.

She hadn't been able to bear his happiness in his marriage. Just before their youngest child, a daughter, had been born, Nakia had made sure the midwife was replaced with a woman of her own. Roderick's wife had not survived to see her daughter born. Nakia smiled at the thought. She hated her younger brother as much as he hated her.

She would have to keep a closer watch on these nobles, though. If rebellion came, they would be the first to join.

The people in the Commoner's Room generally spent less money for frivolities but their costumes looked no less outlandish than the nobles. She marveled at her people's creativity; after all they were an extension of her will. None of this would be possible without her.

A purple unicorn danced with an orange and pink sea squid, a stag with a white doe, a red dragon with a peacock, forest gods cavorted with sea goddesses. Painted bodies and people covered with all manner of fabric and feathers.

Small trees, vines and flowering bushes lined the room and again many large fountains and pools, several of which cooled people's feet. She didn't doubt that by morning several brawls would break out and continue in those same pools, partly fueled by large amounts of summer wine. The heady mixture of fortified wine and herbs, made every autumn to celebrate the following summer was drunk only on Midsummer's Eve.

"Come," she told the Sorcerer. "I want to check with the pooka on their progress of finding the girls. And to make sure the boy is well guarded. You need to check on that burglar."

He nodded and said, "I still think you should reconsider that child. He should simply be killed. Inhaling the souls of both girls is dangerous enough. To add a third is madness." He exhaled loudly. She could feel his fear in voicing such an opinion.

"No. I am strong enough. The Opal will help me consolidate the souls because I am the rightful ruler. She will protect and help me. You know as well as I that there is a rebellion churning away here and I must be powerful enough to destroy it and the people responsible. These souls came into my realm for a reason. The Opal told me the girl's soul would be for me. If it is, then so are the others. I must take them, conquer them and make them mine. Then I will have the dragons as well." She turned to leave the room.

The Sorcerer sighed and followed her. As she knew he would. There was much to resolve before the ritual. The girls must be found. Nothing could be left to chance. She must also align the future by making a decision concerning a consort tonight.

Chapter 28 — Ronan

Ronan entered the upper floor of the palace. He noticed with relief that no pooka stood guard. Perhaps that meant he would find Mira up here and they could search for the soul and Dylan without interruption. The servants would be at their own party.

He slipped into the antechamber of the Queen's Quarters, then entered her bathing room.

There stood Amanda. She still had no soul, but Ewan had seen to it that she found a bath and clean clothes. Even so, she looked even stranger than when he had last seen her. Amanda's hair was disheveled and her eyes wild.

She ran to him, threw her arms around his neck and said, "Beloved."

"I have met your sister, Mira, but not you." He tried to peel her arms from around his neck. She was resistant.

"I love you."

"Oh? What is my name?" he asked, while continuing the attempt to untangle himself from her.

"Ah, what's in a name that a rose should smell so sweet?" She slid her leg seductively up the outside of his thigh and wrapped it around his waist.

His forehead wrinkled in puzzlement while he tried to keep his balance. Amanda must have gotten hit by a faerie curse. The faeries were notorious at Midsummer for their love curses. He wrestled with her, trying to extract himself from the inappropriate embrace.

"Well, it's something like that, romantic Shakespeare, Romeo and Juliet," she added.

He continued to push her away. "Have you seen Mira?"

"Mira, who cares about Mira?" she asked, unwrapping her leg and standing on the floor, although she kept her arms around his neck.

"I do. Have you seen her?" he asked again, finally getting her arms loose and pushing her back.

"You don't need her. You need only me," she said, sliding her arms up his sleeves.

"I need to find your sister," he disentangled himself and ran from the room, back to the main hallway.

"No, please don't go. I want to be with you," she yelled, running after him.

Ronan heard her footsteps behind him, but turned a corner before she could see where he went. Escape was the coward's way out, but he could do nothing for her. The curse would wear off before the evening ended.

He entered the Commoner's Room first. The crowd had grown since he left on his search. He wove through the dance floor avoiding the boisterous couples searching the room. No sign of Mira anywhere.

Ronan spotted Amanda walking into the far door where he'd first entered the room. She saw him also and yelled. The hungry look on her face told him everything. She ran across the dance floor towards him, crashing into people and even knocking a woman down.

Ronan didn't wait to see more. He slipped out the first available door and into the Noble's Room.

This room was much less crowded. Mira wasn't there either.

His heart sank. He'd need to return to the Queen's Quarters and look again. As he turned to leave Lord Montaine greeted him.

"Ah, Ronan, you've grown since I saw you last."

"Hello, Sir. It has been seven turns since my father took us to visit you. How goes your fishing this season?" Ronan remembered and liked the man, but the timing was inconvenient.

"Oh, same as usual. The sea gives us much and takes almost as much in return. We lost two large ships and far too many men in the last storm of the winter."

"I am sorry to...,"

"Beloved, why did you run away?" Amanda asked breathlessly, wrapping her arms around his waist. "I'm not letting go of you now!"

Ronan looked at Montaine and said, "Faerie curse."

Montaine roared with laughter. "Were I you, I would take advantage of that."

He said, "Afraid I cannot. I love her twin sister," he said, laughing at the irony.

"No law against having two lovers."

"I do not think her sister would approve."

"I am not going to share you," said Amanda. "You are mine, all mine.

"Excuse us," said Ronan, walking out onto a balcony, dragging Amanda with him.

Ronan heard Lord Montaine's bellowing laugh behind him.

Once on the balcony, Amanda disentangled herself and moved to face Ronan.

"What do you want, Amanda?"

"You."

"I will not make love to you. This curse will wear off."

"It's not a curse."

"Earlier today you wanted my brother, Ewan."

"I don't remember him," she said, looking confused.

"Come on. We need to find Mira. She is looking for your soul and for Dylan."

"Dylan?"

"Dylan, your son."

"I think I saw him."

"Where?"

"Upstairs, close to where I saw you. He had a gross, yellowy, slimy thing that screamed at me."

"Was it your soul, Amanda?" Ronan asked, even though he knew thinking under a faerie curse was nearly impossible.

She looked thoughtful. Finally she said, "Yes, I think it was, but it scared me."

"Come, we must go find him."

"I'll follow you anywhere."

They made their way back to the Queen's quarters. He worried about Mira's continued absence. What could have happened to her?

Chapter 29 — Mira

Mira's eyes slammed open. Where was she? What was she supposed to be doing?

Standing slowly, she leaned against the wall, waiting for the whirling in her head to wear off. She kept trying to focus her eyes on one small spot to stop the dizziness. Someone came around the corner.

She forgot about focusing on anything but the most beautiful man she had ever seen. His golden curly hair looked like the sun and beneath the purple silk he wore, muscles rippled beautifully.

He came towards her, "Mira, are you well?"

"I don't think so." She floundered, lost in his smiling, blue eyes. Her mouth moved clumsily and she felt awkward. "I think I fell asleep here and woke up feeling very strange. Who are you?" Mira asked in the most flirtatious voice she could summon up.

"I am Ewan," he said, graciously. "I met you on the road and Amanda rode into the city with me."

"Amanda?" She massaged her scalp in an attempt to clear her foggy mind. Her hands found the horn. The horn she couldn't figure out. Was that why she felt so strange? Looking at Ewan, she forgot everything and drowned in his eyes. She started to tip over and he reached out to steady her.

"Yes, I am looking for your sister now. She was supposed to meet me at the feast and I cannot find her. One of the pooka said they saw someone who looked like her up here, chasing my brother. But it must have been you."

"Your brother?"

"Ronan. He is missing."

"Oh, I met him once, I think." She ran her hands up his arms and caressed the lean muscles.

"Do you need to sit down somewhere?"

"Yes, on your lap."

"No, that will not work," he said, blushing. "I do not seem to be making much progress finding either Amanda or Ronan. There is a waiting room, back around the hall. Let us sit there. We can talk. Perhaps they will find us."

She walked unsteadily, leaning heavily on Ewan's arm. Faking small, weak steps, she grabbed his waist, falling once or twice so he would catch her. They shuffled down the hallway.

He smelled divine. His presence was as intoxicating as a fine wine. Chardonnay, perhaps. Rich, full bodied, with a fruity start and a slightly oaky finish that lingered on the tongue. She clung to his muscular shoulders, her lips reaching for his by the time they reached the waiting room.

He gently pushed her down on a chair, then sat himself a good distance away. Mira gazed into his eyes. "Did anyone ever tell you how beautiful you are?"

"What has beauty got to do with anything?" he asked. "You are very beautiful as well, but really, what use is it? It does not guarantee you the lover you want. It will not make you happy, or powerful. It does not mean anything. It is just nice."

"True. It's just nice, but irrelevant. Still, it's nice to have a lover who's beautiful, who you find desirable and attractive, right?"

"Yes, it is."

"And you said I was beautiful, right?" She leaned over and put a hand on his thigh.

"Yes, I did," he said, looking suspicious.

"And I think you're absolutely over the top gorgeous." She slid over onto his lap.

He looked towards the doorway, then attempted to push her off, but she wrapped her arms around his neck and held on.

"There's nothing to be nervous about. I'm attracted to you and you're attracted to me. It's obvious. We should be lovers." She caressed his nearest ear with her index finger.

"It is obvious to me that I want Amanda and you are under a faerie spell. You will feel differently by tomorrow. I better go find her," said Ewan, pushing her off his lap and getting up.

"No, please stay. I know I'm not very good at this."

"It is not your manner. I simply want Amanda." He walked towards the door. "I need to go now. If you see Amanda or Ronan please tell them I am looking for them. Have you found Dylan yet?"

"Dylan?"

He stopped, sighed and said, "I think you need some help. You seem lost."

"Love will do that to you," she said, walking over and putting her arm around Ewan's waist.

"Hello Ewan, can I help you?" asked a black robed man who seemed to appear out of nowhere.

He looked sinister beneath his slimy smile. The man's energy seemed all wrong somehow, like a kid who's had way too much candy, except more subdued.

"Glad Midsummer, High Sorcerer," said Ewan. "I found this woman wandering disoriented in the hallway and brought her here to sit down. Something is wrong with her."

The man touched her. She recoiled from his energy. "Aah," he said, "she has the breath of faerie about her. I thought I smelled their stink earlier. There is another who looks much like this one who also has been touched. She was chasing your brother." The Sorcerer stared at her horn. She felt afraid, but didn't know why.

"How strange," said Ewan.

"She called him beloved."

"Oh dear," said Ewan. "The faerie have been busy."

"I will take care of this one while you go about your celebrating," said the Sorcerer.

Mira clung to Ewan. She didn't want to stay with this man.

"Since the faerie curse cannot be undone, I will take her with me. I am sure you have better things to do. I might as well be of some use. I will return her to the party and see if someone is searching for her," Ewan said.

"As you wish, my Lord," said the Sorcerer. He covered his anger quickly, but Mira sensed it.

She felt a strong urge to mask her power, so she concentrated on filling her entire being with lust for Ewan.

Ewan took her arm and led her from the room. She felt so grateful. That man was horrible. She'd seen him once before and never wanted to see him again.

Unfortunately, the Sorcerer was following them from the room. She saw two pooka standing guard across the hallway. The Sorcerer called them over and she overheard him say, "Please go to her chambers and ask the Queen to meet me in her bath. Tell her, it is very urgent."

Ewan laughed as they walked further down the hallway.

"What's so funny?" asked Mira.

"He is probably trying to get the Queen here, hoping the faerie curse still lingers and she will catch it. Everyone knows she is going to name her consort tonight. He would love to have that kind of power."

"So you think it's just a curse that's made me fall in love with you? You think it won't last." She glared at him, putting her hands on her hips.

"That is what I know. Now, let us go find Amanda and Ronan. And Dylan."

"Why would I want to find any of them?" she asked, pouting.

"Because I want to, and you profess to be in love with me. Surely you want to please me," he said putting his hands on her shoulders and gazing into her eyes.

"You certainly know how to manipulate people."

"Turns and turns of practice watching people use me." He laughed and it sounded like the lovely trilling of a chickadee to her.

As they spied into rooms along the corridors, Mira asked, "How long does this supposed curse last, so I can prove to you my love is real?"

"Probably till the deep of night. Ah, here we are," said Ewan. "These are my father's rooms. Let us go inside and see if we can get you cleaned up and find a costume for you. You will blend in better."

She eagerly followed him into the elegant rooms, a seating room was surrounded by several bedrooms. Each bedroom had a separate bathroom. Ewan pushed her into one and poured hot water from a warmer into the stone tub. He added cold water, showed her the soap and towels and said, "You know what to do. I will search for a costume for you." He closed the door more firmly than was necessary. Mira fumed, but eventually stepped into the water.

She soaked in the tub, enjoying the luxuriant bubbles from the soap and finally washed her terribly filthy hair. She dried herself and wrapped a green towel around her, deciding that looked sexier than simple nakedness. She found a brush and set about trying to untangle her hair, staring into a mirror at the horn growing on her forehead. It would have been quite pretty, if a horn growing from one's forehead wasn't so bizarre.

There was a knock at the door and Ewan said, "I found the perfect costume for you."

She opened the door and he thrust in a wad of fabric topped with an elegant mask.

"Come in and help me," she said, "I need your help."

"I think not," he said, laughing, and closed the door again.

She took off the towel and put on the silky red, brown and white fabric. It was a shirt and pants with white patches like a pinto horse. The mask was a glittery, horse's head, but it wouldn't fit over her horn.

Mira came out of the bath room carrying the mask. She saw Ewan sitting on a couch. He waved her over and she became hopeful. Instead of romance, however, he pulled out a knife. Taking the mask, he cut a hole. When he finished she put it on.

It fit over her horn, so much so that the horn looked like it was part of the mask. A perfect disguise. She took it off, then leaned over to put her arms around him and tried to sit on his lap, again.

He waggled the knife at her teasingly. "The faerie enjoy hitting us with their enchantments when we celebrate Midsummer's Eve," he said. "Every turn some of us are caught by them. They have their jest and it all wears off."

"This isn't a curse. I love you."

"Yes, it is a curse. I am sorry. I would never have wished this on anyone. It happened to me many turns ago. Our sister had just left us, I was very sad about it. At Midsummer, I was unlucky enough to become bewitched by the faerie. I fell in love with a very handsome and popular woman. I think I was sixteen at the time, gawky and awkward. She spent the whole evening laughing at me, as did all her friends and admirers," said Ewan

"It must have hurt you a great deal."

"It was a long time before I could look at another person with love."

"I'm sorry. Let me make it up to you," she said, caressing his face.

"That is the way the faerie play." He stood, backed away from her and left the room.

She followed him through the hallways of the palace. They came to the public area where musicians played string and pipe instruments. Mira noticed one that looked like a cross between a ilean pipes and a bass and made a haunting, plaintive sound which captivated her. They wove their way through the crowd of people dancing, drinking and laughing. She clung to Ewan's hand and he allowed her to.

They stopped near his father, Roderick, who was talking to a couple of men in costume. At least they looked like costumes. The men wore masks, but she wasn't sure how people dressed for parties here. Things didn't become any clearer. Some people were dressed in satin suits like Ewan and long ball gowns; others wore rough cottony clothes like she had worn earlier. Still others wore fantastically colored and shaped clothing with padding and extra peculiar appendages. She couldn't stop staring at the colorful gathering, and basking in Ewan's warm glow. She felt dizzy whenever he looked at her.

A few beings who didn't look real were out on the dance floor as well. Pooka looked strange enough. She saw creatures wearing hooded capes in bright colors, who had pale oval faces with red, burning eyes. She didn't have any name to call them. It seemed impolite to ask. Another type of entity with faces like possums, bulbous bodies and long tales ornamented with many gold bands, danced wildly and other than fur, wore no clothing. There were a couple other types of creatures as well, she turned to ask Ewan about them.

He was deep in conversation with his father. "The Sorcerer said he saw Amanda chasing Ronan. I can only assume the faerie cursed her as well," said Ewan.

Roderick replied, "Is it not interesting that so far, the faeries' only prey have been outlanders and twins?"

"That we know of," Ewan said.

"That we know of," Roderick repeated.

"Does that mean something?" Ewan asked his father, clearly annoyed.

"I am not sure," Roderick said. "We will have to wait and see how the evening plays out, will we not?" Roderick smiled and walked away into the crowd.

"Sometimes my father makes me so angry," said Ewan, glaring at his father's retreating back.

"What was that about?" she asked, beginning to caress his upper arms.

"He has got some juicy piece of information and he is not telling me."

At that moment they were bumped together by a man in a hurry. He looked gorgeous with long dark hair and warm, brown eyes. He would taste like a deep, complex pinot noir. Then Mira looked at Ewan again and became lost.

"Mira," the stranger asked, "is that you?"

She looked at him again, "Who're you? And Amanda! You're here too!"

"It's me, Ronan."

"What are you doing?" asked Amanda.

Who was Ronan? The name sounded familiar. "I'm following this lovely man around, and I will continue all night and tomorrow and the next day until he believes I love him."

Ronan opened his mouth, then closed it again.

"Faerie curse," said Ewan. "And you?" he asked his brother.

"Faerie curse," said Ronan.

"Why do you even care about her?" asked Amanda, with disgust. "I've always been more beautiful than her."

"Amanda love, do you understand what is going on?" asked Ewan.

"Don't Amanda love me, you toad. Ronan, come away with me," said Amanda trying to drag him towards the door.

Ronan looked at Ewan and at Mira. "What should I do? The curse is especially strong with Amanda, since her soul is missing."

"Be gentle with her until the curse wears off," said Ewan.

"Mira, where is Dylan?" asked Ronan.

"Dylan, who is Dylan?" she asked.

"He's Amanda's son. You went to look for him."

"I have no idea. When I woke up there was only you," she said to Ewan.

"Where were you?" Ronan asked

"Where was I?" she asked Ewan, moving closer to him, thrilled by the warmth of his body.

"In the hallway outside the private audience rooms," said Ewan.

Amanda clung behind Ronan, her arms wrapped possessively around his waist, her head resting on his back.

Ronan looked Mira directly in the eye,"I will meet you just after deep night in the Tower. I will find Dylan, and Amanda will find her soul, and there will be time for many explanations." He turned to Ewan, "Make sure she is there. I will bring your Amanda."

Ronan walked away, dragging Amanda after him, Amanda flashed them a brilliant smile. Ewan began chuckling.

"What's so funny?"

"I think my big brother is sweet on you."

"Who cares?" she asked, though wondering fleetingly if she should.

"I suspect you will find he knows more than you think he does," said Ewan.

Chapter 30 — Mira

Mira tingled where Ewan touched her as they danced. All her concentration was focused on looking at him and on not falling down. Underneath the heavy mask, she felt rapture. He had a very seductive voice. All she wanted was to get him naked and alone.

Ewan would allow her to touch him if she didn't go too far, but anything that went beyond casual and he stepped beyond her reach.

The dance ended. Ewan asked someone if the Queen had chosen her consort yet.

"Not yet, we are all waiting to see who it is," the man said.

Ewan turned to her and said, "The Queen seems to have disappeared. Perhaps we should go back to her section of the palace and see if the faerie have caught her as well?" He laughed mischievously.

"I'll go wherever you go," she said. Maybe they could find somewhere to be alone. She followed him up stairs and down hallways, thankful for not living in this palace. She'd never find her way around. Maybe that was the point, it kept out intruders because they got lost.

Mira could feel Ewan concealing the two of them, but she already felt safe hidden within her costume. He wore a purple jeweled, eye mask.

His magic felt smooth as silk. Subtle. She noticed a man and woman sitting in the audience room, facing away from the doorway. Ewan pulled her quickly past the door and next to the wall before they could be noticed by the couple, then put a finger to his mouth to silence her.

As they listened, Mira found she could recognize the two from their voices alone. The Queen and her sorcerer. She couldn't quite make out what they said, except the Queen was angry about being delayed from returning to the feast. The Sorcerer seemed to be pleading with her about something.

Then she caught a familiar scent. The sweetest flower.... She heard giggling, but could see nothing unusual.

She didn't know whether to plug her nose or run.

Mira felt sleepy and almost dropped to the ground when a rush of energy jolted through her. Her mind became clear. Her memory returned completely.

Ewan passed out. She caught his arms and helped him slide to the floor. She was glad he lay unconscious, because her behavior over the last few hours made her face burn. He'd been so kind to her and all she'd tried to do was screw him.

Peering through the doorway she could see the Queen and the Sorcerer unconscious on the floor. She needed to get Ewan out of there. Grabbing his arms, she clumsily dragged him down the hall, wondering if the Sorcerer called the curse or if the faerie had struck again.

There was another audience room off the hallway and she hauled Ewan into it and maneuvered him up onto a chair with great difficulty. Shutting the door, she sat in another chair and took off her mask to cool down a bit. Ewan weighed a lot, all muscle too. No wonder Amanda liked him. He might even be good for her. She didn't know how long he'd be out, but he would probably need looking after. She didn't want him to have to go through everything again, like he had at sixteen.

The curse had abandoned her, completely. The second exposure negated the first curse. She no longer felt in love with Ewan and fully realized what needed to be done.

The only things she remained confused about were Ronan and what he said in the ballroom. How could he have recognized her under the mask? How did he know Amanda had lost her soul and that Mira was looking for both it and Dylan? Amanda might have told him, although Mira didn't believe her sister could be in her right mind between the faerie curse, overdosing on the potion and the vacant hole in her being.

She hoped Edward was free and was all right. She'd have to ask another pooka guard.

Anxious, she got up and paced back and forth. She had regained the rest of her disjointed memories by the time Ewan stirred. Mira tried to cover his eyes. Maybe if he didn't see her, the curse wouldn't work. "Ewan, stop struggling."

He knocked her hands away and just looked at her smiling. "Mira, why did I not see it before? You are wonderful."

"Ewan, you've been zinged with a faerie curse."

"No, that is not possible. It has just taken me a long time to realize that I love you," he stood and reached out to touch her. She backed away and he fell forward onto the floor.

"Yep, see you're still dizzy. It's just a curse. It got both the Queen and the Sorcerer as well."

Ewan sat up and looked at her strangely, as if he was trying to remember. "You have the most amazing green eyes."

"Nope, won't work, don't try it."

Ewan stood slowly this time, then slid back onto the chair looking very relaxed. One leg sprawled out, the other crossing it, he leaned back. His purple silk costume fit his body tightly showing off the curves of his muscles. He took off the mask, looked at her with those blue eyes and brushed his hand through his curly, golden hair.

She almost drooled before coming to her senses. Then she laughed. Ewan held surprisingly powerful magic. She hadn't noticed it before because he kept it focused inward. Glamour. He did glamour. He made himself perfectly seductive. Anyone would want to be with him, listen to what he said. It wasn't just sexual, he seemed brilliant and fascinating. Perfect for a noble family.

His face looked confused. "Why are you not taking advantage of this situation?" He stood again, grabbed her hand and pulled her close, putting her arms around his neck.

"What do you mean?"

"You are in love with me and I have fallen under your spell now. You can do anything you want with me," he said, nuzzling her neck.

"The bewitchment on me seems to have worn off when the second curse came around. It counteracted the first one." She pushed him away gently.

"Oh. So, you are not in love with me anymore?" He looked devastated.

"Yeah, but look at it this way, I could have left you out there with the Queen and the Sorcerer and let you take your chances. That menage a trois would have been interesting."

"What is that?" asked Ewan. "I am unfamiliar with the language."

"A threesome."

"Ghastly. Thank you for getting me out of there."

"You seem pretty coherent for just getting hit by the faerie."

"Perhaps I only caught the edge of the curse," he said, thoughtfully. "Or perhaps I got it so badly when I was young that I have some immunity. Everyone is affected differently by faerie. I truly do not know. The curse is still present and strong, yet I can think and remember."

"As soon as you're ready, I need to go look for Dylan."

"Did not my brother say he would look for him?"

"This is a kidnapped child. There can't be too many people looking for him!"

"We need to be at the Tower of the Black Opal at deep night. That is what he said?"

"Yeah," said Mira.

He stood alone, a little shaky, but after a time, could walk if she assisted him. Mira knew he faked it, as she had. They put their masks on and left. They avoided the audience room which contained the Sorcerer and the Queen.

They snuck into the Queen's Quarters, through the bathing room and went through the Queen's private bedroom and into her study. All mysteriously free of pooka guards.

The study lay torn apart. Nearly every book from the floor to three feet was torn off the shelf and pitched to the floor. It looked like the work of a three year old tornado.

One of the bookcases had spun sideways and the gap exposed a passageway to another room. The bookcase opening was wide enough that someone could enter the room from both in front of and behind it. Mira entered the room, marveling at the amazing books and tools of magic inside.

She saw broken glass on the floor and a chair pulled up backwards to a table. That also looked like Dylan's work. A golden platter sat in front of the chair. She tried to sense what had lain there. It could have been Amanda's soul. Gone. The soul had suffered in this room and its essence lingered here. She felt afraid. Too much time had been wasted under the faerie curse. Where could Dylan have gone?

She walked to the open window and felt the storm brewing. It came off the ocean. The air blew humid, but cool. Incoming clouds grumbled in the distance, lightening flashed in the darkness and thunder rumbled. Huge shadows flew across one of the moons. The thump, thump of dragon's wings came to her between the thunderclaps. Panic brewed within her. What time was it?

They needed to be done by sunrise. She must find the soul, get out of the palace and, if possible, out of the city with Amanda, Dylan and maybe Edward. Either that or somehow get the Queen to step down. If not, the dragons were going to annihilate everyone near.

She wondered if Barinthus knew where Dylan was. Probably. Too bad she couldn't talk to him. It would be really useful right now. She could use some help. Time was short.

Turning to Ewan she asked, "I don't suppose you know anyone who can call dragons do you?"

Ewan thought for a moment. "Ronan calls dragons if they're nearby."

"I don't think we'll be able to find him soon enough."

A rustling noise came from the other room. She looked for a place to hide. A huge Dark Goddess statue. She pulled Ewan behind it. He cuddled up to her, obligingly. Two pooka entered the room.

"I told you. The Queen is not here. I have been out on the balcony and have not seen her reenter her rooms. Where have you come from?"

"I was waiting for her in the servant's quarters. She was to go wish the elders 'Glad Midsummer'. Where can she be to have left the feast for so long? What has happened here?"

Mira knew it was probably very stupid, but did it anyway. She stepped from behind the statue. "Excuse me," she said. "Did you say you're looking for the Queen?"

The pooka looked startled, but only for a moment. "Yes," they said in unison. Then the darker one said, ominously, "Others are searching for you as well."

Mira told them where she'd last seen the Queen, without disclosing the faerie curse. "Please," she asked, "Can you tell me if Edward is all right, is he free?"

"Edward is free," said the dark pooka.

"Can you tell me where he is?"

"I have not seen him for a while, however he asked us to tell you he would be in the Opal Tower at deep night."

"Do you know what time it is?" asked Ewan.

"Deep night approaches," said the lighter colored pooka.

"We better go to the tower. It will take some time," said Ewan.

"We need to find Dylan."

"Who is in there?" said a demanding voice. "Who is in my private room?"

The pooka turned towards the Queen's voice, "It is us, your Majesty. We have been searching for you."

The Queen! Mira could hear her wading through piles of books. She pulled Ewan through the backside of the swiveled bookcase as the Queen and her Sorcerer went through the front side.

They didn't hear the exchange between Queen and the pooka, but as she backed out of the room, Nakia saw Mira and Ewan.

Mira made for the door she and Amanda had left through earlier. Ewan tried to scramble out of the study through the piles of books and fell. She heard the Queen take a deep breath in horror.

"It is not possible. You cannot be here."

Mira shivered and ran back to help Ewan get up. The Queen must have recognized her. Mira's hand shook as she gave it to Ewan.

"Who, my dear?" asked the oily voice of the Sorcerer.

"The girl you took the soul from. Darling, get her."

Mira ran and Ewan followed, sprinting down the hall. She heard the Sorcerer yell, "Thieves, catch them!"

She kept running. There was no way to fight the Sorcerer. Mira felt the Queen's spell coming her way and she and Ewan put up protective shields as they ran. Mira's energy had grown enormous, boosted by the help of the Black Opal. Thudding footsteps of pooka came behind her, although she realized it must have been a halfhearted chase on their part. They could easily have caught them, but pretended to fall as if hit with magic.

She hoped Ewan knew where they were going and the Queen didn't. He took her up a flight of stairs and they ran through what seemed to be servants' quarters. A roaring party was going on. The servants celebrated Midsummer's Eve in their own raucous fashion and there were many pooka as well. The party looked like more fun than anything she'd seen below.

They made their way through a hallway that seemed to run the length of the castle. Then Ewan ran down four flights of stairs and came to a door.

On the other side stood a huge spiral staircase. They were about one-third of the way up to the tower. Looking down into the bowels of the palace, she could see the bone columns in the cavern below. She took off her mask, it was simply too hot and she wasn't hiding from anyone anymore. Ewan also removed his.

They ran up the interior of the tower circling round and round. She could hear echoes of voices. Amanda calling Ronan. Dylan calling Mira. Edward calling Mira. It sounded as if they all headed towards one huge gathering.

Her chest tightened with fear and exertion. This wasn't happening like she wanted it to. The Queen and Sorcerer chased them. Dylan and the soul might be up there, or maybe not. Even if the soul was found, how could she get it back into Amanda without Aste?

Chapter 31 — Nakia

Queen Nakia Ophalion threw the ancient Nebaia statuette onto the floor of her hidden room and watched it shatter into red shards sharp as glass. Her Sorcerer left the room to confer with the pooka.

Rage rose up inside her and she felt it spill out every pore of her body. Nakia had destroyed half the room of breakable treasures before she could control herself. She stood looking down at splintered glass, clay and crystal, her body trembling with anger. She did a clearing spell and shoved all emotion away.

The pesky faerie curse still remained, but she could manage that. Picking up a pendant which held a smooth chunk of the Black Opal in its center, she stroked it, watching the light flicker within the stone.

How could the soul have been stolen? The pooka guarded the outer hallways, although not inside her rooms. She herself had put wards up on the doorway of this room. Nakia examined the edges of the revolving bookcase and felt what remained, shreds of the wards were still there, but had been blasted apart by a stronger power.

She felt the child's magic. He had been here first.

"Sorcerer!"

"Yes, my Queen," he said, appearing from outside her study.

She touched his hands and stroked his cheek, "Go to Taraya's chamber and see what has become of her. The child has escaped."

He bowed and was gone.

The girl and Ewan had shed Nakia's impotent attacks as well as the Sorcerer's powerful magic like rain falling off a slanted roof. How had the girl gained such adeptness? Ewan did not have that much, his only gift was glamour. Or was it?

She absently scratched her forehead. The sheath grew looser daily as her horn eroded. Soon it would be gone. Tonight, she had needed to use glue to keep the sheath on.

Where would the girl have run? The Sorcerer had told Nakia the girl was the sister, not the one with the missing soul. The soulless one must be nearby. Nakia could feel the empty husk of the girl close to her twin.

Nakia now knew the taste of the one who belonged to the soul she wanted. The child must be with them. Soul lust wrapped its dark tendrils around her own diminished soul.

And Ewan. What had Ewan to do with this? That must mean Roderick would be involved as well, and probably Ronan.

It had come. They would try to take the throne from her tonight. On Midsummer, a time no one would suspect such rebellion.

They could be only be one place.

The Sorcerer entered, gingerly touching her arm. "Taraya was senseless. She said one moment she played with the child and the next I released her from the spell. The boy must have hidden his power this whole time. He is dangerous and devious." Her Sorcerer looked into her eyes and she could see the worry in them.

"Follow me, I know where they are, bring as many pooka as you can gather. There will be a battle. They mean to try to take the throne tonight. Instead, I will take the outlanders' souls and try to think of a fitting torture and death for my brother and his sons."

She gently set the pendant down on the long table and calmly slipped a silver dagger into her sleeve. Then she turned and moved through the room, lifting her long skirts so they wouldn't catch on the fragments of her rage.

Her brother would regret this. She would ensconce all three souls in her body and would not only be invincible, but joined with the dragon as well. Through him she would control all the dragons. Her power would have no limits.

The Sorcerer followed her down to the cavern, gathering pooka along the way. By the time they reached the lift in the Tower wall, the Sorcerer had gathered twenty pooka. Most of them ran up the tower stairs to look for stray rebels. Six rode the lift up with the Nakia and her Sorcerer. One of them took the wheel and turned it, sliding the lift upwards.

As they rose, she felt the Black Opal calling to her and welcomed it within. She also felt that lost soul and its body, the child, the sister, as well as several individuals who shielded themselves from her. She would know soon enough who all her enemies were.

The lift arrived.

Queen Nakia flung the doors open and flowed into the room. "What, none of you liked the party downstairs?"

Chapter 32 — Mira

Mira and Ewan entered the Black Opal Tower followed by several pooka. Another door opened and the Queen waltzed into the room. Followed by her Sorcerer and six pooka guards. From a third door on the other side of the tower, more pooka appeared.

Mira saw Aste standing among the crowd of people. Aste glanced at her, nodded in greeting, then returned her hawk-like attention to the Queen.

Mira sensed overwhelming power in the room, most of it from the Black Opal. The Queen and her Sorcerer held a great deal of magic; flaunting it like strutting peacocks. Ronan masked his, as did Roderick.

Aste stood holding Dylan. She seemed healed, at least well enough to stand and hold thirty pounds of squirming toddler. A stranger stood beside her. The man held an aura of potency which seemed to be equal to hers.

The pooka stood silently in the background, their energy swirling about them like water flowing around boulders. They conducted more power than any of the humans. In contrast, Amanda stood drooping and depleted. The infusion had stripped her bare of energy and almost of life. Ewan stood with his glamour intact, still lost in the faerie curse. Edward was absent.

Mira realized they were playing a game here. She felt impatient, but didn't want to start things either.

The tower room looked truly spectacular. The side walls were made of panels with huge glass windows, alternating with spaces open to the wind. The ceiling was also made of glass. Rainbows gleamed everywhere, even at night. The massive Black Opal hung suspended and slightly above the center of the open floor. The Opal looked even more magnificent up close and she could see flecks of different colors pulsing deep within it. The stone created its own light. As she moved past it, the colors and flecks flickered and shifted. Everyone stood on a metal cat walk ten feet wide which connected to the wall around the entire circumference of the round tower.

Mira could see through the small grating of the floor, down into the cavern. The cat walk extended to within three feet of the widest parts of the Opal. She could see over the top of the Opal to the other side. Nearby, a wide, clear platform extended out from the catwalk to touch the Opal.

She became aware of thundering. Storm clouds had arrived. Lightening was not far off and the fresh, salty air blew in off the sea. Dragons circled the Tower. Their wings slapped the wind and occasionally they trumpeted. The Opal didn't seem to be holding off this storm.

Barinthus landed in an open panel of the window as did an orange dragon and a silvery-white one. Mira felt the energy in the Tower shift. Fear floated through the air in an almost tangible way.

"My you are a grumpy group of people for Midsummer. Is this a new faerie curse I am unaware of?" Queen Nakia asked innocently. No one answered.

Mira saw glowing lights surrounding the Tower and realized faerie gathered, showing themselves. They began to perch in the open windows. As they became still Mira could discern their various shapes and sizes.

She watched the Queen move closer to Aste, who put Dylan on the ground behind her. "I will take that," she said to Dylan, reaching towards him.

Mira noticed Dylan held a glowing, golden orb. It pulsed and the tendrils rippled like a jellyfish. As the Queen came closer, the soul screeched and flailed in torment. Amanda's soul!

"No," he said, with all the defiance of a three year old.

Mira waited anxiously for someone to do something. No one spoke or moved to help Dylan. It would have to be her. "Stop," she said, rushing around the cat walk towards Dylan.

"Are you going to stop me girl? Tell me, shall I take your soul as well as your sister's? Oh, and the child's too?" asked the Queen, smiling. She advanced on Mira.

Queen Nakia stopped. Her eyes focused on Mira's horn.

Mira was surprised to see the rage erupt on the Queen's face. Mira was unprepared for the Queen's attack. She grabbed Mira's arm and thrust her free hand towards Mira's belly.

Mira struggled to get away, but the Queen was physically much stronger. She realized Nakia was trying to suck her soul out. It felt like a hurricane hovered over her stomach.

Mira gathered all her frustration at not being supported by her family, all her self doubt and fears, everything she'd gone through to get here. It all got rolled up into a huge ball of energy centered in her belly. She pushed all that power out at the Queen.

Queen Nakia fell backwards. Her eyes wide with shock. Two pooka grabbed her roughly and pulled her to her feet. Other pooka restrained the Sorcerer.

The Queen looked confused. She clearly hadn't expected Mira's power, or the pooka to rebel against her.

Mira felt her own power radiating outward. Aste came to Mira and nodded toward the Queen, "You must finish this."

Mira walked out onto the glass ledge and put both hands on the Opal. She heard several sharp intakes of breath behind her. She spoke, knowing the Opal gave her the right words to say. "Giver of life, sustainer of life, remover of life, we return this woman's power to you. It is time she ends her reign and another ruler is chosen."

Mira turned and walked to stand next to Nakia. The faeries hummed in an eerie manner and the pooka joined in.

The Black Opal began to vibrate until Mira thought it might move out of the steel net which supported it. The Opal moaned and formed a tunnel of charged energy which looked like a tornado funnel. The tip crackled and snaked its way to Queen Nakia. Its luminous vortex stabbed her and she screamed out, trying to escape.

Mira could feel the stone taking back what little magic Nakia had left. It removed what made her Queen, her sense of self. The deposed Queen, Nakia, looked as if she would cry with loss. As the Opal broke off contact and became quiet, Nakia recovered somewhat.

Mira watched her jaw tighten and eyes narrow with anger. She nearly snarled as Roderick removed the crown from her head, a pendant from around her neck and a ring off her finger. As he stepped back the cone of fabric on her forehead fell off revealing a black scar. Mira realized with horror that Nakia once had a horn, like she did now, but Nakia's refusal to relinquish power rotted it away.

"Brother," Nakia spat, "you have waited a long time for this. You will be assassinated before the next waning moon."

Roderick merely smiled. "Nakia, I never had any desire to be King of this land. If I had you would have been gone long ago. But I know one who is more worthy to rule," he said looking at Ronan.

"That must be decided later," said Ronan, nodding towards Aste.

Aste and the stranger stood in front of the Sorcerer. The Sorcerer stared at them defiantly. "You cannot do it. You do not have the authority or the right."

Aste lowered her voice and it sent chills down Mira's spine. "I have every right. I made you. Not only did I give birth to you, you wretched creature, but I taught you most of what you know. You took what I taught, twisted it and turned it to evil.

"Angus, do not struggle, it will only be harder for you," said the man.

"Donal, you were ever her favorite, Little Brother, but you have no skill here, go back to your safe little shop."

Donal smiled gently and said without malice, "I have enough skill to help her unmake you, Big Brother."

Mira stood watching the three of them. So these were Aste's two sons. She could see the physical resemblance. But where Donal's face seemed open and honest, Angus, the Sorcerer looked closed and cruel. Donal pulled something out of a bag he wore and handed it to Aste.

A flash of fear passed over the Sorcerer's face. Aste struck the Sorcerer before he could work a spell. She held a glass jar full of some amber liquid and began chanting in an unknown language.

Nakia lunged towards Aste, but the pooka held her, "You cannot," she said. "Have mercy on him, he is your son."

"My son has given no mercy and shall get none," said Aste, her face emotionless.

"The time for mercy is past," came the deep voice of Barinthus from one of the open panels. Multiple blasts of wind blew inward from all sides. Bolts of electricity flew outward from the clouds haloing the tower. It felt like being in the center of a ball of lightening. Mira's hair swam in the static. The purple light of the Opal was punctuated by blasts of brittle white, casting eerie shadows everywhere. Dragons landed in each of the open panels, some of them looking familiar, and some she had never seen before.

Nakia became silent upon seeing the dragons, but Mira could see her mind working. Nakia was trying to figure out how to come out of this alive, and maybe regain her power.

Aste continued chanting. The air around her flashed as if sparks sprang from her skin. Her son, Donal concentrated on holding the circle she created. Mira watched the amber liquid in the glass bottle Aste held, slowly turn to a purple color. The Sorcerer looked anguished.

The pooka murmured angrily. "The Sorcerer has gone too far. He took power from the Black Opal, that is only for the King or Queen to do. He drained off her power. He must be put to death."

Aste said, "What I will do to him will be worse than death, you will see. He did take from the Opal, but has not drained her power. No one can touch the Opal without her permission. She entrapped him. Her power is unlimited. She comes from the land. I will return this power to the Opal." She resumed chanting.

Mira began to worry. She moved back, against the outer wall, wrapping her arms around herself. If the Sorcerer violated the Opal, then what did she do? She had wallowed in the stone's power. Would she be punished too? Surely Aste would notice it. Mira felt as if she glowed with purplish light.

"As I have made you, so I unmake you. No magic have you left. Only a memory of what you once held and squandered, do I leave with you. You will also be bound forever to this worthless woman and she to you. This faerie curse will last your entire lives. The land is my witness." Aste said and drew a sign of protection in the air. She then took the glass bottle over to the center. Aste poured the liquid onto the Black Opal, who reabsorbed it immediately, steaming with purifying heat.

No longer the Sorcerer, Angus looked empty. The pooka let go of him and he stood, in shock. One of the pooka searched him for weapons and took away a knife hidden beneath his robe.

Aste turned her attention to Nakia, who snarled at her. Aste looked at Roderick, then Ewan, then Ronan.

Ronan nodded. Donal pulled a small bowl out of his bag. Ronan held it while Donal poured clear liquid from a bottle into it. Then Donal took the bowl. Aste pulled a small knife from a sheath on her belt, took Ronan's arm and made a small cut. Donal held the bowl out for her and she dipped the knife in it. Mira could see the blood swirling in the liquid. Aste wiped the knife on her skirt, then sheathed it.

She took the bowl and walked towards Nakia. "Queen you were made by your father's death. Queen you were, unworthy, made evil by hoarding power. The people of this land unmake you with the blood of your kin. Queen you are, no more." Aste flung the bowl's contents in the Queen's face drenching her and Nakia screamed in rage.

Ewan said, quietly, "I think it is time to return Amanda's soul."

Mira realized he held her in his lap as sat on the catwalk near the Opal. Amanda lay barely conscious. Ewan looked pale and frightened.

Dylan walked to Amanda and set her soul on her belly. He stood near her and faeries fluttered around him.

"Not yet," said Aste. "We must remove this evil before we begin healing."

"This is my home. No one shall remove me," said Nakia.

"Please do not hurt her," begged Angus. "I enacted this evil plan. She has done nothing wrong."

Nakia looked at him in wonder. "You would risk yourself for me?"

"Yes, my Queen," he said.

"Brother, have you nothing to say to me?" Nakia asked Roderick.

"Goodbye Nakia. May you find peace," he said.

Nakia sighed and shrugged off one of the pooka. She walked closer to Angus and took his hand and patted it. "It will be all right, my love. We will be fine," she said, with a voice so kind, Mira found it hard to believe.

"I know," he said, beaming at her.

Then everything happened at once. Nakia twisted and wrenched free from the other pooka. She slipped a small, silver dagger from her sleeve and lunged screaming, at Amanda still laying on Ewan's lap. "This is all your fault! You should have had a stronger soul."

Though two faeries attempted to pull Dylan back, he squirmed loose.

Dylan bolted between Nakia's blade and his mom. Nakia's knife stabbed him. The momentum of Nakia's rush tumbled Dylan over the edge of the catwalk.

Against the outer wall, Mira watched and screamed in horror as he fell into open space.

Two pooka grabbed Nakia as she tried to get away. Mira ran for the edge. Ronan caught her so she wouldn't follow Dylan. Amanda's soul shrieked.

A vacuum formed where Barinthus sat. Mira could see him on the outside of the tower below, trying to break in through window after window, each one lower, attempting to find one large enough to fit through. The tower shuddered with each collision. He bellowed in pain and fear. Great gashes formed on his shoulders.

Dylan's fall seemed to last forever. Faerie raced to try and catch him, but he fell faster than they flew. Mira was powerless to do anything except watch. She couldn't even breathe as she hoped Barinthus would reach him in time. Dylan landed directly between the columns of old bones she had stood beneath earlier. He was dead before Barinthus broke through enough stone to reach him. The dragon lay beside him making horrible, guttural noises Mira would never forget. A host of faerie flew around them, looking like a cloud of dark birds, keening and screeching in anguish.

"Dylan," she whispered and turned into Ronan's chest. His arms closed around her.

She heard a slap as Aste hit Nakia. "You are unspeakable," Mira looked up to see wounds opening on Nakia's arms and face, bleeding freely. It looked as if someone had taken knives and cut open her skin. Aste wasn't doing it. Amanda was sitting up, cradling her soul and almost breathing fire at Nakia. Nakia screamed, writhed and covered her face. Mira realized with a shock that Amanda was using magic to attack Nakia.

"Amanda, stop," said Aste, quietly. "You must save your strength to accept your soul back in your body.

Ewan picked Amanda up. She struggled, although Mira saw she didn't have much strength left.

Aste walked over to one of the dragons. "Would you be willing to carry Nakia and Angus to the Island of Lost Souls, where they can be contained and do no more harm until their fate is decided?"

"Certainly. We will guard them well," snarled the chartreuse dragon covered with spines.

A golden yellow dragon covered with wrinkles, who looked ancient, picked Nakia up roughly with his claws and flew off. The chartreuse one took Angus. Several other dragons followed, but many stayed. Others joined Barinthus below, mourning. It hurt Mira just to hear the bellowing. She stayed in Ronan's arms, sobbing.

"Come, it is time," said Aste, touching Mira's arm. "We must return your sister's soul to her before she is lost as well."

Mira nodded, feeling numb and said, "Amanda drank the whole potion."

"Yes, I can see that. That will make this much more difficult, but I think with your abundant power added to mine, we can do this."

Aste motioned for the pooka to bring one of the benches, sitting against the glass wall, closer to the Black Opal.

Donal picked up Amanda's soul as Ewan lay Amanda, now unconscious, on the bench.

Aste took a bottle of herbal oil out of her bag and removed Amanda's shoes and unbuttoned her shirt. She began chanting and anointed Amanda's forehead, each of her drooping arms, her feet and lastly her chest and belly with the oil.

Aste turned to the Black Opal and began an invocation.

Chapter 33 — Mira

The power within the room grew. It became thick. Aste's body moved as if in slow motion. Mira could practically stir the air, sculpt it with her hands. The Opal resonated with Aste's power, enhanced and returned it. Aste turned to Mira. They joined hands over Amanda's unconscious body.

Mira could feel the Opal's energy filling the empty void inside her that Dylan had left. She needed to focus her intense emotion on Amanda now.

Aste raised an eyebrow when she touched Mira's power. Her secret of communing with the Black Opal was out, although Aste didn't look angry about it. Rather she looked secretly pleased about something.

Mira turned her attention to the work of healing of her twin, Amanda. Love for her sister surfaced. They knelt on either side of Amanda, one hand on her arm, another on her thigh, trying to call up her life force. Mira felt it as a faint trickle.

She felt something brush her arm and turned to see Ronan holding the silver branch from the Pearl World. How had he gotten that? Mira looked at Aste, who motioned her to take it. She took the branch and lay it on Amanda's chest. Amanda's energy immediately surged. Ronan retreated to the background.

Aste stood and reached to get the soul from Donal. He handed it to her, then went to kneel touching Amanda's feet. Everyone else in the room seemed to have made a circle around them.

Aste lay the golden, gelatinous-looking soul, on Amanda's belly, just below the silver branch. The soul heaved a great sigh and wrapped its tentacles around Amanda's body. Aste knelt, held her hands above the soul and began to chant again. Mira felt a growing connectedness fill the room. It overwhelmed her and she could barely think, only sense and respond.

As she watched, Aste's hand sank closer and closer to Amanda's belly. Her twin's body was slowly sucking its soul back inside. The silver branch vibrated, turning a grayish color.

Finally Aste pulled her hands from Amanda's belly and lay one on Amanda's arm and the other on her thigh, mirroring Mira. "It is done," she said. "We must wait and let Amanda come back into herself."

The three of them held the circle for Amanda. Ewan came to join them, cradling Amanda's head. They did this for what seemed a long time to Mira's aching knees.

Everyone stood silently, except for the pooka, who began a haunting song. She had never heard anything like it. The only music Mira could compare it to were some of the original recordings of Scottish Mouth Music she had once heard. After while, the faerie joined in and every now and then a dragon would make a punctuation with wings or tail slapping. She could still hear the dragons down in the cavern mourning Dylan, and Barinthus' loss of a partner. Their song wove in and out of the pooka's tune. It was the eeriest lamentation she ever heard. She wanted to cry again, but held the circle instead. Mira knew she needed to be useful.

Eventually, Amanda's energy shifted and went down a notch or two. If felt as if her heart slowed, relaxed and beat at a normal pace. She stirred and opened her eyes, then struggled to move, but they pinned her in place.

"Relax Amanda, you're safe," said Mira.

"What's going on?"

"We've just returned your soul to you."

"I had the strangest dream. There was this beautiful woman with white-blond hair. She cradled my soul and healed me."

"You have absorbed the power of the World of the Enigmatic Pearl," said Aste. "Mira brought a branch with her. The spirit of that land came into this room. She helped heal you and you will always carry a part of that land within you now."

Amanda lay there, her mouth open in astonishment. Ewan stroked her hair. Amanda looked at him and smiled. It was the first genuine smile Mira had seen on her twin's face in a very long time. She looked relaxed and almost glowed with vitality. "Can I sit up?"

"Yes, if you feel like it," said Aste.

They helped her to sit. What remained of the branch fell to the floor, turning to dust which was picked up in the breeze.

Mira must have looked disappointed, she certainly felt that way.

Aste said to her, "That world is not for you. It is possible you may visit it, but you must realize it is this world to which you are connected."

"What do you mean?"

Amanda hugged Ewan, then she screamed out "Dylan" and began sobbing.

She had seen him fall, then, thought Mira as a new wave of grief flooded through her. Her sadness doubled now that she could feel Amanda's pain as well.

Aste took Mira's arm and led her over to one of the now vacant windows. "You will find in time what Dylan did is not without reason. The Black Opal called him home just as clearly as she called you to her. She invited you to join with her and you accepted. That is an honor given to very few of us. This land has chosen you. You felt drawn to the Opal enough to want to join with her. It is tradition for the Opal to choose both King and Queen. You bear the horn of the Unicorn Queen. You belong to this world, but the choice to stay and serve is of course yours."

"But I did exactly what the Sorcerer did, I stood between the pillars in the cavern and absorbed the Opal's energy. So how am I different from him?"

"He did not merely stand there, he used magic to steal vitality from the Opal, uninvited. I take part of the blame for that," Aste said, wrinkles tightening around her eyes. "When he was a child with no one else to look after him, I took him down there and he watched me commune with the Opal, asking for guidance. I think it awoke in him hungers he should not have had; his lust for power overruled his good sense."

"If I decide to stay and be part of this world, can I ever go home?" Mira asked, brushing the hair out of her eyes.

"It is possible you may go, although you may find it is no longer your home. It is also possible that this is truly your world and the portals may not open for you. You carry the Opal's power and the unicorn's magic, as well as your own."

"If I am able to leave, can I come back?"

"Certainly, this is not The Wizard of Oz. You may come back here and live if you want."

"How do you know about The Wizard of Oz?"

"Can you keep a secret?" asked Aste deviously. She waited until Mira nodded yes. "I have Ethernet."

"You what?"

"I pick up signals through one of the portals. So, I know a fair amount about what goes on in your world," said Aste. "Although now my home has burned I will have to acquire a new system.

Mira shook her head in disbelief. "Do you have a treadmill? I had a dream while I was at your home. You wore gaudy workout clothes, had short cropped hair and worked out on a treadmill while watching TV."

"Well, one must keep up one's health and it gets awfully snowy where I live. Very difficult to keep in shape. Yes, this wig," Aste said fingering the long, gray hair, "and those clothes are all for show. But what is a Witch or a Magician if not a good actor?"

"I have a lot to learn," said Mira, looking at Aste in amazement.

"You have got time, my dear. Plenty of time. You have learned some of the most important lessons already," said Aste.

"Like what?"

"You tell me."

"To trust myself and my instincts. Have faith in myself. That those you love are more important than most anything."

"Aah, those are the best of lessons."

"I just realized, I haven't seen Edward, although I heard him on the stairs earlier. Where is he?" asked Mira.

"Edward?" asked Aste, puzzled.

"Edward, the pooka, we met him on the road."

"Oh, that Edward. If I wanted to find him I would ask Ronan." said Aste.

"Ronan, why?"

Three blasts of wind buffeted the room. The golden dragon and two others landed in open windows of the Opal Tower.

The golden dragon bowed at Aste and said, "We have deposited them on the Isle of Lost Dreams and left two guard dragons on them. They await the human's final judgment. We have no judgment left to pass. Their power has been removed and Nakia is Queen no more. The dragons are satisfied with this and will not declare war."

"Thank you," said Aste, bowing in return. "Your help is much valued. So is the peace between our nations."

"Who will be your ruler now?" he asked.

"Roderick is next in line," said Aste.

Roderick stepped forward, "I do not want this honor. It has never been my wish to rule and I fear I would make a poor ruler. I would pass this on to my eldest, Ronan. He is well suited to be a King."

"Father, I am not ready."

"Nonsense," said Aste. "No one with any sense is ever ready to rule."

Ronan looked at her and grudgingly nodded in agreement.

Aste continued, "I have noticed you over the turns. Watched you travel back and forth over the land and help this woman in need, solve that man's problem, save imperiled animals, persuade stubborn men to go the opposite direction they wanted to, as well as do whatever you could to nurture this land. It took me a while to connect all your actions since you did much of it anonymously. If you became King your actions would become known and more effective."

"You are right, as usual. I am merely afraid," he said, shrugging. "Afraid I am not strong enough, smart enough or courageous enough to be King."

"Your willingness to challenge your shortcomings makes you enough," Aste said. "Go, walk out on the edge and touch the Black Opal. She will decide if you are to be King."

Ronan hesitated, catching Mira's eyes with a strange look on his face. She didn't know how to interpret it. Then he walked out onto the floor which extended to the Opal. He stopped just short of the Black Opal, bowed and said something she couldn't hear. Then he reached out with both hands and touched the stone. Mira felt the echo of the stone's welcome through her whole body. Her skin tingled then relaxed as the Opal asked Mira to let Ronan in.

She breathed deeply and visualized doors opening in her mind. She could hear and feel everything that passed between him and the Opal. Did anyone else feel this or was it just her? The stone showed Mira how to open her spirit further and allow Ronan to communicate with her silently.

She felt him brush her soul. Apprehension gripped her. She didn't want to let this near stranger into her soul, but when the Opal asked again, Mira let the anxiety pass over her. Acceptance waited within. She was astonished to discover that he let her into his soul as well. She had felt drawn to Ronan since she first met him. Perhaps they could become good friends. Maybe more, said her body.

After what felt like hours, but more likely only minutes, she watched Ronan fall to his knees. Was he crying? His face looked full of bliss and he glowed with life, all weariness washed away.

Roderick moved next to Aste and said, "Perhaps we should go down to the feast and make an announcement, since it must have become clear Nakia is not announcing her choice of consort." Grinning, his whole face was lit up.

"Yes, you are right. You should take Ronan and Ewan and make the announcement. There will be much joy in the city tonight. In the entire land, when the news travels."

"Will you come down with us? Your presence will be helpful."

"Let me check on Amanda. If she is well, then we will all come for a short time."

Roderick went to congratulate his son. Aste knelt and touched Amanda's hand. Donal stood talking with three of the pooka guard. Most of the pooka had already left.

Mira felt out of place and couldn't see where she did fit into all this. The contact with Ronan and the Opal felt so intense all her emotions were heightened and on edge. Another wave of grief threatened to consume her or fracture her completely. She tried pushing it all to the back of her mind, but it wouldn't stay. Think of something else, she told herself. She wondered where Edward could be. She missed his quiet company and support. Why did she feel this way?

She had made it to the city and returned Amanda's soul back to her. She found her magic and her own strength. Here she stood on the brink of a fairy tale ending, her prince, or rather King, staring at her and all she could do was cry. She had lost Dylan and perhaps Edward. Her thoughts drifted back to what Aste said.

On one level, Mira knew Aste was right. She belonged here, belonged to this land and to the Black Opal. She certainly couldn't go home with a horn coming out of her head. But could she be Queen? Did Ronan even want her as Queen?

Chapter 34 — Ronan

Ronan stood facing the Black Opal. He had dreamt of this for turns, never believing it could actually happen. His heart beat wildly. Sweat dripped down the back of his neck and his hands felt cramped. What if the Opal rejected him, found him wanting?

He stepped forward and said to the stone, "Sacred stone of our people, I ask you to judge me. Can I learn what is needed to be a useful King, a wise King? I will follow whatever choice you make."

The Black Opal pulsed slightly. He walked closer and placed his palms on the stone, noticing again the scales on the back of his hands.

He felt overwhelmed by a wave of empathy and power from the Opal.

"Welcome, my Son! I have been training you to be King for many turns."

Ronan understood now why the Queen had lost her magic. The Black Opal had cut her connection with Nakia and the power the Sorcerer wrenched from the stone was not given openly. No wonder the Queen went insane. To have been given this much love and joy freely and then have it withdrawn would be enough to make anyone mad. Would he be able to give it up when his time came?

He saw images of Mira connecting with the Opal. The stone had drawn Mira in and joined with her. He could feel Mira's fears and her attempts to release them. He felt thrilled at her physical attraction to him, but also sadness for her doubts about whether she would enjoy just being with him. She did not think there could be much common ground between the two of them. Ronan disagreed. He also felt her deep grief for Dylan and worry for Edward.

"She is the Queen," the Opal told him, "although, Mira does not understand this yet."

He felt elated the Opal agreed with him about Mira, and longed to join with her body, mind and soul.

The Opal reminded him of the myth:

"He who is claimed by the dragons, bows to the Black Opal.

She who is chosen by the unicorns, blessed by the Black Opal."

The Black Opal continued, "You, of course are the Dragon King, my son."

Drained from the past few days, Ronan sank to his knees, still touching the stone as she gave him the secrets he needed to rule the kingdom. He knew Mira had been given different knowledge as the Opal wanted her to do other work. The Opal conveyed information into his mind until he felt it might burst. He was surprised by much of it, especially that the Opal communicated with the Enigmatic Pearl and the Flaming Ruby. He asked for wisdom and the Black Opal provided. Ronan surrendered himself completely.

The stone also filled his heart with the capacity for more compassion and patience than he had ever possessed. As a gift, she poured his heart full of bliss. He felt tears stream down his face.

He knew Mira felt this as well. She was bound to the stone and now to this land. She could refuse to be Queen, just as he could refuse the Kingship. He hoped that would not be her choice.

Ronan dropped his hands from the stone. He felt full, exhausted and completely rested all at the same time. He wiped his face and stood. Turning, he saw Roderick, beaming, step forward to hug him and clap him on the back.

"I knew this was the way it should be, you King and not me," said his father.

"I was not so sure," said Ronan.

"Nonsense, and congratulations. You will make a fine King."

"Thank you Father. I will do my best and I will need your help."

"What, do I not get a life of leisure now?" he asked, mockingly.

"No, no, no. I have many plans for you."

"Hmmph," said Roderick.

Ronan watched Aste check on Amanda. Ewan sat with Amanda's head in his lap, stroking her long red hair. How like Mira she looked and yet she was so different in action and her vital force.

He glanced at Mira standing by one of the glass walls. She looked very small and alone. Her face was filled with grief. He should have made sure Nakia was under more restraint. He should have moved, not been frozen with horror. Maybe he could have prevented Dylan's death.

The Black Opal whispered to him, "This was meant to be. The child did what he came to do in this life. Dylan touched and healed many. It was his time to surrender and complete the cycle of life. His soul has other adventures to move on to. That is the way of things."

He knew Mira was trying to understand her place in all this. He knew where she belonged, and needed to confess about Edward. She had only met him as Ronan once and had no idea how well they knew each other. He needed to get her alone and have a long talk with her. Tonight. No, now.

He began to walk towards her when Roderick touched his arm. "We must go down to the feast and tell the people what has happened."

Ronan thought both Mira and he should both be there to announce their leadership, but she had not accepted yet and perhaps did not even understand what the Opal offered.

"Wait," he said to his father."

Ronan walked to Mira, put his arms around her and said, "We will talk, I must go and speak to the people."

She nodded, "I must go see Dylan." Tears streamed down her face.

"May I come with you, before I return to the Celebration?"

"Please," she said. "I don't think I can face this alone. I should never have brought him. He would still be alive if...."

Chapter 35 — Mira

Mira started to follow the others towards the stairway door when she saw a soft, green lump. It lay near the edge of the catwalk where Dylan had fallen. It was Dylan's stuffed dinosaur, Freddie, a fancy, flying one with sparkles, looking very much like a dragon. She stuffed it inside the waist of her pants to give to Amanda later. She wiped her face with the soft fabric of her unicorn mask.

Part of her wanted nothing more than to join Barinthus and the other dragons in mourning. Another part of her felt afraid to start crying again. Would there be any end to it? She was only eighteen, but had already lost Dad, then Mom, then Aunt Rita and now Dylan. Mira wanted to go home and be comforted, but she had no home anymore and no one to comfort her. She shoved her emotions back down and followed the others.

Behind her, Ronan said to the two pooka, "Can you send for the Healers to wash Dylan's body and prepare him and the cavern for the mourners that will come?"

"It is done," one of them said, bowing. They left by the other door.

She felt surprised at his sensitivity, considering everything else that had happened tonight.

Mira numbly followed Amanda and Ewan down the steps. The tower reverberated from the dragons' howling. Amanda was doing well, considering. She had come out of the healing with an enormous amount of vitality. Her twin wasn't ready to cry.

Two-thirds of the way down, Roderick, Donal and several pooka went towards the ballroom to make things ready. The rest of them continued to the catacombs. Ronan had followed behind and took her arm after she stumbled.

The descent ended and Mira had to move forward.

She and Amanda went to Dylan's body. Mira tried to look past the blood. It ran everywhere and Dylan was broken and mangled. She blocked that out, not wanting to remember him like that.

She squatted next to Amanda, putting an arm around her. Amanda touched Dylan's face and looked at Mira. "I've been horrible to him since my soul was stolen, haven't I?"

"You had no choice," she said. "He understood. He was such a smart kid."

Amanda nodded. They sat down for a while, both of them working hard not to start the endless crying. Mira stroked Dylan's curls. She felt aware Barinthus and several other dragons watched them, giving Amanda and her space to grieve alone. The dragons were better at grieving. They wailed, moaned and cried, then probably got on with their lives. Both she and Amanda came from a family where you cried only when you were alone. Not in front of others. She couldn't remember crying at Dad's funeral.

Amanda shifted and said, "We should go. They're waiting for us."

Amanda was right, but Mira didn't feel up to going to the gathering. Still, she nodded and stood, pulling the unicorn mask on over her head and the horn. She wanted to remain invisible and still wasn't sure how she felt about the horn sticking out of her forehead.

Joining the others, they walked back up several flights of stairs. Ronan assisted her again, his touch warm and gentle. She noticed he had green, iridescent scales on the backs of his arms and hands. It didn't look like part of a costume since he didn't seem to be wearing one. She wondered if he had the scales when she met him before. She wanted to bask in the tenderness of his eyes, but felt afraid of crumbling into little pieces that could never be put together again. At least no one could see her crying inside the mask.

They reached the ballroom that Ewan had called the Commoner's Room. The Midsummer's Eve party had only become more raucous. The music louder, the lighting brighter, the magic more out of control and the dancing more wild. Most of the magic was glamour , people making themselves other, or more, than they actually were. So much glamour hung in the air, it made her nauseous. Despite the bath earlier, she was still dirty and smelly. She never felt less glamorous and couldn't find it in her to summon up a charm to change that. Never in her life had she felt so tired.

When Roderick and Ronan stepped onto the dais, she heard cheers and whistles, many of them from young women. Eventually, Roderick did what he could to bring the crowd to something resembling quiet.

He said, "This evening, or I should say early this morning Queen Nakia of the Black Opal had a change of heart. She has decided to give up the crown. She and her sorcerer have departed."

The crowd went wild at this news. Mira could see no one who felt upset by the announcement, although she supposed it wasn't a wise political move to disapprove of a change in rulers.

When the crowd calmed down, Roderick continued, "The crown was offered to me, but I am much too lazy to be King."

There was much laughter at this, obviously the man knew his audience.

"I suggested the crown be passed on to my eldest, Ronan and the Black Opal has overwhelmingly accepted him. Now he needs your approval."

Clapping, yelling and screaming followed. Mira felt like she was at a rock concert. People stomped their feet and yelled "Ronan! Ronan! Ronan!"

He stepped forward and stood next to his father. Aste and Ewan joined them as did several pooka. Mira, Amanda and Donal remained off the stage and to the side.

Mira was trying to be invisible, helped somewhat by her costume. She felt numb. Partly from helping heal Amanda, but mostly from the loss of Dylan. Plus, she needed sleep. She put her hand over the bulge in her waistband and fondled the toy dinosaur.

She missed most of Ronan's speech. Something about returning vitality to the land and making peace between all the living beings. He was very magnetic. Quiet, dark and very handsome. Very much like Ewan, except Ronan personified the moon where Ewan represented the sun.

Why had he avoided telling her his name when they first met? Probably because he decided I looked repulsive, she thought. Why did she care? She really didn't understand why, but she did care. She wanted Ronan to like her. To be as attracted to her as she felt drawn to him. It wasn't just desire. She felt as if he carried a missing part of her soul that she needed to be whole.

Mira rubbed her eyes beneath the mask. She chalked all such thought up to exhaustion and grief. She must be in shock.

When Ronan finished his speech and the applause died down, a voice came from a young man in the audience. One of Roderick's men. "The Queen was planning to name a consort tonight. The least you could do, King Ronan, is to name one of these young ladies as your Queen and see if the Opal accepts her, so you can let the others off the hook and the rest of us stand a chance."

That produced a huge roar of laughter from the crowd. She thought Ronan would blush, but instead he laughed. "I would be glad to, for your sake alone Samuel, and I do have someone in mind, but I can guarantee she would geld me if I did not speak to her alone first. So I am sorry I cannot oblige you. Tonight."

She wondered if he really did have someone in mind or if it was simply an evasion. She felt even smaller and more insignificant than before. Did she really want an unattainable King? Did she want to stay here? Grief and fatigue added to her confusion. The Opal had offered her something, but Mira wasn't clear what. Work as a Healer, the antithesis of what the Sorcerer had been.

The crowd laughed again and there was a toast. It looked like alcohol and she could use that. She pushed the mask away from her mouth to drink, but kept the top part on. She didn't want to face anyone. Drinking wine made her even more tired, but it tasted delightful. She'd been up since early morning of the day before when she and Edward had entered the catacombs. Now dawn had come again. She'd gone through exhaustion, past feeling silly, gotten a second wind and then lost it. She felt ready to drop for the tenth time, and couldn't remember when she last ate.

Amanda looked at her and asked, "Are you okay?"

"I need to eat. And sleep," she said.

"As soon as Aste comes down here, we'll take care of that," said Amanda. "And thank you for getting me here and healing me," she added.

"I could never have done otherwise." She saw the grief in her sister's eyes and knew Amanda purposely avoided talking or thinking about Dylan.

Amanda put her arm around her shoulder and hugged her. Mira returned the hug and said, "It's good to have you back."

"It's good to be back. I feel terrific. Physically, at least," Amanda said.

Aste stared at them. As the speeches and toasting ended and the partying resumed, Aste came down off the dais and walked up to her. "Mira, my dear, I have completely forgotten about you, I am sorry. The healing took a lot out of you. I should have attended to you as well."

She shrugged. "It's just been a really long, bad day, or two. Maybe a bad week."

"The palace has quarters for guests, let us get you set up for the night. You need some food and rest. This celebration will continue for hours, even days." She nodded to the throng who had put Ronan on their shoulders and carried him throughout the palace.

She followed Aste and a pooka to yet another part of the palace that looked unfamiliar. Mira took off her mask and sat down. A small feast sat out on a table. Mira, Donal and Aste ate. Mira ate as much as she could before falling asleep propped up on her elbow, listening to Aste and Donal talk. Aste led her off to one of the guest rooms.

"Sleep as long as you need. Food will be in the common room we just left, when you awake."

Alone, she undressed and found a small bathroom that had a peculiar flushing toilet. She washed her face with water from a pitcher, but was unable to find the oomph or desire to take a bath in the large tub. There was clothing draped over the edge of the bed that might be a nightgown, bathrobe or something, but she didn't care. She dropped onto the bed naked, pulled the covers up, and although exhausted, found it difficult to fall asleep.

She had missed something important. It had to do with Ronan and the Opal and herself. The harder she grasped to catch the thought, the further it fled from her. Finally, it slipped away completely and she fell asleep.

Chapter 36 — Ronan

Ronan found himself shadowed by pooka guards wherever he went. Smiling pooka guards. They looked very pleased about the change in rulers.

The announcement had caused the wildness of the Midsummer Festival to leap into full swing with the party continuing on past dawn. The entire palace became the center of chaos as it should be on Midsummer, and had not been in far too many turns, he thought.

After the party died down a little, he went to look for Mira, and found his brother and Amanda. Ewan told him Mira had long since retired to bed. At his clear disappointment, Ewan laughed and said, "We finally share the same taste in women, brother. I am happy to see that it is she you referred to during your little speech."

Ronan laughed and smiled. He could say nothing else.

"Congratulations. And I can truly say I am glad you are King and not me. You are the only one fit to rule in our family. So you better marry her and have many children so the crown can go to them, because I would be a terrible king. And Father, well, you already know," said Ewan.

Ewan grabbed Amanda's hand and pulled her out onto the dance floor. Ronan watched them for a few minutes, realizing Amanda was holding back her terrible grief by ignoring it. When she let the barricade down, the outpouring of pain would be overwhelming. He hoped Ewan would be there to help.

Ronan had paid close attention in the catacombs as the sisters sat by Dylan's body, neither of them shedding a tear. Aste had explained to him that the two came from a family where grieving generally happened in private. He marveled at their strength. Ronan's own grief at Dylan's death would have to wait as well, he needed to celebrate with his people tonight. He hadn't known the child as long or loved him as deeply as Mira and Amanda, but his own tears would flow. He sighed deeply and moved off through the crowd.

He found himself pulled aside by various people interested in keeping their political ambitions intact or coming into new favor. Making no promises, Ronan said only that he would do his best to be fair and that all backbiting and politicking within the court would be at an end. He would not tolerate it. Word about that needed to travel quickly.

The faeries continued to wreak havoc wherever they could. Normally they bewitched isolated couples, but now he saw large groups of the crowd drop to the floor. Everyone not wanting to be the object of someone's affection ran from the general area. Those wanting the opposite flocked to the downed bodies. At least half the celebrants must now be under the spell of faeries. Ewan and Amanda disappeared. Aste did not come back down after finding Mira a bed. Finally, only a handful of people remained. Roderick, Stephen and a number of others. Ronan slipped off as quietly as he could, pooka following him.

Up in the Queen's quarter, he turned to one of them and asked, "Where am I going? I do not even know where to sleep." His father's rooms would be full of other guests since Ronan had never wanted to sleep in the palace.

They laughed at this, thought it was a hilarious joke. He did not. He had been up now longer than Mira and felt exhausted and overextended.

They took him to the visitor's quarters until the housekeepers could find time to purge and redecorate to his simpler tastes. Or until he claimed another section of the palace as his sleeping quarters.

When he finally found a bed and undressed, it took him a long time to fall asleep. It must be midday and there was work to be done, but he needed a little sleep to continue. He tossed, fitfully, thinking mostly about Mira and how best to tell her about Edward.

He wanted to find a way to explain so she would fall in love with him. He actually considered using magic, but she would see through that. She had far too much insight for him to sneak magic past her.

No, he would have to be straight forward and honest. Explain that he fell in love with her. That he needed her strength and compassion to help him rule this land and wanted her by his side as his lover, not just as Queen or Sorceress.

When sleep finally came he dreamt of her. She sat on a beautiful black unicorn. The faeries had bewitched her and she would not come down. He told her of his love. Mira told him she preferred the unicorn and freedom. The unicorn ran off, carrying her away.

He could not remember any more of the dream upon waking. The dimming light told him evening was coming. He had only slept a short while, but felt eager to get on with his work. He bathed quickly and found fresh clothes laid out. They were much more regal looking than he would have liked. He put them on anyway and ate rapidly.

Ronan left word with one of the pooka to bring Mira to him when she woke. He spent a long time going through Nakia's papers in her office and uncovered a great, many ugly secrets. Clearly she had not feared being spied upon. She wrote down everything, bits of information to be held over various people's heads, bribery and threats. He found an elaborate plan laid out for taking control of the Worlds of the Enigmatic Pearl and the Flaming Ruby. It was very detailed and she clearly needed the dragons to carry it out. He also spoke to several of Nakia's advisors and stripped more than one of them of their titles, land and rank, even imprisoning a couple who enjoyed their work too much.

Mira never strayed far from his thoughts. He kept wondering how best to approach her and earn her trust, friendship and love. His dream of the night before haunted him. Would she prefer freedom to him?

Before dinner he went up to the Black Opal Tower, searching for the right words to say to her. The wind whipped through the top of the tower, clearing his mind.

He did not have to touch the Opal this time. She greeted him when he entered the room. He presented the stone with his problem.

The answer she gave him, The choice must be left to her. Be truthful.

He hoped the advice would work. He did not know if he could let her go. Not that he ever had her, except in his mind. What if she went back to her own world, so very far away? What if she did not come back? What if she connected with an old lover? What if she had an accident?

Worry consumed him. He calmed himself and breathed in the fresh, salty air coming off the sea, while watching the life of the city wind down again, perhaps a little later today than normal. After the Midsummer Celebration everything slowed down for a few days. Sea birds cawed as fishing boats came in with their catch. Dragons flew, trumpeting their own excitement about the renewal of the land. Palace staff rushed about, preparing for the inauguration.

How could he govern without her? The Black Opal had revealed that she held the key to healing the land and its people from Nakia's devastation. Ronan held moderation and balance. Mira was the spark and the fire.

Ronan could sense her presence before she arrived. He heard the Opal's welcome and felt Mira's surprise at that.

The door closed and he turned to look at Mira. Her long red hair was worn down as he had rarely seen it. Her beautiful, pearl colored horn glistened in the twilight. She wore silky white and green streaked pants and a shirt that made her green eyes even more luminous than normal. Eyes that he wanted to truly see him.

He almost lost his nerve. He would do almost anything to keep her. Tell her whatever she wanted to hear. Ronan closed his eyes and ran his hand through his long hair, smoothing it out of his face. He wondered if he had even combed it this morning; he knew he forgot to shave.

"The pooka said you wanted to speak with me," she said.

"Yes, I do." He smiled. "I have been spending some time trying to solve the problems Nakia left behind," he said, shaking his head. "But that is not why I called you." He motioned toward the bench beside him, "Would you like to sit down?"

"Sure."

Ronan watched her perch uncomfortably on the edge of the bench. "I owe you a few explanations," he said, sitting down beside her.

Mira's eyebrows wrinkled, "You don't owe me anything."

"Oh, but I do. When I first met you, I tried to balance being as helpful as I could to you, while leading my father and his men astray. They were once again illegally hunting the black unicorns. Ewan and I had come along as trackers, trying to desperately lead them off in the wrong direction when we met you. I would liked to have taken you to Aste's and brought you all the way to the City myself."

"It wasn't necessary," she said. "Although I'm glad you weren't really part of the hunting party."

"No, and my father will not be hunting unicorns again either. I plan to keep him too busy." He nervously brushed the hair out of his face. "The rest, well, this is very hard to explain. When I was a child I discovered I had a gift. Few people know about it. I am able to shape-shift with ease and to stay in those shapes for long stretches. I had a mentor, a pooka, who helped me polish those skills as a young boy." He paused making sure she followed him.

She nodded.

He continued, "There have been times in the last fifteen turns when I shape-shifted so I could do things that were not exactly legal, but were the right thing to do. I was on one of those missions last week, trying to forge an alliance between the dragons and a certain faction of people in this city who thought Nakia should step down. I ran into you while I searched for the High Dragon." He paused, waiting for her to understand.

"I know I should get this, but I don't remember running into you."

"I am Edward."

Mira seemed completely without words and glared at him. She said, "That's very difficult to believe."

"I know it is," he said. "I am not sure if I will be able to change fully now that I have become the Dragon King," he said, showing his hands to her. She took them and examined the scales and ridges on the back, tracing them gently with her finger. "I will try to change, because you must believe me."

He rose and walked away from her, turning his back, then removed his clothes. She gasped as he took his shirt off. He knew she was reacting to the sight of scales covering his back. While continuing to undress, he worried that she felt repelled by them.

Ronan focused on the change and found he could still become pooka where there were no scales. The scaled parts of him stayed the same. His ears grew long, his body taller and covered with fur, even the shape of his eyes changed. Finished, he moved to her side.

"And you were able to stay this way all the while, running by my horse's side."

"Yes, when one is masquerading as a pooka, one adopts the philosophy, body and soul of a pooka as far as possible."

Mira crossed her arms. She looked at him, her eyebrows drawn together, and said icily, "So, I told you all my deep, dark secrets and you were someone else all the time."

"Not quite someone else. Edward exists within me and I within him. But yes, I withheld truth from you and for that I am sorry. For many turns my life has not been my own. I thought I was working to help my father get the crown. Now it appears that all along he was working to get me the crown. Still my life will not be my own either, but at least that part will be out in the open. I am done with hiding."

Returning to the pile of clothes, he made himself Ronan again, breathing hard and wincing with the pain of changing so quickly in such a short space of time. He dressed hastily.

"So after you met up with the dragons, why did you stay with us?" she asked.

He could hear the coldness in her voice. What could he say to melt it? "I would like to say that your cause and my own were the same; which turned out to be true, but my intentions were not that honorable." He nervously looked down, wanting to escape her freezing gaze. "The truth is I fell in love with you and could not bear to leave. I did not want to become Ronan again, because you trusted Edward. You talked to him, told him your secrets and relied on him. I did not want to lose you." He sat on the bench beside her.

She remained silent, inscrutable.

He continued, "I wanted to talk to you last night, but could not get you alone and I knew your grief overwhelmed you. When I saw you nearly collapse during the toasts, I wanted to leave and carry you away. To care for you. As the new King, I could not leave." His hands became tight fists, remembering the frustration.

She struggled with what he said. Emotions flowed across her face, died and seemed to be replaced by competing emotions. "How did you escape from the Sorcerer?" she asked.

He could tell she needed more time to understand things. "The pooka guard arrived and recognized me at once, they have always known about my abilities and are amused by them. The Sorcerer continued to search for you, while they took me to a cell. The pooka helped me escape and get into the palace. I became Ronan again and began to search for you."

He stood up and walked towards the Black Opal, then came back and sat by her. "When I communed with the Black Opal, I was encouraged to talk to you about this. I will give you all the time you need to assimilate what happened and work things out. I realize you come from another world, that you have a life there and people you love, who love you. But would you consider living in this land? Could you consider being my Witch, my Consort, my Queen?"

She looked astonished. "I hardly know you. You know me, but I've only met you twice, briefly. We've hardly talked."

"Yes, you are right. It is a preposterous request. I would never have dared to make it, if the Opal had not encouraged me."

"I also communed with the Black Opal yesterday," she said.

He was not surprised, "I know she chose you, but when?"

"After you were captured, I was chased all over the catacombs and got lost. Eventually, I returned to the cavern and felt called to stand between the pillars. I bathed in her light and presence."

"So she chose you."

"That's what Aste said."

"What will you do about it?" he asked.

"I haven't decided yet. I need to go home and talk to Mom and my Aunt Rita. Tell them about Dylan. See if Amanda needs me. After that I don't know. Perhaps come back here." She looked at him and said, "But I have this horn. How can I go home with this?"

He took her hand. "I do not know, but it is beautiful." Pushing a tendril of hair off her face, he said, "Tell me at least that I have a chance to win your heart."

"You have a chance."

"That is as much as I could ask for," he said, quietly.

Chapter 37 — Mira

Mira walked though the formal palace gardens after dinner. Lanterns hung everywhere making the garden glow beautifully. Large, white moths the size of her hand flitted in and out of the light. She found a wildish section, full of herbs and scraggly trees. She sat on a gnarled wooden bench, noticing how drained she felt from the last several days.

Her bath this afternoon had been spent crying. Tears had run down her face for Dylan, for her Father, who left her by killing himself when she was ten, for Amanda, but mostly for herself. Now that she had done what needed doing, where was she? Here in this strange land with a horn growing out of her head and no clue what to do next.

She sat and breathed in the scents of lavender and old roses. What should she do about Ronan? Part of her felt furious with him. She sat and broke twiggy stalks of wormwood as she fumed. How could he have spied on her all that time, pretending to be Edward? Well, at least that explained who defended them in the battles with Nakia's assassins. He was a shape-changer, not a pooka.

She stood and walked over to the wall of climbing roses. The fragrance filled her with lightness. In the end she would probably forgive him. He had done incredible things to keep them all safe and help them get to the City. She didn't think they would have made it without him.

Another part of her felt thrilled to hear him say he loved her. Even though she didn't know him and he didn't really know her. When she went inside herself and asked the Opal about it there came a resounding sense of rightness and completion. She had been in a couple of really bad relationships, chosen the wrong guys, it was difficult to trust herself in choosing any man.

She moved out of the herb garden, intending to make her way into the palace and find Amanda. Freddie was stuffed in her pocket and Amanda would want him. The paths in the garden curved through hedges almost forming a labyrinth, echoing the design of the catacombs. She finally came to a large open space covered with lawn. In the middle of it sat Barinthus.

He said, "I have been waiting for you," and flashed his green scales. Mira could see the gashes on his head and shoulders had been smeared with an iridescent purple paste.

"Will you be all right?" she asked.

"I shall carry the loss of him with me always, but his coming was a welcome sign that the world changes."

"What do you mean?"

"His coming to us, joining with me, meant it is time for us to connect with humans again. The reign of the Dragon King, and perhaps the Unicorn Queen, is here. It is time to open the barriers we have put up between our peoples. When you healed the unicorn it was a sign. There will be hatchlings among us. The unicorns are beginning to recover from the horrible massacre and we can finally forgive ourselves for our part in it. With time they will cover the plains again. They carry the wild magic. It will be a beautiful sight. This is a momentous time in our land." As they talked Barinthus led them down a wide stone path, the width of a two lane road.

"I didn't realize any of this," she said, walking beside his head. She knew so little about this world. The thought of the plains covered with unicorns sent shivers up her spine. She wanted to be here to see that.

"You will stay here. With Ronan?"

"I don't know," said Mira. "I don't know him."

"Of course you do, he is Edward. How can you not know him after all you have been through together?"

"I just learned he is Edward," she said, stiffening.

"Humans sometimes amaze me. You become so insulted about small things that the larger part flies right past you. He loves you and I sense you love him. I could see that the first time I met you. Together you form a whole, Dragon King and Unicorn Queen. So many of your people are incomplete without a partner. Please consider staying with him, for both your happiness."

"I will consider it."

"Will you come with me to visit Dylan's body one last time?" he asked.

"Yes, I will." She had not noticed, but the walkway led them towards the Tower.

The Tower wall had a huge arch built into it at ground level. Workers were still clearing away the rubble from where Barinthus broke it open the night before.

"Before the enmity between humans and dragons this garden was a place for us to land and spend time with people. This Tower entrance was built for us so we could enter the palace. Queen Nakia walled it up when she became afraid of us. We could always have opened it, but chose not to."

They entered into the cavern.

She felt amazement at the change in the room. The light drifting in made the three columns of bones almost sparkle.

Dylan's body lay on the stone platform between the columns. The purple phosphorescence of the Black Opal bathed him. The room was filled with people, pooka, faeries and dragons. Many of the dragons and faeries perched on window ledges up the entire height of the Tower. They sang together, not quite so mournful as yesterday, more hopeful, she would say.

As they entered, a path opened to let them through to the front. She found Amanda, Ewan and Aste. Amanda gave her a hug, eyes swollen from crying. Mira reached into her pocket, pulled out Freddie and gave him to Amanda. Her sister took the cuddly dinosaur and hugged it, thanking Mira with her eyes. She clutched it to her chest and began sobbing. Mira couldn't help but start crying again.

Ronan appeared and she felt him standing next to her, even though they didn't touch. The keening of the dragons and faeries rose to a high pitch, reminiscent of a Gregorian Chant. The light from the Opal changed to orange. Heat rolled off the platform and Dylan's body began to burn. She felt shocked, not knowing what else to expect. His body turned red, orange, yellow, green, blue, then purple again as it transformed to ash. In the smoke that rose, Mira watched three faeries dance and could have sworn she saw Dylan's soul flying there, laughing. His soul looked like a red and gold dragon and the smell of pinon pines wafted through the air.

She felt herself drooping, Ronan put his arms around her for support. She turned into his chest, quietly crying.

"His body is at peace now. His soul will return when it is time and where he is needed," said Ronan.

She heard a scraping noise and saw two men sweeping Dylan's ashes into a stone urn. They brought the urn to Amanda and she hugged the jar.

Amanda said, quietly, "I will always love you, little one." Then she handed the urn to Barinthus who took it with his supple front feet and handed it to the three faeries. They fluttered onto his back to sit. She said, "I would be honored if you would spread his ashes over the land where he came into his own."

Barinthus nodded, "It will be done. The land is honored by your gift." He streamed up and then out through the archway followed by all the dragons and faeries. It was as if a glittery, rainbow river flooded throughout the cavern, cascading upwards into the sky.

Mira numbly followed the humans and pooka up stairs and into the ballroom for a wake. She felt aware of Ronan holding her hand and guiding her. He pulled a chair out for her and occasionally reminded her to eat and drink. Her mind still seemed caught in the sights, sounds and smells of the funeral.

Chapter 38 — Mira

Mira sat in the formal palace garden with Aste. Stretching her legs in the warmth of the day, toes poking out of the tan sandals she wore, below the fluttery, summer dress made of gauzy, green material. She tried to savor what the day offered her.

The courtyard had massive fountains and ponds with a huge population of water birds and fish. Much of the stone work, wall statues and benches in this part of the garden were carved out of slippery, black stone. It felt silky and smooth to sit on. And warm, as if it absorbed heat from the air. Very comfortable. It made her realize how much tension she stored in her body. She felt the pressure of so many things that needed resolution.

The garden was filled with the sweet scent of a flower she didn't recognize, but it smelled tropical and strong. The day looked as bright as any she had seen here, with no clouds in the sky, just an occasional dragon coming or going. Apparently this still wasn't normal because whenever it happened, anyone in the garden, guests or gardeners stood and stared as if they'd never seen a dragon before. She sighed. Dragons would always make her think of Dylan.

"It wasn't always this way, you know. There used to be a great partnership between humans and the dragons," said Aste. "However, dragons hate deception and lies, thus they broke the alliance with Nakia."

"What will happen to her and Angus?"

"I do not know. Either Ronan will make a decision or he will convene the High Council. The High Council have not been called together for a very, long time. Nakia disbanded them shortly after the massacre when she chose not to share her power, she made her own council. Either way, things will not turn in her favor."

Mira had so many questions, she didn't know where to start. The more she learned the more confusing everything was. She became distracted by the sound of hoof beats and a feeling of overwhelming joy in running. Five horses raced towards them. No, they were unicorns. A bay led the way. Mira recognized her as Shadow, only because she felt the mare's mind. Shadow whinnied and slid to a stop in front of her. Mira stood and touched her neck. Upon the mare's forehead grew a beautiful, tortoiseshell horn with swirling ridges sculpted into it.

Shadow snorted, Thank you for releasing us. Many of us chose to hide as horses who have little magic, after the Queen tried to crush us.

"You are most welcome." She felt so happy to see Shadow.

Shadow tossed her head and said, We have decided to live in this lovely garden for a time. Humans and unicorns should mingle. I will come back and visit, but now it is time to run. She briefly touched horns with Mira, then raced off, leading the others.

Mira recognized the gray as Amanda's horse, the strawberry roan who had been the packhorse and the black as the horse Aste had ridden. The other unicorn, a tall bay stallion, she didn't know; although Shadow referred to him as Pinecone.

Mira asked Aste, "Why do all the creatures of our myths live in this world?"

"These are not creatures, but thinking, feeling beings. As are the horses they pretended to be. As was the cow we ate for dinner last night. Your world categorizes many things as non-sentient for its own convenience. It also will not admit to the existence of many beings, so they would be invisible to you, in the same way people who are not trained to clean up after themselves cannot see dirt or dishes that need washing. I would guess they live here because we acknowledge their existence and our grass is sweeter."

"Why is this world beneath or inside my world?"

Aste looked amused. "Who is to say if you were to go slipping through a garden gate sideways that you might not find a portal to a new world 'above' yours? I would be careful about assigning a specific placement of any world in relation to the others. That is the logic drilled into you by your educational system. Everything must have a rational and scientific explanation." She shook her head and smoothed her long skirt. "Do not misunderstand me. Science has brought your world many wonderful things, but it also brings a kind of blindness. If the current theories cannot explain something, it is often dismissed. The worlds are more closely connected than you realize. Passing from one to another is as simple as going into another room, provided you know where the door is and how to open it," said Aste.

"But how did the portal open when we went through?" she asked.

"Some are always open. Perhaps Nakia opened all the portals in that area or maybe the eagle opened it. I do not know."

"How will we get back?"

"I will make sure the way is open for you," said Aste.

"How will I come back here if I choose to return?"

"If?" asked Aste, raising an eyebrow.

"All right, when. Probably," she said.

"You can email me and I will open the portal for you."

"You're joking," said Mira looking at Aste's smug expression. "Okay, you're not joking."

"Most certainly not. Wickedwitch@paganmissive. The internet is one of your world's wonderful things. Once you learn more, I will teach you how to open the portals yourself," said Aste. "Have you spoken with Ronan about Edward yet."

"Oh yeah." She looked at Aste and crossed her arms. "You knew all the time, didn't you?"

"Yes, but it was not my secret to tell. I trusted his motivation to be well intended."

"How long have you known?"

"About his ability to shape-change?" asked Aste.

Mira nodded.

Aste said, "I am not sure. I knew about it when I was here at court. I do not remember how long ago that was."

"How old are you?"

"Truly I have not kept count. It is not important to me. My eldest son Donal is fifty-three," she shrugged.

There came a flurry of activity in one of the fountains as two geese had a spat about something.

Aste asked her, "What else did Ronan talk to you about?"

"He asked me to be his consort, whatever that means."

"In your world you would call it a life partner, a spouse. What did you answer?"

She tucked her hair back behind her ears. "I told him I'd think about it."

"Will you?" asked Aste.

"Yes, but I'm going to think about it for quite awhile. I've had enough jerky boyfriends. And my emotional state right now is unbalanced, at best. I don't want to end up in another mess. I don't trust my judgment yet."

"Love is always messy, but I do not think Ronan would qualify as 'jerky'," said Aste. She picked a daisy and rolled it back and forth between her hands, making it twirl. "Have you considered that none of this was an accident?"

"What do you mean?" Mira asked, feeling she knew what Aste would say.

"I do not believe in coincidences. What if you were brought here by the Black Opal with the intent that you replace Nakia?"

She took a sharp, short breath and leaned against the bench's back, staring at Aste. Did the Opal engineer the Queen's madness, the theft of Amanda's soul, meeting Ronan, everything? "Are you serious?"

"Yes."

"Even Dylan's death?" Anger rose within her.

"I do not pretend to understand all the implications of his death. I am not saying every detail was planned. I am merely speculating the Black Opal set things in motion for you to come here and become Queen."

"What if you're right?"

"It is possible you may not be able to go back through the portal. You are joined with the Black Opal in a way few of us ever are."

"I might be stuck here?" she asked, trying to slow her breathing.

"I would not look at it that way, but essentially, yes," said Aste. "I know Nakia tried to leave a few times, she had grand plans of invading other worlds. It seems the Opal no longer allows the chosen ruler to leave. That has not always been so. Her father ruled three different worlds simultaneously, and traveled between them."

She sat looking at the ground. She had always hated feeling trapped, pushed into things. She had fought it her whole life, between Aunt Rita and her mom. Back in her world, what would she do about the horn? She couldn't cut it off, knowing what it symbolized. What if she had to stay here? There was no requirement that she marry Ronan. Mira could do what she wanted, go where needed and learn. But replacing Nakia, being a Queen, a ruler, was truly beyond her. She felt absolutely unprepared to do such a thing.

She shook her head to clear it. Who was she kidding? Of course she would marry Ronan. She'd be crazy not to. Lately she woke every morning warm from dreams about him. She would take her time about this, but felt clear they would be a couple. "If I am not allowed to leave, then I guess I'll be staying in this world, won't I? But I don't have a clue how to be a Queen."

"Few people do. Nakia was one of them. I suspect it is something you learn as time goes on. Have you considered what you want to do here?" asked Aste.

"There's so much I want to see and learn, I don't know where to start."

"At the beginning of course."

"I'm not sure how much patience I have for starting at the beginning. I never have been good at that. I always want to jump right in the middle."

"Well, that comes from a fear there is not enough time and a desire to learn everything at once. Time acts differently in each world. It flows more slowly here and you can allow yourself the luxury of slowing down to learn things thoroughly from the start," said Aste.

"Perhaps you're right. Aunt Rita says I'm always too impatient and that's why my spells fail so often."

"Your Aunt Rita sounds like a very wise woman," said Aste. She stood and they began to stroll through the garden, passing hedges with doorways cut into them.

"Do you think I will see Amanda again, if I stay?"

"Ah, Amanda, I think she will become a great traveler."

"What do you mean, a great traveler?" asked Mira.

"I think she and Ewan will journey a great deal. He has always moved about in this world. I suspect he will return with Amanda to your world for a time and then who knows?" said Aste, smiling.

"You're not telling me everything you suspect, are you?"

"No, but I will tell you this, Amanda has the breath of the Enigmatic Pearl imbedded in her soul. She will seek out that world. Who knows what will happen? I truly do not, but it will be an interesting tale to hear."

"I must get ready to go and see what happens. You said we can leave from here and return through the cedar tree, right?"

"Yes, if the Opal allows you to leave."

"I don't know how to say goodbye to you. We owe everything to you and I've learned so much...." She didn't have any of the right words and it almost made her choke to say anything.

"That is because this is not goodbye. You will return here because you have much more to learn from me as well as from this world, but mostly to learn from yourself. The Black Opal will call you home," said Aste. "All you need do is choose to answer."

They walked into the palace and descended downwards along several stairways until they reached a long corridor. The cold dankness of the earth enveloped them. The skull-lined passageway ended at the great, underground cavern.

There she saw Amanda standing beside Ewan. Amanda wore the same clothes as when she entered this world, cutoff jeans, a T-shirt and her yellow sweater. However, instead of being barefoot, she now wore white sandals. Ewan, dressed all in black with boots, looked like a normal guy, except twice as gorgeous. He hugged Roderick and then Ronan, who was shadowed by two pooka. As she and Aste approached, Ronan turned to them and smiled.

He took her aside and said, "I will miss you terribly, I hope you hurry back." From a pocket in his pants he pulled a blue-black heart-shaped stone set in intricate, silver filigree on a long silver chain and put it around her neck. The pendant shimmered with a rainbow of colors. "This piece left the Black Opal long ago, before the tower was built and has been handed down over time. I wish you to have it. Perhaps it will draw you back sooner," he said, kissing her on the lips.

She had never been kissed like that. If felt sensual and warm; her entire body woke up, shaken to the core. She clung to him, her head spinning. More kisses like that would be worth coming back for.

She said, "Thank you. I just don't seem to have any of the right words today."

"Words are not important right now," he said, putting his hand above her heart and pulling her hand to his heart. He drew them closer and his forehead rested against her horn as they both breathed deeply. Beneath all her neurotic fears about failed relationships, she felt such a deep connection to him.

Finally, he put her hand on his arm and led her back to the others. She joined Amanda and Ewan.

"Amanda, it's possible I won't be able to go through."

"What are you talking about?"

"The Opal might not let me leave," she said, hugging her sister. She caught Ewan's eye and he nodded. Mira could tell he had the same thought, probably from Ronan.

"That's not possible. You have to come home with me," said Amanda, breaking off the hug and grabbing her arms.

"It may be that I am home." She looked into Amanda's eyes to make it clear to her. Amanda sighed. Mira nodded to Aste.

Aste directed them to stand beneath the three bone columns. Aste began chanting and walked around the outside of the columns. She burned some mixture of herbs in a large, cupped stone.

Mira smelled cedar and pine, but something else more exotic and elusive. She felt the energy of the Black Opal pulse and, interestingly enough, the heart pendant on the chain pulsed with it. She automatically tuned her energy to that pulse, feeling connected to the Opal, to the land.

Amanda grabbed one hand and Ewan the other, together the three of them formed a circle. The Opal's light turned buttery yellow like their sun. A whirr of wind swirled around her. Her body tingled and she almost felt dizzy. This felt nothing like the other portal. The wind swirled fog around them and all they could see was each other. Amanda had a look of wonder on her face and laughed. Ewan looked like he was setting out on a great adventure. Mira felt like she shouldn't be here, didn't want to leave.

The fog cleared and the wind stopped. She could see the inside of the great cedar stump, but couldn't move. Surrounded by the sharp, pungent scent of cedar, she looked for the hole where they first entered into another world, but could find no sign of any opening.

The ladder she had used to get down inside still stood there. Amanda, the athlete, followed by Ewan, climbed the ladder, whooping all the while.

Mira stood frozen, unable to speak or move. A huge lump formed in her throat.

Amanda turned as she climbed over the top of the stump. "Mira c'mon." Then Amanda began to fade and Mira heard her call faintly, "I'll come back and see you." The inside of the stump faded completely.

Mira found herself back inside the Black Opal Cavern, alone with Ronan. He looked simultaneously full of joy and grief.

Chapter 39 — Nakia

Nakia sat on a large flat stone, watching the dragon. The monstrous red beast basked in the light of the Opal, seemingly asleep. She smoothed her ball gown and eagerly watched the progress of the morning, her mind racing with plans. The dragon never moved, except for breathing.

"Angus," she said, "do you not think we should explore this island if it is to be our prison?"

"Why yes, my Queen," he said, catching her point.

"Your Queen, no longer," she said, rising stiffly and walking towards the water.

"You will always be my Queen," he said, softly.

"Please, call me Nakia. I will call you Angus," she said, touching his arm gently. She felt touched by his words. It had been a long time since she could trust anyone. Had she ever trusted anyone?

She picked up a rock and threw it into the water. Bending to pick up another, she glanced at the still sleeping dragon.

They casually walked along the beach, putting space between them and the dragon. When it felt far enough that the dragon couldn't overhear them, she whispered, "Are there herbs here to make a draught of incapacitation for a dragon?"

"I am not sure, but I will look. I don't seem to remember much. When Aste took away my power...."

"Yes, I know, poor dear. If you can remember the herbs, perhaps I can find them."

"What then?"

"I'm not sure. A boat or raft. We will need to make one."

"The nearest island is far away."

"If we do not find one, we will die at sea. Far preferable to what my nephew or the High Council will decide on as our punishment. We must find a portal to another world."

He was silent, thinking. "How much of your power did they take?" Angus asked hesitantly.

She picked up a shell and examined it, "I'm not sure. I have no stones to enhance what little remains and the Opal has bled away my vitality for turns, surely you knew that."

"I suspected," he said, softly.

"I still hold some, but very little. Although, I have felt a renewal, as life is renewed in the land. But I still have my knowledge. They did not take that from me."

"Wormwood makes dragons sleepy. I know there are two other herbs that would help." He looked confused. "We can make a fire and burn them. It is when they breathe the smoke they fall asleep."

A roaring filled the sky and a blue dragon appeared, landing next to the red one. A guard change.

"You go talk to them, I must find some bushes and empty my bowels," she said slipping into the woods. "When you go, begin to collect wood for a raft. Leave it hidden among the trees."

She walked into the forest heading towards an exposed, gravelly slope which could be seen from the beach. That's where wormwood would grow, if there was any to be found.

She would not give up.

"What news from the city?" she heard Angus ask of the blue dragon who had just arrived.

"Quiet! Do not bother us with your questions."

The dragons continued speaking in their own language. She could not understand them.

Nakia scraped her arm as she slipped and fell on the slope. Soon her green ball gown would have to be torn to make it shorter. It did not work either on the beach or in the woods.

There was no wormwood on this sunny cliff side. She would have to try elsewhere. The red dragon flew past, on its way to the mainland. Nakia's mind had cleared since arriving on the island. She hadn't realized how much influence the Opal had over her. The stone had driven her mad. She felt more whole now than in many, many turns.

Climbing down, she made her way back to where the dragon was. She picked a couple of wild apples from a tree. At least they would have lunch.

She heard a rustling behind her and turned to see Lord Montaine and another man.

"How did you get here?" she whispered, trying to keep her mouth from dropping open.

"I would be a poor island man indeed if I did not have a boat or two," he said with a sly smile.

"How did the dragons not see you?"

"My Jeffrey is a cunning magician," he said. "Are you coming?"

"I need to get my Sorcerer away from the dragon."

"We came in two boats. Jeffrey will wait for the Sorcerer and join us later."

She hesitated. Could this be some sort of trap? She did not want to be separated from Angus, but couldn't be sure that Jeffrey would actually bring him. Both she and Angus were so defenseless. "I cannot repay you, Lord Montaine. Rufus."

"I ask no payment," he said, yet she felt some concealment there. He expected something. She would need to be careful.

"I will come." She followed him through the underbrush, trying to reach Angus with her mind. 'Follow, follow' went her thoughts to him.

She hoped he heard.

Chapter 40 — Mira

Despite the bad news of the day, Mira felt blissful. It was Lammas, otherwise known as first harvest. She and Ronan had just been married. According to tradition the marriage lasted for a turn and one day and then could either be renewed or ended. This felt permanent. They would remarry every turn.

The unicorn population was recovering and black unicorns from the forests of Analla had returned to the plains with foals that were bay, roan, even pinto and appaloosa. Shadow visited her each evening and assured Mira that she carried a white foal, from the bay stallion who had been Ronan's Pinecone.

Dragon eggs had hatched and the hatchlings had left their parents for the sea. The dragon's recovery was well under way. Ronan planned to make the court nomadic as it once was. The better to be in touch with peoples and beings throughout the realm. All of it felt like waking after a long winter to see spring bursting out everywhere.

Mira focused on the bad news as she wrote the email to Amanda. Ronan had meant to bring Nakia and Angus before the High Council, but poof, the two of them had vanished. How they got off the island was still a mystery. They were sighted near a coastal town. Apparently Nakia still had enough magic left to use the portals, or perhaps her magic had rejuvenated along with the land. Aste traced her as far as the World of the Enigmatic Pearl.

"You and Ewan must go to the World of the Enigmatic Pearl immediately! Ewan is blood to Nakia and can track her. Ronan and I will not be allowed to leave. Roderick broke his leg and cannot go. Aste will come as soon as she is free. Nakia will attack that world and begin to move out into the others. You must leave before her trail is cold. Aste will open the portal for you."

Mira hoped Amanda would answer soon. The memory of the serene, beautiful place burned in her mind. She could not let it be destroyed by that madwoman.

The Jeweled Worlds Series is continued

in Book 2 — The Enigmatic Pearl

ABOUT THE AUTHOR

Linda Jordan writes fascinating characters, funny dialogue, and imaginative fiction. She creates both long and short fiction, serious and silly. She believes in the power of healing and transformation, and many of her stories follow those themes.

In a previous lifetime, Linda coordinated the Clarion West Writers' Workshop as well as the Reading Series. She spent four years as Chair of the Board of Directors during Clarion West's formative period. She's also worked as a travel agent, a baker, and a pond plant/fish sales person, you know, the sort of things one does as a writer.

Linda now lives in the rainy wilds of Washington state with her husband, daughter, four cats, eighteen Koi and an infinite number of slugs and snails.

Visit her at: www.LindaJordan.net

Metamorphosis Press website is at:
www.MetamorphosisPress.com

Her other work includes:
~*The Enigmatic Pearl: The Jeweled Worlds Book 2*
~*The Flaming Ruby: The Jeweled Worlds Book 3*
~*Elements: 5 Stories for Young Adults*
~*Infected by Magic*

If you enjoyed this story, please consider leaving a review and telling other like-minded readers about it. Thank you!

Get a FREE ebook!
Sign up for Linda's Serendipitous Newsletter on her website:
www.LindaJordan.net
and get a free copy of *Infected by Magic*

Made in the USA
Columbia, SC
08 March 2023

13440374R00200